Praise for the novels of
New York Times bestselling author

RACHEL VINCENT

"*Twilight* fans will love it."
Kirkus Reviews on *My Soul to Take*

"A high-octane plot with characters you can really care about. Vincent is a welcome addition to this genre!"
Kelley Armstrong on *Stray*

"I liked the character and loved the action. I look forward to reading the next book in the series."
Charlaine Harris on *Stray*

"Highly recommended for adults and teens alike."
—*Book Bitch*

"Fans of those vampires will enjoy this new crop of otherworldly beings."
—*Booklist*

"*My Soul to Take* grabs you from the very beginning."
—*Sci-Fi Guy*

"Wonderfully written characters… A fast-paced, engrossing read that you won't want to put down. A story that I wouldn't mind sharing with my pre-teen… A book like this is one of the reasons that I add authors to my auto-buy list. This is definitely a keeper."
—*TeensReadToo.com*

Also available from ***Rachel Vincent***

Published by

Soul Screamers
MY SOUL TO TAKE
MY SOUL TO SAVE

Coming soon…

MY SOUL TO STEAL

Visit www.miraink.co.uk

my SOUL to Keep

RACHEL VINCENT

Published in Great Britain 2011
MIRA Books, Eton House, 18-24 Paradise Road,
Richmond, Surrey, TW9 1SR

ISBN 978 0 7783 0410 4

47-0511

Printed in the UK
by CPI Group (UK), Croydon, CR0 4YY

ACKNOWLEDGEMENTS

Thanks most of all to No.1, who takes over so many real-life duties so I can live and work in my own little world.

Thanks to Rinda Elliott, for one honest opinion after another, to the Deadline Dames, for camaraderie, and to Jocelynn Drake and Kim Haynes, for friendships I grow more grateful for every year.

Thanks, as always, to my agent, Miriam Kriss, for making things happen.

And thank you to my editor, Mary-Theresa Hussey, and to Elizabeth Mazer and everyone else behind the scenes. Without your patience and enthusiasm, this book would never have made it on to the shelf.

To Amy, Michelle and Josh.
My memories of you from high school make the
nonfantasy elements of Kaylee's life feel so real to me…

THE WHOLE THING STARTED with a wasted jock and a totaled car. Or so I thought. But as usual, the truth was a bit more complicated....

"SO, HOW DOES IT FEEL to be free again?" Nash leaned against my car, flashing that smile I couldn't resist. The one that made his dimples stand out and his eyes shine, and made me melt like chocolate in the sun, in spite of the mid-December chill.

I sucked in a deep, cold breath. "Like I'm seeing the sun for the first time in a month." I pushed my car door closed and twisted the key in the lock. I didn't like parking on the street; it didn't seem like a very safe place to leave my most valuable possession. Not that my car was expensive, or anything. It was more than a decade old, and hardly anything to *oooh* over. But it was mine, and it was paid for, and unlike some of my more financially fortunate classmates, I'd never be able to afford another one, should some idiot veer too close to the curb.

But Scott Carter's driveway was full long before we'd arrived, and the street was lined with cars, most much nicer than mine. Of course, they all probably had more than liability coverage....

Fortunately, the party was in a very good section of our little Dallas suburb, where the lawn manicures cost more than my father made in six months.

"Relax, Kaylee." Nash pulled me close as we walked. "You look like you'd rather gouge your own eyes out than hang for a couple of hours with some friends."

"They're your friends, not mine," I insisted as we passed the third convertible on our way to the well-lit house at the end of the cul-de-sac, already thumping with some bass-heavy song I couldn't yet identify.

"They'd be yours if you'd get to know them."

I couldn't help rolling my eyes. "Yeah, I'm sure the glitter-and-gloss throng is waiting for *me* to give *them* a chance."

Nash shrugged. "They know all they need to know about you—you're smart, pretty, and crazy in love with me," he teased, squeezing me tighter.

I laughed. "Who started *that* vicious rumor?" I'd never said it, because as addictive as Nash was—as special as he made me feel—I wasn't going to toss off words like *love* and *forever* until I was sure. Until I was sure *he* was sure. Forever can be a very long time for *bean sidhes,* and so far his track record looked more like the fifty-yard dash than the Boston marathon. I'd been burned before by guys without much staying power.

When I looked up, I found Nash watching me, his hazel eyes swirling with streaks of green and brown in the orange glow from the streetlights. I almost felt sorry for all the humans who wouldn't be able to see that—to read emotion in another's eyes.

That was a *bean sidhe* thing, and easily my favorite part of my recently discovered heritage.

"All I'm saying is it would be nice to get to hang out with my friends and my girlfriend at the same time."

I rolled my eyes again. "Oh, fine. I'll play nice with the pretty people." At least Emma would be there to keep me company—she'd started going out with one of Nash's teammates while I was grounded. And the truth was that most of Nash's friends weren't that bad. Their girlfriends were another story.

Speaking of bloodthirsty hyenas...

A car door slammed in the driveway ahead and my cousin, Sophie, stood next to Scott Carter's metallic-blue convertible, her huge green eyes shadowed dramatically by the streetlight overhead. "Nash!" She smiled at him, ignoring me in spite of the fact that we'd shared a home for the past thirteen of her fifteen years, until my dad had moved back from Ireland in late September.

Or maybe *because* of that.

"Can you give me a hand?" As we stepped onto the driveway, she rounded the end of her boyfriend's car in a slinky, sleeveless pink top and designer jeans, a case of beer clutched awkwardly to her chest. Two more cases sat at her feet, and I glanced around to see if any of the neighbors were watching my fifteen-year-old cousin show off an armload of alcoholic beverages. But the neighbors were probably all out, spending their Saturday evening at the theater, or the ballet, or in some restaurant I couldn't even afford to park near.

And most of their kids were at Scott's house, waiting for us to come in with the beer.

Nash let go of me to take the case from Sophie, then grabbed another one from the ground. Sophie beamed at him, then shot a haughty sneer at my plain jacket before turning on one wedge-heeled foot to strut after him.

I sighed and picked up the remaining box, then followed them both inside. The front door opened before Nash could pound on it, and a tall, thick senior in a green-and-white-letter jacket slapped Nash's shoulder and took one of the cases from him. Nash twisted with his empty arm extended, clearly ready to wrap it around me, but found Sophie instead. He sidestepped her—ignoring her plump-lipped pout—and took the case from me, then stood back to let me go in first.

"Hudson!" Scott Carter greeted Nash, shouting to be heard over the music. He took one of the cases and led us toward a large kitchen crowded with bodies, scantily clad and shiny with sweat. In spite of the winter chill outside, it was hot and humid indoors, the hormone level rising with each new song that played.

I took off my jacket, revealing my snug red blouse, and almost immediately wished I could cover myself back up. I didn't have much to show off, but it was all now on display, thanks to the top Emma had picked out for me that afternoon, which suddenly seemed much more daring than it had in the privacy of my own room.

Nash set the remaining case of beer on the counter as Scott slid the first one into the refrigerator. "Kaylee Cavanaugh," Scott said when he stood, having apparently noticed me for the first time. He eyed me up and down while I resisted the urge to cross my arms over my chest. "Lookin' good." He glanced from me to Sophie, then back, while my cousin tried to fry me alive with the heat of her glare. "I'm starting to see the family resemblance."

"All I see is you," Nash said, pulling me close when he realized Sophie and I weren't happy with the comparison.

I smiled and kissed him impulsively, convinced by the slow churn of colors in his irises that he meant what he said.

Scott shoved the last case of beer into the fridge, then slapped a cold can into Nash's hand as I finally pulled away from him, my face flaming. "See? Family resemblance." Then he headed off into the crowd with Sophie, popping the top on a can of his own. Three steps later they were grinding to the music, one of Scott's hands around his drink, the other splayed across my cousin's lower back.

"Wow, that was…unexpected," Nash said, drawing my gaze from the familiar faces talking, dancing, drinking, and…otherwise engaged. And it took me a moment to realize he meant the kiss.

"Good unexpected, or bad unexpected?"

"Very, very good." He set his can on the counter at my back, then pulled me closer for a repeat performance, one hand sliding up my side. That time I didn't pull away until someone poked my shoulder. I twisted in Nash's arms to find Emma Marshall, my best friend, watching us with an amused half smile.

"Hey." Her grin grew as she glanced from me to Nash, then back. "You're blocking the fridge."

"There's a cooler in the other room." Nash nodded toward the main part of the house.

Emma shrugged. "Yeah, but no one's making out in front of it." She pulled open the fridge, grabbed a beer, then popped the can open as she pushed the door shut with a toss of one shapely hip. It wasn't fair. Emma and her sisters inherited crazy curves—a genetic jackpot—and all I got from my relatives was a really gnarled family tree.

There were times when I would gladly have traded all

my *bean sidhe* "gifts"—did a glass-shattering screech and the ability to travel between the human world and the Netherworld even count as gifts*?*—for a little more of what she had. But this was not one of those times. Not while Nash's hands were on my waist, his taste still on my lips, and the greens and browns in his eyes swirling languorously with blatant desire. For *me.*

Em drank from her can, and I grabbed the car keys dangling from her hand, then showed them to her before stuffing them into my hip pocket, along with my own. She could stay the night with me, and I'd bring her back for her car in the morning. Emma smiled and nodded, already moving to the music when someone called her name from the living-room doorway.

"Hey, Em!" a voice called over the music, and I turned to see Doug Fuller leaning with one bulging arm on the door frame. "Come dance with me."

Emma smiled, drained her can, then danced into the living room with Doug's hands on her already swaying hips. Nash and I joined them, and he returned greeting after greeting from the glitter crowd writhing around us. But then he was mine. We moved with the music as if the room was empty but for the stereo and the heat we shared.

I had stolen Nash from a room full of his adoring devotees with nothing but the secret connection we shared. A connection no other girl could possibly compete with.

We'd combined our *bean sidhe* abilities to bring my best friend back from the dead and to reclaim a damned soul from the hellion who'd bought it. We'd literally saved lives, fought evil, and almost died together. No mere pretty face could compete with that, no matter how much gloss and mascara she applied.

An hour later, Em tapped my shoulder and pointed toward the kitchen. I shook my head—after a month without him, I could have danced with Nash all night—but after Emma left, Nash kept glancing at the kitchen door like it was going to suddenly slam closed and lock us out.

"Need a break?" I asked, and he smiled in relief.

"Just for a minute." He tugged me through the crowd while my heart still raced to the beat, both of us damp with sweat.

In the kitchen, Emma drank from a fresh can of beer while Doug argued with Brant Williams about a bad call during some basketball game I hadn't seen.

"Here." Nash handed me a cold soda. "I'll be right back." Then he pushed his way through the crowd without a backward glance.

I looked at Emma with both brows raised, but she only shrugged.

I popped open my Coke and noticed that Doug and Brant's argument had become a whispered conversation I couldn't follow, and Emma hadn't even noticed. For several minutes, she prattled about her sister refusing to lend her a blouse that made Cara look lumpy, anyway.

Before I could decide how to respond, someone called my name, and I looked up to find Brant watching me.

"Yeah?" Obviously I'd missed a question.

"I said, 'Where's your boyfriend?'"

"Um…bathroom," I said, unwilling to admit that I wasn't sure.

Brant shook his head slowly. "Hudson's falling down on the job. You wanna dance till he gets back? I won't bite." He held out one large brown hand for mine, and I took it.

Brant Williams was tall, and dark, and always smiling. He was the football team's kicker, a senior, and the friendliest jock I'd ever met, not counting Nash. He was also the only other person in the house I would dance with, other than Emma.

I danced with Brant for two songs, glancing around for Nash the whole time. I was just starting to wonder if he'd gotten sick when I spotted him across the room, standing with Sophie in an arched doorway leading to a dark hall. He brushed a strand of hair from her forehead, then leaned closer to be heard over the music.

My chest ached like I couldn't breathe.

When he saw me looking, he stepped away from Sophie and scowled at my partner, then waved me over. I thanked Brant for the dance, then made my way across the room, dread building inside me like heartburn. Nash had ditched me at a party, then showed up with Sophie. Deep down, I'd known this day would come. I'd figured he'd eventually look elsewhere for what he hadn't had in the two and a half months we'd been going out. But with Sophie? A flash of anger burned in my cheeks. He may as well have just spit in my face!

Please, please be imagining things, Kaylee....

I stopped five feet away, my heart bruising my chest with each labored beat. Yes, Sophie had a boyfriend, but that didn't mean she wouldn't try to take mine.

Nash took one look at my face, at my eyes, which were surely swirling with pain and anger I couldn't hide, then followed my gaze to Sophie. His eyes widened with comprehension. Then he smiled and grabbed my hand.

"Sophie was just looking for Scott. Right?" But then he tugged me down the dark hall before she could answer, leaving my cousin all alone in the crowd. "We can talk in here," Nash whispered, pressing me into a closed door.

The full body contact was promising, but I couldn't banish doubt. "Were you talking to her the whole time?" I asked around the hitch in my breath as his cheek brushed mine.

"I just went outside to cool off, and when I came back in, she cornered me. That's it." He fumbled for the handle near my hip, and the door swung open, revealing Scott's dad's posh office.

"Swear?"

"Do I really need to?" Nash stepped back so I could see his eyes in the dim light of the desk lamp, and I saw the truth swirling in them. He didn't want Sophie, no matter what she might do that I hadn't.

I felt myself flush. "Sorry. I just thought—"

Nash closed the door and cut my apology off with a kiss. He tasted good. Like mint. We wound up on Mr. Carter's burgundy leather couch, and I had just enough time to think that psychiatrists made *waaaay* too much money before Nash's mouth found mine again, and thinking became impossible.

"You know I'm not interested in Sophie," he whispered. "I wouldn't do that to you or Scott." He leaned down and kissed me again. "There's only you, Kaylee."

My entire body tingled in wave after wave of warm, exhilarating shivers, and I let my lips trail over the rough stubble on his chin, delighting in the coarse texture.

"Oh, blah, blah, *blah,*" a jaded voice said, drenching our privacy with a cold dose of sarcasm. "You love him, he loves you, and we're all one big, happy, sloppy, dorky family."

"*Damn* it, Tod!" Nash stiffened. I closed my eyes and sighed. The couch creaked beneath us as we sat up to see Nash's undead brother—fully corporeal for once—sitting backward in Mr. Carter's desk chair, arms crossed over the top as he watched us in boredom barely softened by the slight upturn of his cherubic lips. "If you don't quit it with the Peeping Tom routine, I'm going to tell your boss you get off watching other people make out."

"He knows," Tod and I said in unison. I straightened my shirt, scowling at the intruder, though my irritation was already fading.

Unlike Nash, I had trouble staying mad at Tod lately because I considered his recent reappearance a good sign. We hadn't seen him for nearly a month after his ex-girlfriend died in October—without her soul. And when I say we'd *not seen* him, I mean that literally. As a grim reaper, Tod could choose when and where he wanted to be seen, and by whom.

But now he was back, and up to his old tricks. Which seemed to consist entirely of preventing me and Nash from having any quality alone time. He was almost as bad as my dad.

"Shouldn't you be at work?" I ran one hand through my long brown hair to smooth it.

Tod shrugged. "I'm on my lunch break."

I lifted both brows. "You don't eat."

He only shrugged again, and smiled.

"Get out," Nash growled, tossing his head toward the door. Like Tod would actually have to use it. One of the other perks of being dead, technically speaking, was the ability to walk through things. Or simply disappear, then reappear somewhere else. That's right. I got swirling eyes and the capacity to shatter windows with my bare voice. Tod got teleportation and invisibility.

The supernatural world is *so* far from fair.

Tod stood and kicked the chair aside, running one hand through short blond curls that not even the afterlife could tame. "I'm not here to watch you two, anyway."

Great. I scowled at the reaper, my eyes narrowed in true irritation now. "I told you to stay away from her." Emma had met him once, briefly, and we'd made the mistake of telling her what he really was. He'd been watching her covertly before, but after Addison's death and his obvious heartbreak, I'd assumed that had stopped.

Tod mirrored his brother with his arms crossed over his chest. "So you won't let me go near her, but you'll let her get in the car with some drunk jock? That doesn't even kinda make sense."

"Damn it." Nash was off the couch in an instant and I followed, whispering a thank-you to Tod as I passed him. But he'd already blinked out of the office.

I trailed Nash down the hall and through the packed living room, accidentally bumping a beer from a cheerleader's hand on the way. We ran out the front door and I wished I'd stopped to find my jacket when the frigid air raised goose bumps all over my skin.

We paused at the end of the walkway, and I spotted Emma near the mouth of the cul-de-sac, a brief glimpse of long blond hair. "There." I pointed and we took off again. We got there just as Doug pulled his passenger's side door open. He had Em pressed against the side of the car, his tongue in her mouth, his free hand up her shirt.

Emma was totally into it, and though I didn't think she'd have gone so far in public if not for the beer, that was her business. But getting in the car with a drunk crossed the line from stupid into dangerous.

"Em," I said as Nash slapped one hand on Doug's shoulder and pulled him backward.

"What the hell, man!" Doug slurred as his hand pulled free from Emma's bra hard enough that the elastic slapped her skin.

"Kaylee!" Emma smiled and fell against me, and I glared at Doug. She didn't know what she was doing, and *he* was being a complete asshole.

"Em, you know how it goes." I wrapped one arm around her waist when she stumbled. "Come together, stay together…"

"…leave together," she finished with a wide-eyed, pseudo-serious expression. "But we didn't come together, Kay…"

"I know, but the last part still applies."

"Fuller, she's drunk." Nash angled him so that Doug fell into his own passenger's seat. "And so are you."

"Noooo…" Emma giggled, blowing beer breath at me. "He's not drinking, so he gets to drive."

"Em, he's wasted," Nash insisted, then glanced at

me and tossed his head toward the house. "Take her back in."

I started walking Emma up the sidewalk, trying to keep her quiet as she told me how nice Doug was. She wasn't just drunk, she was *gone.* I should have watched her more closely.

A minute later, Nash caught up to us as I was lowering Emma onto the porch. "Did you get his keys?" I asked, and Nash frowned. Then, as he turned to head back toward Doug's car, an engine growled to life and a sick feeling settled into the pit of my stomach. Nash took off running and I leaned Emma against the top step. "Tod?" I called, glancing around the dark yard, grateful there was no one around to see me talking to myself.

"What?" the reaper said at my back, and I whirled around, wondering why he always appeared behind me.

"Can you sit with her for a minute?"

He scowled and glanced at Emma, who stared up at us, blinking her big blue eyes in intoxicated innocence. "You told me to stay away from her."

"Hey, I remember you," Emma slurred, loud enough to make me wince. "You're dead."

We both ignored Em. "I know. Just watch her for a minute, and don't let her get into any cars. Please." Then I raced after Nash past the entrance to the cul-de-sac, confident Tod would watch Emma. That he'd probably been doing it all night, though he'd catch hell for missing work.

Ahead, streetlights shone on the glossy surface of Doug's car, gliding past like a slice of the night itself. Then, as I caught up to Nash, Doug leaned suddenly to one side, and his car lurched forward and to the right.

There was a loud pop, followed by the crunch of metal. Then the crash of something more substantial.

"Shit!" Nash took off running again and I followed as that sick feeling in my stomach enveloped the rest of me. "Oh, no, Kaylee…"

I knew before I even saw it. The street was lined with expensive, highly insured cars belonging to people who could easily afford to replace them. But the drunk jock had hit mine. When I got closer, I saw that he'd not only hit it, he'd rammed it up onto the sidewalk and *through* a neighbor's brick mailbox.

My car was *crunched*. The driver's side door was buck-led. Bricks and chunks of mortar lay everywhere.

Behind us, Scott's front door squealed opened and voices erupted into the dark behind me. I glanced back to find Tod—now fully corporeal—ushering Emma away from the crowd pouring into the yard. When I was sure she was okay, I turned to my poor, dead car.

Until I noticed that Doug Fuller had yet to emerge from his.

Crap.

"Help me with him," Nash called, and I rounded the

car as he pulled open the completely unscathed driver's side door of the Mustang. Doug's head lolled on his shoulders, and he was mumbling drunk nonsense under his breath. "...with me. Somebody else in my *car,* dude..."

Nash leaned inside to unlatch the seat belt—what kind of drunk remembers to buckle up?—but he couldn't fit between his friend and the steering wheel, which had been shoved way too close to Doug's chest. "Kay, could you get the belt?"

I sighed and crawled across his lap, wedging my torso between the wheel and his chest as I felt around for the button. "Scared the *shit* out of me..." he mumbled into the hair that had fallen over my ear. "He was just *there,* outta nowhere!"

"Shut up, Doug," I snapped, seriously considering leaving him in the car until the cops arrived. "You're drunk." When I had the belt unlatched, I backed out of the linebacker's lap and he exhaled right into my face.

I froze, one hand braced against his thigh, and that sick feeling in my stomach became a full-body cramp. Ice-cold fingers of horror clenched my heart and shot through my veins. Emma was right. Doug hadn't been drinking.

Somehow, Eastlake High School's completely human first-string linebacker had gotten his big, dumb hands on the most dangerous controlled substance in the Netherworld.

Doug Fuller absolutely *reeked* of Demon's Breath.

"ARE YOU SURE?" Nash whispered, brows drawn low as, behind him, a big man in a grease-stained coat hooked the front of my smashed car up to the huge chain dangling from the back of his tow truck.

"Yes. I'm sure." He'd already asked me four times. I'd only had two brief whiffs of Demon's Breath a month earlier, but that bittersweet, biting tang—more like an aftertaste than a true scent—was emblazoned on my brain, along with other memorial gems like the feel of nylon straps lashing me to a narrow hospital bed.

"Where would he even get it?" I murmured, zipping the jacket Nash had gotten for me as a motor rumbled to life on the street and the big chain was wound tighter, raising the front of my poor car off the ground.

"I don't know." Nash wrapped his arms around me from behind, cocooning me in a familiar warmth.

"Humans can't cross into the Netherworld and hellions can't cross into ours," I murmured, thinking out loud while no one else was close enough to hear me. "So there has to be some way to get Demon's Breath into the human world without bringing the hellion who provided it." Because the name was a very literal description: Demon's Breath was the toxic exhalation of a hellion, a very powerful drug in the Netherworld. And evidently a hell of a high in our world, too.

But Demon's Breath could rot the soul of a reaper who held it in his lungs for too long. Did the same hold true for humans? Had Doug breathed enough of it to damage his soul? How had he gotten it in the first place?

"I'm gonna take a look around," I whispered, and Nash shook his head.

"No!" He stepped closer to me, so everyone else would think he was comforting me over the loss of my car. "You can't cross over. Hellions don't like to lose, and Avari's going to be out for your soul for the rest of your life, Kaylee."

Because I'd escaped with mine when we'd crossed over to reclaim the Page sisters' souls.

"I'm just going to peek." Like looking through a window into the Netherworld, instead of actually walking through the door. "And anyway, Avari won't be there." I frowned. "Here." Or whatever. "At Scott Carter's party."

The Netherworld was like a warped mirror image of our own world. The two were connected at certain points, wherever the bleed-through of human energy was strong enough to anchor the Netherworld to ours, like a toothpick through layers of a sandwich.

"Kaylee, I don't think—"

I cut him off with a glance. I didn't have time to argue. "Just stand in front of me so no one can see me. It'll only take a second."

When he hesitated, I stepped behind him and closed my eyes. And I remembered death.

I thought back to the first time it had happened—at least, the first time I remembered—forcing myself to relive the horror. The certainty that the poor kid in the wheelchair was going to die. That dark knowledge that only I had. The shadows that churned around him. Through him.

The memory of death was enough, fortunately, and the scream began to build deep in my throat. A female *bean sidhe*'s wail heralds death and can suspend the deceased's soul long enough for a male *bean sidhe* to redirect it. But my wail would also let me—and any other *bean sidhe* near enough to hear me—see into the Netherworld. To cross into it, if we wanted to.

But I had no desire to go to the Netherworld. Ever again.

I held the scream back, trapping it in my throat and in my heart so that Nash heard only a thin ribbon of sound, and no one else would hear a thing.

Nash took my hand, but I could barely feel the warmth of his fingers around mine. I opened my eyes and gasped. Scott Carter's street had been enveloped by a thin gray film, like a storm cloud had settled to the ground. My world was still there—police, tow trucks, an ambulance, and a small crowd of onlookers.

But beneath that—deeper than that—was the Netherworld.

A field of olive-colored razor wheat swayed in a breeze I knew would be cold, if I could have felt it, the brittle stalks tinkling like wind chimes as they brushed together. The sky was dark purple streaked with greens and blues like bruises on the face of the world.

It was both beautiful and terrifying. And blessedly empty. No hellions. No fiends. No creatures waiting to eat us or to breathe toxic breath on Doug Fuller, even if we'd found some kind of hole in the barrier between worlds.

"Okay, it's clear. Let it go," Nash whispered, and I swallowed my scream.

The gray began to clear and the *wrong* colors faded, leaving only the upper-class suburban neighborhood, somehow less intimidating to me now that I'd seen what lay beneath. The Netherworld version of Scott's neighborhood looked just like mine.

I wrapped my arms around Nash, discomforted by the glimpse of a world that had once tried to swallow us both whole. "However he got it, it didn't come straight from the source," I said, then I let go of Nash to face the real world.

Only a few brave—and sober—partyers had stayed once word got out that the police were on their way, and the stragglers were gathered around Scott on his front lawn, watching the cleanup from a safe distance. The cops knew there'd been a party, and they obviously knew Scott had been drinking. But so long as he stayed in his own yard and didn't try to get behind the wheel, they were clearly willing to look the other way, thanks to his elite address and his father's considerable influence in the community.

Emma wouldn't be so lucky. She and Sophie had taken refuge four doors down, in Laura Bell's living room. Laura—Sophie's best friend and fellow dancer—had only let Emma in because Nash used the male *bean sidhe*'s vocal Influence to convince her.

But just in case, we'd sent Tod to watch out for Emma. Invisibly, of course.

Nash's arms tightened around me as a uniformed policeman clomped across the street toward us. "Miss—" he glanced at the notebook in his hands "—Cavanaugh, are you sure you don't need a ride?"

"I have one, thanks." I let him think Nash was my ride so I wouldn't have to mention Emma or her car.

The cop glanced at Nash, and my heart fell into my stomach. He'd finished his one drink hours earlier, but suddenly I was afraid the cop would make him walk the line or breathe into something. But when Nash didn't flinch beneath the appraisal, the cop's gaze found me again.

"You want me to call your parents?"

I hesitated, trying to look like I was seriously considering that option. Then I shook my head decisively. "Um, no thanks." I waved my cell for him to see. "I'll call my dad."

He shrugged. "They're hauling your car to the body shop on Third, and the guys there should have an estimate for you in a couple of days. But personally, I think an angry word from your lawyer could get this Fuller kid's parents to buy you a new one. He looks like he can afford it—" the cop shot a contemptuous glance over one shoulder "—and I'm willing to bet a year's pay that kid's baked hotter than an apple pie. They're taking him to Arlington Memorial, so make sure your lawyer gets a look at his blood-test results."

I nodded, numb, and the cop glanced at Nash over my head. "Get her home safely."

Nash's chin brushed the back of my head as he nodded, and when the cop was out of hearing range, I twisted to find Nash's irises swirling languidly with none of the urgent fear skittering through me.

"Do you think the blood test will show anything?"

"No way." Nash shook his head firmly. "There's not a human lab built that can detect a Netherworld substance, and that cop lacks the necessary equipment to do it himself." He tapped my nose and smiled reassuringly, and for a moment, I felt like a supernatural bloodhound. "You ready to go?"

"I guess." I stared as the tow truck pulled away with my car, and a second one backed slowly toward Doug's Mustang.

Doug sat on the floor of the ambulance, legs dangling over the edge, and as I watched, another officer held out a small electronic device with a mouthpiece on one end. Doug blew into the breathalyzer, and the cop glanced at the reading, then smacked the device on the palm of his hand. Like it wasn't working.

It probably showed at least one beer, but nowhere near enough to account for his current state. Nash was right; neither humans nor technology could detect Demon's Breath. I wasn't sure whether to be happy about that, or scared out of my mind.

We knocked on Laura Bell's door as the ambulance pulled away, followed closely by the second wrecker pulling Doug's car. Laura led us through a large, tiled foyer and into a sunken living room full of dark colors and expensive woods.

Emma sat in a stiff wingback chair, looking lost and half-asleep. When I reached to help her up, Tod popped into view a foot away and I nearly jumped out of my skin. Would I never get used to that?

"She's fine," Tod said as I knelt to look into Emma's heavy-lidded eyes, and I knew by the lack of a reaction from anyone else—including Nash—that no one else could see him. "She just needs to sleep it off. And to get away from these squawking harpies you call friends."

In fact, I did *not* call Sophie and Laura friends, but I couldn't explain that without looking crazy to everyone who didn't see the invisible dead boy. So I scowled at the reaper as I helped Emma up, and Nash wrapped her other arm around his neck.

"Hey, Sophie, do you want a ride?" I asked as we passed my cousin, standing with her hand propped on one denim-clad hip.

She sneered at me with shiny pink lips. "Didn't Doug just wrap your rolling scrap pile around a mailbox?"

"In Emma's car," I said through gritted teeth.

Sophie sank onto the couch and crossed one skinny leg over the other. "I'm staying with Laura."

"Fine." They deserved each other. "Thanks for watching her," I said to Tod.

"Someone had to." But before I could answer, the reaper popped out of existence again, presumably gone back to the hospital, where he was no doubt overdue.

"Just get her out of here before my parents get home," Laura said, assuming I was talking to her. "They don't like me hanging out with drunk sluts." I bit back a dozen replies about the irony of her friendship with Sophie and settled for slamming the door on our way out.

I called my dad on the drive home, but he was working overtime again, and I got his voice mail. I hung up without leaving a message, because somehow "my car got rammed by a linebacker high on Demon's Breath" just seemed like the kind of thing he'd want to hear in person.

It was almost midnight—my official curfew—when I pulled into my driveway, and Emma had fallen asleep in her own backseat. Nash carried her inside and put her on my bed. I took off her shoes, then curled up next to Nash on the couch with a bowl of popcorn and a sci-fi channel broadcast of the original *Night of the Living Dead*—a holiday classic if I'd ever seen one.

My front door opened just as the first zombie ripped its way into the farmhouse on-screen, and I jumped, dumping popcorn everywhere.

My father trudged through the door in faded jeans and a flannel shirt, an entirely different kind of zombie thanks to shift after shift on an assembly line, trying to keep us both clothed and fed. Then he stopped and backed onto the porch again, and I knew exactly what he was looking for.

"Where's your car?" Dread warred with the exhaustion in his voice as he tossed his jacket over the back of a living room chair.

I stood while Nash began dropping stray kernels into the bowl. "Um, there was a little accident, and—"

"Are you okay?" My dad frowned, eyeing me from head to toe for injuries.

"Yeah, I wasn't even in the car." I stuffed my hands into my back pockets because I didn't know what else to do with them.

"What? Where were you?"

"At a party. When Doug Fuller left, he accidentally… hit my car."

My dad's dark brows furrowed until they almost met. "Were you drinking?"

"No." *Thank goodness.* I wouldn't put it past him to whip out a plastic cup and demand a urine sample. I swear, he would have been a great parole officer.

My father studied me, and I could see the exact moment he decided he believed me. And with that settled, his gaze fixed behind me, where Nash now stood with the bowl of spilled popcorn. "Nash, go home." The most common words in his verbal arsenal.

Nash handed me the bowl. "You want me to take Emma home?"

"Emma…?" My dad sighed and ran one hand through his thick brown hair. "Where is she?"

"In my bed."

"Drunk?"

I thought about lying. I had no idea how he would

react, even if I wasn't the one drinking. But Em smelled like beer; my lie would never float.

"Yeah. What was I supposed to do, toss her the keys and wish her luck?"

My dad sighed. Then to my complete shock, he shook his head. "No, you did the right thing."

"So she can stay?" I couldn't believe it. He didn't even sound mad.

"This time. But next time, I'm calling her mother. Nash, I'm sure we'll see you tomorrow."

"Yes, sir." Nash squeezed my hand, then headed for the door. He would walk to his house, two streets away, like he'd done every time he'd come over since I'd been grounded. Including several times when my father'd had no idea he was there.

"What happened?" My dad locked the door behind Nash, then sank into his favorite armchair as I settled onto the couch, trying to decide whether or not to tell him the whole truth. About the Demon's Breath. He was being pretty cool so far, but the Netherworld element was guaranteed to push him over the edge.

"I told you. Doug Fuller hit my car."

"How bad is it?"

I sighed, mentally steeling myself for an explosion. "He wrapped it around a neighbor's brick mailbox."

Air whistled as he inhaled sharply, and I flinched.

"He was drinking, wasn't he?" my father demanded, and I almost smiled in relief. Part of me had been sure he'd know about the Demon's Breath from my posture, or my expression, or some kind of weird *bean sidhe* parenting telepathy I didn't know about. But he thought it was just regular teenage drama, and if I wasn't mistaken, he looked a little relieved, too.

I was not going to burst his bubble. "I don't know. Maybe. But he *is* about as smart as a tractor."

"Where'd they take the car?"

"To the body shop on Third."

My dad stood and actually smiled at me, and I could almost taste his relief. He was thrilled to finally be faced with a normal parent's problem. "I'll go look at it in the morning. I assume this Fuller kid is insured?"

"Yeah. The cops gave me this." I held out the form with Doug's contact information and his insurance company's number. "And he said his dad would pay for it."

"Yes, he *will*." My father took the form into the kitchen, where the light was better. "Go get some sleep. You and Em are working in the morning, aren't you?"

"Yeah." From noon to four, we'd be selling tickets and serving popcorn at the Cinemark in the never-ending quest for gas money. Which we spent going to and from work. It was a vicious cycle.

Dismissed, and feeling like I'd just been pardoned from death row, I changed into my pj's, brushed my teeth, and lay down next to Emma in the bed. And as I listened to her breathe, I couldn't help thinking about how badly everything might have turned out if she'd actually gotten into that car.

I'd already lost Emma once and had no intention of losing her again anytime soon. Which meant I'd have to find out how her boyfriend got his human hands on Demon's Breath—then make sure that never happened again.

"KAYLEE, COME ON IN!" Harmony Hudson brushed blond curls back from her face and held the door for me as I stepped into her small, neat living room, stuffing my freezing hands into my jacket pockets. "Do we have a lesson this morning?"

"No, I just came to see Nash."

"Oh!" She smiled and closed the door, cutting off the frigid draft. "Then you must have served out your sentence."

"As of yesterday."

Nash had been grounded, too, but he only got two weeks, to my four. I think he would have gotten more if he'd still been underage, but it's hard to ground an eighteen-year-old. And punishing Tod wasn't even an option, considering he was fully grown and technically dead, and had unlimited access to the Netherworld. She couldn't even keep him in one room—not to mention corporeal—long enough to yell at him.

"He's still asleep. What did you guys do last night, anyway?"

I dropped my duffel on the faded couch, going for nonchalance, though I hated withholding information from her even worse than from my father. "Party at Scott's house. Doug Fuller rammed my parked car with an '08 Mustang."

"Oh, no!" Harmony stopped in the kitchen doorway, holding the swinging door open with one palm. "You're insured, right?"

"Liability only." That's all I could afford, working twelve hours a week at the Cinemark. "But Doug's parents are loaded, and there's no way they can say I'm at fault. I wasn't even in the car."

"Well, that's good at least, right?" I nodded, and she waved one hand toward the short hallway branching off from the opposite side of the living room. "Go wake up van Winkle and see if you can get him to eat something. I'm making apple-cinnamon muffins."

Harmony was always baking something, and always from scratch. She was really more like a grandmother than a mom, in that respect, though she looked more like Nash's older sister. She was eighty-two years old, with the face and body of a thirty-year-old.

So far, slow postpuberty aging was the only real

advantage I'd discovered to being a *bean sidhe*. My father was one hundred thirty-two and didn't look a day over forty.

Nash didn't answer when I knocked, so I slipped into his room, then closed the door and leaned against it, watching him sleep. He looked so vulnerable in his boxers, one side of his face buried in the pillow, one leg tangled near the bottom of his sheet.

I knelt by the bed and brushed thick brown hair from his forehead. The room was warm, but his skin was cool, so I started to cover him up, but before I could, his face twisted into a grimace, his eyes still squeezed shut.

He was breathing too fast. Almost panting. His teeth ground together, then he made a helpless mewling sound. His arms tensed. He clenched handfuls of the fitted sheet.

I watched Nash's nightmare from the outside, trying to decide if I should wake him up or let the dream play out. But then his eyes flew open and he gasped, his gaze still unfocused. He scuttled over the mattress, bare chest heaving, and stood against the far wall, staring across the bed at me. His irises churned in terror for several seconds before recognition settled into place and by then my own heart was racing in response to his fear.

"Kaylee?" He whispered my name, like he wasn't sure he could trust his own eyes.

"Yeah, it's me." I stood as his breathing slowed and he started to calm down. "Nightmare?"

He rubbed both hands over his face, and when he met my gaze again he was calm, back in control of his expression. And of his eyes. "Yeah, I guess."

"What was it about?"

"I don't remember." He frowned and sank onto the mattress. "I just know it was bad. But the waking up part is good so far…"

Nash pulled me onto his lap. "So, what's with the personal wake-up?" He swept my hair over one shoulder and suddenly I was acutely aware that he was half-naked and now very close. "Phone calls just aren't as satisfying anymore?" he whispered, trailing feather-soft kisses down my neck.

He leaned us both back, and before I even realized what had happened, I was lying on his bed, his weight pressing me into the mattress. His lips trailed down my neck again and his hand roamed over my shirt, and all I could think was that I didn't want to stop him. He'd waited long enough. I wanted to just let it happen…

My next exhale was ragged, and I couldn't control my racing pulse.

"I, uh…" What was I saying? What did he ask? Suddenly it didn't seem to matter.…

His hand slid beneath my shirt, but his fingers were freezing on my skin, and the shock woke me up. Irritated, I pulled Nash away and sat up to frown at him. "Are you Influencing me?"

He shrugged, a heated grin turned up one side of his mouth. "Just helping you relax."

"Don't Influence me, Nash!" I stood, struggling to sustain my anger with his voice still slithering through my mind. "Don't ever do that to me when I'm not singing for someone's soul." Sometimes his voice helped me quiet my *bean sidhe* wail, but that's not what this was. Not even close. "I hate losing control. It's like falling off a cliff in slow motion." Or being sedated. "And that's not what I came in here for," I insisted, waving one hand at the bed.

Nash scowled, and that tremendous, irresistible false calm deserted me, leaving only the chill of its sudden absence and his obvious irritation. "How am I supposed to know that? I wake up and you're in my bedroom with the door closed. What was I supposed to think? That you want to play Scrabble?"

"I…" I frowned, unsure how to finish that thought. Had I sent him some kind of signal? Was I wearing my "I'm done with my virginity, please get rid of it for me" T-shirt? "Your mom's in the other room!"

"Whatever." He sighed and pulled me closer by one hand. "Forgive me?"

"Only if you promise to play nice."

"I swear. So, what's up?" He leaned back on a pillow propped against his headboard, hands linked behind his skull, putting himself on display in case I changed my mind.

"You said you'd give me a ride."

His eyes swirled with mischief, and my cheeks blazed when I realized what I'd said. "Um…you're the one who said no."

"A ride to *work*." I'd just discovered the cause of spontaneous combustion. Surely I'd burst into flames any moment.

"I guess I could do that, too."

"I'm serious!" But not too serious to let my gaze wander. After all, I was being invited to look… "I need a lift to work, and I was hoping we could make a stop first."

"Where?"

I closed my eyes and took a deep breath. "Doug Fuller's."

"Kaylee…" he began, and I could already hear the protest forming. He sat up and I let one leg hang off the bed. "Whatever Fuller's into is none of our business."

"He's taking *Demon's Breath*," I whispered with a nervous glance at the closed door, hoping his mother was still in the kitchen. "How is that none of our business?"

"It has nothing to do with us." He stood and snatched a shirt from the back of his desk chair.

"Don't you want to know where he got it? He could have killed someone last night. And if he takes any more of it, he'll probably kill himself."

Nash sank into his desk chair. "You're overreacting, Kaylee."

"No, you're *under*reacting." I scooted to the edge of his bed. "What happened to looking out for your friends?"

"What am I supposed to do?" He shrugged, frustration clear in the tense line of his shoulders. "Go up to Fuller and say, 'Hey, man, I'm not sure where you're getting secondhand air from a demon you don't even know exists, but you need to lay off it before you kill yourself'? *That's* not gonna sound weird." He kicked a shoe across the room to punctuate his sarcasm.

I crossed my arms over my chest, struggling to keep my voice low. "You're worried about sounding weird in front of a guy who's getting high off someone else's breath?"

"Why do you care, anyway?" Nash demanded. "You don't even like Fuller."

"That doesn't mean I want to watch him die." Especially considering that his impending death would send me into an uncontrollable, screaming *bean sidhe* fit, forcing us to decide whether or not to try to save him. "And I won't let him take Emma with him."

Nash's scowl wilted, giving way to confusion. "What are you talking about?"

"They were all over each other last night, Nash. While he was high on Demon's Breath. And it probably wasn't the first time. She could be accidentally inhaling what he exhales."

Horror flitted across Nash's face, greens and browns

twisting in his irises, then he closed his eyes and reset his expression before I was even sure of what I'd seen, effectively locking me out of his thought process.

I leaned against his headboard and fiddled with his pillowcase. "Tod says it's highly addictive and ultimately *deadly* to humans. What if she gets hooked on it, too? What if she already is?"

Nash sighed and sank onto the bed, facing me. "Look, we don't even know that Fuller's actually addicted, okay? We just know he took some last night. And to even be exposed, Emma would have had to suck air straight from his lungs, right after he inhaled. And the chances of that are almost nil. Right?"

"How do you know? He was still exhaling enough for me to smell it on him, and they've been all over each other for the past two weeks. Are you sure she couldn't have gotten even a tiny bit by kissing him?"

"I seriously doubt it, Kaylee." But before he regained control of his eyes, I saw the truth in the nervous swirl of color. Nash wasn't sure. And he was scared.

He exhaled heavily, then met my gaze again. "Okay, we'll find out if he knows what he was taking and where he got it. But if he doesn't know, don't tell him what it is, okay? No more full disclosures to friends. Emma was plenty."

"Fine." I wasn't exactly eager to tell anyone else I wasn't human, anyway.

"You have to be at work at noon?" I nodded, and he

pulled off the shirt he'd just put on, then tossed it at his open hamper like a basketball. "We'll leave as soon as I get out of the shower."

"After breakfast," I corrected on my way to the door, smiling over my victory. "Your mom's making muffins."

In the kitchen, I waited for Nash in a rickety chair at the scratched, round table, watching Harmony wash dishes.

"So are you enjoying your freedom?" She glanced at me over her shoulder as she set a metal bowl in the dish drainer.

I shrugged. "I haven't experienced much of it yet."

She dried a clean, plastic-coated whisk, dropped it into an open drawer, then leaned against the counter and eyed me in blatant curiosity. "Was it worth it?"

"Was it worth being grounded?" I asked, and she nodded. "Yes. And no. Getting Regan's soul back was totally worth it." Four weeks of house arrest were nothing compared to the eternity she would have suffered without her soul. "But there was nothing we could do for Addy." And every time I thought about that, my stomach pitched like I was in freefall, a mixture of guilt and horror over my failure.

"Do you still hear from Regan?" Harmony asked when I didn't elaborate.

"Not very often. I think it's easier for her to try to forget about what happened with Addy." About the fact that her sister had been damned to eternal torment because she died without her soul. With nothing to release upon her death but a lungful of Demon's Breath.

And suddenly I had an idea… "Do you think Regan will be okay? Because of the Demon's Breath, I mean. Tod said it's really dangerous."

Harmony nodded absently, opening the oven door to check the muffins. "It certainly can be. Demon's Breath decays your soul. It rots the parts of you that make you you."

Okay, that's not terrifying….

"But on the surface, it acts a bit like a very strong hallucinogenic drug. It'll make you see and hear things that aren't there."

Which would explain why Doug thought someone had been in the car with him…

Harmony continued, sounding every bit like the nurse she was. "It's also highly addictive, and even if it doesn't kill you quickly, long-term use can lead to brain damage and psychosis."

I swallowed the huge lump that had formed in my throat and hoped my voice sounded normal. "Psychosis, like, insanity?"

"Simply put, yes. A complete loss of contact with reality." She used a pot holder to pull the muffin pan from the oven, then kicked the oven door closed. "And withdrawal is even worse. It sends the entire system into shock and can easily be fatal, even to someone who survived the substance itself."

"Great..." I whispered. So cutting off Doug's supply might kill him even faster than the Demon's Breath would.

"Oh, no, hon!" I looked up to find her watching the horror surely growing on my face. "Don't worry about Regan. She wasn't huffing Demon's Breath for a high—she was sustained by it in the absence of her soul. That's a totally different ball game. Still very dangerous, for obvious reasons," she conceded with a shrug. "That whole sell-your-soul thing. But very little risk to her, physically."

"Because she didn't have a soul..." My mind was racing. "But if she inhaled Demon's Breath now that her soul's back in place..."

Harmony frowned. "She'd be in very serious trouble."

AN HOUR LATER Nash turned his mother's car onto a brick driveway in front of a huge house with a coordinating brick-and-stone facade. And I'd thought Scott's place was crazy. Whatever Doug Fuller's parents did, they made some serious cash.

"You think he's home?" I asked, and Nash pointed at the spotless, late-model sports car in the driveway, with a rental sticker on the rear windshield.

He turned off the engine and stuffed the keys into his pocket. "Let's get this over with."

Doug answered the door on the third ring in nothing but the sweatpants he'd obviously slept in, then backed into a bright, open entryway to let us in. We followed him to a sunken den dominated by a wall-size television, where a video game character I couldn't identify stood frozen with a pistol aimed at the entire room.

"Sorry about your car." Doug plopped onto a black leather home theater chair without even glancing at me.

"Um…" But before I could finish the nonthought, he waved off my reply and picked up a video controller from the arm of his chair.

"My dad'll pay for the damages. The rental place is supposed to deliver your loaner this afternoon. I got you a V6."

Just like that? Was he serious? I got weird death visions and a supersonic shriek, and Doug Fuller got unreasonable wealth. That was a serious imbalance of karma.

"Trust me—it's a step up."

My fists clenched in my coat pockets. How could Emma stand him?

"Um, thanks," I said, for lack of anything even resembling an intelligent reply. I looked at Nash with both brows raised, silently asking what he was waiting for. He dropped onto a black leather couch and I sat next to him.

"So was your dad pissed about the drug test? You must have been high as a satellite to hit a parked car." Nash slouched into the couch, sounding almost jealous, and that must have been the right approach because Doug grinned and paused his game.

"Dude, I was in *orbit*." He set the remote on the arm of his chair and grabbed a can of Coke from the drink holder. "But the test came out clean, other than a little alcohol. The E.R. doc told my dad I was probably euphoric from shock."

"What the hell were you taking?" Nash leaned forward and took two Cokes from the minifridge doubling as an end table.

"Somethin' called frost. It's like huffing duster inside a deep freeze, but then you're high for hours...."

Chill bumps popped up all over my skin and I shuddered at the memory of dozens of creepy little fiends crawling all over one another in the Netherworld, desperate for a single hit of Demon's Breath—preferably straight from the source.

Nash handed me a can and raised one brow to ask if I was okay. He'd noticed the shudder. I nodded and popped the top on my Coke.

"Where'd you get it?" Nash leaned back on the couch and opened his own soda.

"From some guy named Everett. I think that's his last name. I got a physical next Tuesday, and he swore this frost shit wouldn't show up in a blood test." Doug's focus shifted to me. "Hey, Kaylee, do you know if Em's working tonight?"

"Yeah. I think she's closing." Actually, we'd both be off by four in the afternoon, but I didn't want her hanging out with Doug until I was sure he wasn't going to freeze-dry her lungs with every kiss.

Nash set his can on the minifridge. "You have any more of this frost?"

"Nah. I had an extra balloon, but I sold it yesterday." One corner of his mouth twitched twice, and my stomach flipped. The fiend we'd met in the Netherworld had twitched just like that, from withdrawal. "And I huffed the last of mine last night."

"It comes in a balloon?" Nash frowned and his irises suddenly went still, like he'd flipped the off switch on his emotional gauge.

"Yeah. Black party balloons, like the kind we used to pop in the back of the class to watch Ms. Eddin's substitute jump. Remember, back in eighth grade?"

Nash nodded absently.

"What friend?" I demanded, my hands both clenched around my Coke. "Who did you sell the other balloon to?" But I knew the answer before Doug even opened his mouth. Because that's just the kind of luck I had.

Doug picked up his game controller, his hand twitching around the plastic. "Scott Carter."

My heart dropped into my stomach. I was right. He'd

sold his other balloon to my cousin's boyfriend. And Sophie was cold enough on her own, without exposure to secondhand frost.

"THAT'S JUST GREAT!" I buckled my seat belt as Nash shifted into Reverse. "Doug exposes Emma, then sells half his supply to Scott, who's just going to turn around and drag Sophie into the whole mess. It's an epidemic. How are we supposed to stop an epidemic?"

"It's not an epidemic." Nash twisted in his seat to check behind us while he backed down the driveway. "It's two guys who have no idea what they're into." The car rocked as the tires dropped from the brick driveway onto the smoother surface of the road, then Nash settled into his seat facing forward. "And I really don't think they could expose Emma or Sophie to secondhand Demon's Breath. Or would that actually be thirdhand?" He tried on a halfhearted grin to go with his joke, but couldn't pull it off.

"But you don't actually know that, right? You can't know for sure that they haven't been exposed."

"No, but I don't think—"

"Why are you trying to brush this off? This isn't like having a drink at a party or lighting up behind the shop building. We're talking about humans inhaling the toxic life force sucked out of a demon from another *world.*" Quite possibly the weirdest sentence I'd ever said aloud… "And according to your mom, if they survive addiction—and that's a big if—their scrambled brains'll make Ozzy Osbourne look rational and coherent."

And as far as I was concerned, insanity—including the risk of being locked up in some mental ward—was worse than death, which would simply put an end to the terminal drama and angst of human existence. Unless you were stupid enough to sell your immortal soul like Addy had…

Nash's silence drew my gaze, and I found him staring at me, rather than at the road. "You asked my *mother* about Demon's Breath?" His voice held a hard quality I'd rarely heard from him before, like his words formed the bricks in a wall I was destined to crash into.

"In reference to Regan." I rubbed my palms over the denim covering my legs. "I didn't mention Doug or Emma." At least, not in the same sentence as Demon's Breath. "I'm not stupid, Nash."

"Neither is she!" His palm slammed into the steering wheel and I jumped, then a sharp jolt of anger skittered up my spine. "She knows. You ran your mouth off, and now she knows everything. Great, Kaylee. Thanks."

"She doesn't know. What is *wrong* with you?" I demanded, fighting to keep from shouting.

"Even if she doesn't know yet, if this gets as bad as you seem to think it will, she's going to figure out why you were asking, and then we're both going to be in serious trouble, Kaylee!"

I rolled my eyes. "If this gets as bad as I *know* it will, having your mother mad at us will be the least of our problems." I paused, waiting until my point had a chance to sink in, and when his grip on the wheel eased, I continued, trying to ignore his clenched jaw and tense posture. "We need to know if Scott's tried it yet." Thus, whether Sophie was in any potential danger. "And we have to get that balloon away from him, then figure out where this Everett guy is getting his supply."

Nash exhaled heavily and answered without looking at me. "Yeah. You're right." But he didn't seem very happy about it.

The rest of the ride was quiet and uncomfortable. I was mad at him for getting mad at me, and I didn't know how to deal with any of that. We'd never had a real fight before.

So we rode in silence and I got lost in my own head, trying to figure out how Demon's Breath had gotten into the human world in the first place, and how best to wrestle it from the privileged, demanding hands of the

Eastlake football team without turning both of us into social rejects.

I didn't even realize I'd fallen asleep until I woke up in the Cinemark parking lot with my face against the cold passenger's side window. Confused, I blinked and sat up to find Nash watching me, frowning, his hands clenched around the wheel again.

"You okay?" He looked upset, but made no move to reach for me across the center console.

"Yeah." I stomped on the floorboard, trying to ease the tingling in my left foot, which hadn't woken up along with the rest of my body. "Just worried about this whole frost mess." I glanced at the dashboard clock, surprised to see that my shift started in ten minutes. "And tired, I guess."

Nash nodded, but his worried look held. "Hey, I'm sorry I got mad. I'll find out if Scott's tried it yet."

"Thanks." I smiled, determined to take him at his word. I didn't understand his change of heart, but I'd take it.

"You need a ride home?" he asked as I opened the car door and hauled my duffel into my lap from the rear floorboard.

"Em said she'd take me. I'll call you when I get home."

His grin that time looked more natural. "Is your dad still working overtime?"

"Yeah."

"I'll bring pizza if you pick up a movie."

"Deal."

He leaned in for a kiss, and I kissed him back, trying to believe everything would be okay. "Don't worry about Scott's balloon," he said as I got out of the car. "I'll take care of it."

I CHANGED INTO my ugly red-and-blue polyester uniform in the bathroom, then pulled my hair into a ponytail and met Emma in the box office, where she was already counting the cash in her drawer. Somehow she'd scored us matching shifts selling tickets, which almost never happened. Usually one or the other of us got stuck scooping popcorn or emptying trash cans.

I counted my own drawer in silence, trying to decide whether or not to tell her to stay away from Doug. And what to cite as the reason.

I wasn't sure if she knew what he was taking, and even if she did, I couldn't tell her what frost really was. Not without scaring the crap out of her, anyway. And my policy on Emma and Netherworld stuff was to keep the two as far apart as possible, for as long as possible. How was I supposed to know Netherworld trouble would find her all on its own?

Finally, after two hours, a steady stream of customers, and a snack break during which I'd done little more than nod along with her chatter, she went suddenly silent on the stool next to mine, sitting straighter as she aimed a bright smile through the window in front of us. I looked up to find a familiar face halfway down the line across from Emma's register.

Doug Fuller.

I had to nudge Emma into giving change to an elderly lady taking a small child to see a PG-13 comedy. Emma slid the change and receipt under the window, then glanced at me as her next customer ordered two tickets for a Japanese horror flick. "Doug's here," she whispered.

I ran a debit card through the scanner, then dropped it into the dip in the counter beneath the pane of glass. "I see him." And I didn't like what I saw.

Oh, I understood the attraction. He was tall, and dark, and undeniably hot, and was just edgy enough—he didn't care what *anyone* thought of him, including his own friends—to intrigue Emma. But Doug wasn't just "she's so drunk she doesn't know what she's doing" dangerous. He was "spend the rest of your life in a padded cell" dangerous. And that was the best-case scenario.

"I knew I should have waited to take my break." Emma slid three tickets and a receipt beneath the glass to her next customer, glancing at Doug every chance she got.

"Em, what do you see in him? I mean, other than the obvious." Because for a short-term, nontoxic, casual good time, the obvious would have been plenty.

She shrugged and slid two more tickets under the

glass. "I don't know. He's hot and he's fun. Why does it have to be deeper than that? We're not all looking for a lifetime commitment at sixteen, Kay."

"I'm not..." I started to argue, then gave up. I wasn't sure what I was looking for from Nash, but it definitely wasn't short-term fun. "Em, I don't think you should—"

"Shhhh!" she hissed as Doug stepped up to the counter, his lopsided grin showing off just one dimple, and I knew I'd lost her. She smiled and leaned forward on the counter, and somehow her uniform clung to her curves, where mine only hung from my angles. "Hey."

"Hey. So, you wanna come over after you close?" he said, and the people in line behind him started grumbling.

I slid a debit card beneath the glass on my side of the counter and tried not to groan out loud.

Reason number eighteen that Kaylee should not lie: she never gets away with it.

Em frowned. "I'm not closing—it's a school night. I get off in two hours."

"But Kaylee said..." Doug glanced at me, and I stared at the counter, relieved when the customer behind him moved into my line, giving me something to do.

"She was wrong." Em was mad. Of *course* she was mad. "Meet me at five?"

"Uh, I gotta do something first." His hand jerked on

the counter, and my stomach pitched. "I'll pick you up at seven."

"Okay." Emma smiled for him, but didn't even look at me until he'd stepped out of line, already heading down the steps toward the parking lot. She served her next customer in silence while I handed back change, then both lines were empty for the moment.

Emma turned on me while Doug veered toward the rental I'd seen in his driveway, now double-parked in two handicapped spots on the front row. "What the hell, Kaylee?"

I twisted on my stool, brainstorming damage control that would not come. "I'm sorry. I just… I don't think he's good for you."

"Because he hit your car? That was an accident, and I'm sure he'll pay for it."

"Yeah. He already got me a loaner."

"Then what's the problem?"

I sighed, grasping for some way to explain without… well…*explaining.* My urge to protect her from all things Netherworld was overwhelming, and my gut was all I had to go on at the moment. "He's not safe, Emma."

She rolled her eyes. "I don't want safe. I want fun, and Doug is fun."

"Yeah, he's so fun he tried to haul you off while you were drunk. What do you think would have happened next, Em?"

"Nothing I didn't want to do." She crossed her

arms beneath her breasts. "What? You think Nash is perfect?"

My pulse spiked and I thought about him Influencing his way up my shirt that morning. But Em didn't know about that. "What's that supposed to mean?"

"Nothing." Emma sighed and leaned with both elbows on the counter, watching through the glass as Doug unlocked his car. "I'm just saying guys only come in a couple of models, and Nash didn't exactly break the mold. So lay off my boyfriend until you're ready to take a closer look at yours."

I had no idea what to say to that. So Nash was getting a little pushy. That was nothing compared to Doug breathing toxic fumes all over her.

In the lot, Doug's arm twitched as he pulled open his car door. Emma didn't even notice, but I knew what those twitches meant, and I was pretty sure I knew what he had to do before he picked her up. I had to tell her something—had to at least warn her, if I couldn't keep her away from him.

I took a deep breath and twisted on my stool to face her as Doug pulled out of the lot. "Emma, Doug's into something new. Something really bad. It's called frost."

She frowned, ignoring the customer who stepped up to her window. "What are you talking about?"

"Just listen. Please. It comes in a black balloon, and it *will* kill him. And if you inhale any of it, it could kill you, too. Or drive you insane. For real."

Emma's frown deepened. "You're serious?"

"*So* serious." I looked straight into her brown eyes, wishing she could see the sincerity surely swirling in mine. "Nash and I saved your life once and I'm trying to do it again. If you see Doug with a black balloon or even if he just starts acting weird, go home. Okay? Whatever you're doing, just stop and go home."

The man in front of the glass knocked on the window, but we both ignored him.

Emma's eyes widened and she clutched the counter. "Kaylee, you're kind of creeping me out."

"I know." I took both of her hands when she started to turn toward the window. "But you have to promise you'll go home if he starts acting weird. Swear."

"Fine, I swear," she said as the man knocked harder and a second customer appeared in front of my window. "But I gotta tell ya, you're the one acting weird right now, Kay."

I knew that, too. But at least my brand of weird probably wasn't going to get anybody killed. No one other than me, anyway.

"YOU WANT THE GOOD news, or the bad?" Nash asked as soon as I opened the front door. I took the pizza from him and he pulled the door shut as he stepped inside.

"Bad first." Because I was a "get it out of the way" kind of gal. I set the pizza box on the coffee table and headed into the kitchen for a couple of sodas. He tossed his jacket over one of the chairs around the table in our eat-in kitchen.

"Okay, Carter has tried the balloon, and I think he was still flying pretty high when I got there this afternoon. He was talking fast and leaping from one subject to the next. I could hardly keep up with him."

"But Doug didn't act anything like that. He was slurring and reacting kind of sluggish. And seeing things."

"I know." Nash flipped open the pizza box and sank onto the couch. "It seems to be affecting them both differently. But the good news is that Sophie's at the Winter Carnival committee fundraiser, so the chances of her inhaling anything from him tonight are pretty slim. If that's even possible. She's probably safe until tomorrow."

"This good news isn't sounding so good." I set a Coke can on the end table nearest him.

"Okay, then how 'bout this…" He pulled me onto his lap, and my unopened soda fell from my hand to roll under the coffee table. "I talked him into bringing the balloon to school tomorrow, so I can 'try' it."

My smile reflected his own. "And we're gonna get rid of it before he has a chance to share, right?"

Nash's grin widened, and he kissed me before lowering me to the couch next to him. "That's the plan."

"Okay, I like that part. So, how are we going to get the balloon? Ask Tod to pop in and snatch it for us?"

"Even better." He leaned to one side and dug in his

hip pocket, then pulled out a single key with an electronic lock on a plain silver ring.

I frowned. "You stole Scott's car key?" Yes, it was convenient, and meant we wouldn't have to actually break into the car, which was equally illegal. Still…

Nash shook his head. "I just borrowed it from the kitchen junk drawer. He won't notice it's gone until he locks himself out of his car again, and with any luck, I'll have it back way before then. How else are we supposed to get into his car?"

"Tod can do it without stealing a key."

He raised a brow in challenge, pulling one slice of pizza free from the others. "Does that make it morally acceptable?"

"No, that makes it easier and safer. Tod won't get caught, and we won't be connected to a B and E on school grounds."

"Tod got in trouble for missing too much work," Nash said around a mouthful of pepperoni. "So he's working for the next forty-eight hours straight, with no breaks. Evidently some poor old lady lingered on the wrong side of a second heart attack when the first should have done the job."

Great…

"So unless you know how to pop a car lock, this is our best bet." Nash held up the key, and his nonchalance made me distinctly uncomfortable. Unfortunately, he was right.

Was unlawful entry really any worse than theft, anyway? And did confiscating a toxic Netherworld substance even count as theft?

I nodded reluctantly, and Nash slid the key into his pocket. "You don't trust me."

"It's not about trust. I don't want to get caught breaking into Scott's car."

"We're not gonna get caught. And if we do, he won't get mad. No one ever gets mad at me, Kaylee. I have a way with words…." He leaned closer, teasing me with a short kiss, his mouth open just enough to invite me in. Just enough so that I missed his lips the moment they were gone.

"I got mad at you this morning," I whispered as he angled us back on the couch, reaching down to lift my right leg onto the cushion.

He pulled my left leg up on his other side, bent at the knee, then leaned over me, propped up on his elbows. "Yeah, but you got over it." Nash kissed me, and I got lost in him. I *wanted* to be lost in Nash, to forget about fear, and danger, and death, and everything that wasn't him, and me, and us. Just for a few minutes, to forget about everything else. Nash made that possible. He made that inevitable.

He made me feel so good. Beautiful, and wanted, and needed, in a way I'd never been needed before. Like if he didn't have me, he wouldn't have *anything*.

And I wanted him to have me. I wanted to have him.

But I couldn't. Because what if Emma was right? What if he was like all the others, and once I'd been had, he'd need someone else?

His tongue trailed down my neck and my head fell back on the throw pillow, my mouth open. My eyes closed. His hand slid beneath my shirt and I gripped the cushion under me. I could feel him through our clothes. Ready. Needing.

But Nash was right before—I didn't trust him. I couldn't, because if he wasn't perfect, I didn't want to know about it. Not yet. I wanted to sleep with Nash, but that's not what I needed.

I needed him to break the mold.

"Wait."

"Hmmm?" But then he kissed me before I could repeat myself. His hand slid farther, his cold fingers crawling over my ribs. His mouth sucked at mine, and I couldn't talk. I could hardly breathe.

When his other hand found the waist of my jeans, I turned my head and shoved him with both hands. "I said stop."

He frowned. "What's the problem? I'm not using any Influence."

"I know. Just…slow down."

He sat up and frowned while I tugged my shirt back into place. "If we go any slower, we'll be moving back in time. You've been teasing me for months, Kaylee. Anyone else would already have walked away."

My face burned like he'd slapped me. "I'm not a tease, but you're starting to sound like a real jackass. If you wanna walk, I'm sure you won't have any trouble finding someone a little more cooperative."

Nash sighed, scrubbing his face with both hands. "I don't want someone else. I want you."

Yeah. More of me than I was ready to give. But I wanted him, too. "Let's just watch the movie, okay?"

"Fine."

The ache in my heart eclipsed the other aches I was trying to ignore, but before I could figure out what to say to make it better without giving in, he stood and crossed the room to start the DVD.

I ran my hands through my hair, searching for a change of subject to act as a reset button on the entire evening.

"Doug showed up at the Cinemark this afternoon," I said, grabbing my Coke from the floor. I tapped the top to settle the bubbles. "He's picking Emma up tonight, so I made her promise to go home if he starts acting weird." Hopefully she wouldn't think twice about taking his rental, since she wouldn't have her car.

Nash turned to look at me, his eyes narrowed. "You didn't tell her…"

"What frost really is?" I shook my head. "I just told her that he'd gotten ahold of something bad." I searched his eyes for disapproval, but found only leftover frustration. "I had to tell her something."

"I know." Nash grabbed the remote from the top of the TV and changed the input. "How did Fuller look?"

"Twitchy." I turned and dropped my feet onto his lap when he sank onto the opposite end of the couch, universal remote in hand. "I think he's picking up another balloon tonight." I made a mental note to call and check on Emma before bed, to make sure she sounded like herself and that Doug hadn't gone all psych ward on her.

I sipped from my soda as thoughts—dark possibilities, really—sloshed in my mind like murky swamp water. "Did Scott say anything about Everett? Does he know him?"

"Nope." Nash grabbed the slice of pizza he'd already started on and handed another one to me. "He's never met the guy. He thinks Fuller's holding out on him." He tore a bite from his pizza and spoke around it. "So what do you think a party balloon goes for on the street these days?" Nash grinned, trying to lighten the mood, but the idea of some creepy Pennywise peddling balloons full of Demon's Breath on the corner scared the crap out of me, and I struggled to purge the visual.

What if we'd discovered the problem too late? What if Doug's dealer had already been peddling his product all over central Texas, or worse, all over the state? Or the entire south? After all, what were the chances that we *happened* to go to school with the only human in the area who huffed Demon's Breath?

No, my inner logic insisted. If people were dropping dead or being admitted to mental hospitals in record numbers, we'd have heard about it. This was just starting, which meant it was still fixable. It had to be.

I took a deep breath, then another drink from my can. "I think the real question is, what is Everett? If he's human, where's he getting his supply? And if he's not, what is he doing here?"

Nash shrugged. "Evil, would be my guess. That's kind of a Netherworld specialty."

"Okay, but as far as diabolical Netherworld schemes go, getting a bunch of human teenagers high, hooked, then dead is kind of lame." I looked at my pizza, but couldn't bring myself to actually eat it. "I mean, how good can the repeat business be if the customers are all gonna die?"

Nash chewed some more, apparently giving the idea some serious thought. "Nobody's dead yet."

But we both knew that was only a matter of time.

Or was it?

I dropped my uneaten slice into the box and grabbed the remote, poking the pause button until the image on the screen froze. "Maybe no one's going to die from this. You can't die if it's not your time, right? If you're not on the list?" The reaper's list, which contained the names of everyone whose soul was scheduled to be collected on a given day. Tod talked about the list like it was scribbled by the hand of Fate herself, thus could not be changed.

Of course, being driven insane wasn't much better than death. But at least I wouldn't have to scream for those hauled away in straitjackets.

But Nash didn't look very relieved.

"Kay, it doesn't work like that. Demon's Breath is a Netherworld element. It trumps the list, just like actually crossing into the Netherworld."

My heart hurt like it was being twisted within my chest, and my throat felt almost too thick to breathe through. "So, even if we got in touch with Tod and he got his hands on the master list, he couldn't tell us who's most at risk from this. Or how far it's going to spread."

Nash shook his head slowly. "There's no way to track this, and no way to know who's going to die from it. Not until…"

He didn't have to say it. I knew.

"Not until I start screaming."

"WHAT'S WRONG WITH YOU two today?" Emma speared a cherry tomato in her salad. Which was really just a mountain of iceberg lettuce dotted with croutons and smothered in cheese, ham, and ranch dressing. Emma didn't do health food, and I'd always respected that about her. "You look like you're waiting for a bomb to go off."

Not a bomb. A football player. We'd seen Scott Carter in the hall before first period, and his eyes had a familiar fevered look, yet his breath was too-sweet and *cold,* like he'd been chewing ice. He was high. On frost. At school.

Maybe having him bring it with him wasn't such a good idea, after all....

Before I could come up with an answer, Emma's gaze

strayed over Nash's shoulder and her eyes flashed with something like desire or anticipation, only stronger. More fervent. I twisted on the bench to see Doug pushing his way through a huddle of freshmen in front of the pizza line.

Emma smiled at him, and I wanted to break my own skull open on the white brick wall behind her.

Around us, the cafeteria buzzed with conversation, individual words and voices muted by the steady swell of sound. Our school was a closed campus for the entire first semester, thanks to a fender bender in the parking lot the second week of school, so nearly a third of the student body was crammed into four rows of indoor picnic-style tables. For most of the year, Em and I ate outside in the quad, but in December, even Texas was too cold for all but the truly hardy—and those in desperate need of a secret smoke—to brave the winter chill.

"So, I take it last night went well?" I dipped a corn chip into my cheese sauce, but couldn't bring myself to eat it as I watched her closely for some sign that her attraction to Doug went beyond the usual hormonal tidal wave. But I saw nothing but the hair tosses and challenging eye contact she usually saved for guys old enough to drink. Or at least date her college-age sisters.

"Does she really *like* this ass-wipe?" Tod said, appearing suddenly on the bench beside me.

The corn chip in my hand shattered, but for once I managed not to jump and look like an idiot in front of Nash and Em, who clearly couldn't see the reaper this time. Wasn't he supposed to be a virtual prisoner at Arlington Memorial for another day or so?

But I couldn't ask without looking crazy in front of half the varsity football team sitting at the other end of the table.

"*So* well." Emma's voice went deep and throaty, and I glanced briefly at Tod with one raised brow, silently asking if that answered his question.

He scowled, then blinked out, and I wiped cheese sauce from my fingers with a paper napkin. I knew what I had against Doug, but why did Tod care who Emma liked? I'd assumed he'd let go of his crush on her when Addison had stepped back into—then quickly out of—his life a month ago.

Evidently, I was wrong, and the implications of that settled into my gut like a brick in a bucket of water. How would a grim reaper—someone no longer bound by the limitations of mortal existence—deal with the potential competition Doug Fuller represented?

Oh, *crap!*

Someone was selling Demon's Breath in the human world, and Tod had on-demand access to the Netherworld. Doug had sworn someone had appeared in his passenger's seat on Saturday night when he'd hit my car, and Tod had the infuriating habit of popping in anywhere he wanted, whenever he wanted, to whomever he wanted....

Was it possible?

No. I almost shook my head before I realized no one else knew what I was thinking. Tod wouldn't do that. Not that he'd hesitate to sabotage the competition if he ever decided he was serious about Emma. But he wouldn't do anything to jeopardize his job—because an unemployed reaper was a dead reaper—or Emma, one of the few humans he actually cared about.

Still… I made a mental note to mention the possibility—however slim—to Nash the next time we were alone.

"Hey." Doug dropped onto the bench next to Emma, straddling the seat with his left thigh against her backside. He reached across the table to slap Nash's hand in greeting, then turned to me. "How's the loaner working out?"

"Fine." I dunked another chip and tried to hate Doug quietly, so Emma wouldn't notice. It would be hard to protect her if she wasn't speaking to me.

Doug ran one hand slowly up and down Emma's back. "What are you doing after school?"

"Working. But then I'll be home. Alone."

"Want some company?"

"Maybe…" She bit into a cube of ham speared on her plastic fork, and Doug's hand moved slowly beneath the table, probably working its way up her thigh. Then something behind me caught his eye, and he tossed his head at someone over my shoulder.

I turned to find Scott Carter making his way across the cafeteria toward us, a tray in one hand, his other arm around Sophie's thin shoulders. Scott set his tray down and sank onto the bench next to Doug. Sophie took a bruised red apple from Scott's tray and bit into it, chewing in angry silence while she tried to avoid my eyes.

Or maybe she was trying to avoid being seen with me.

"We still on for this afternoon?" Scott asked Nash, twisting the lid on a bottle of Coke, then tightening it before it could fizz over. "I'm parked on the west side, near the gym." His eyes looked a little clearer, and I could no longer smell the Demon's Breath on him. He was coming down from his initial high, and I couldn't help but wonder how long it would be before he'd need another fix. And what that need would look like on him.

Would Sophie notice something was wrong? Would his teachers? His parents were still out of town....

"Yeah." Nash shoved the last bite of his cafeteria hamburger into his mouth and picked up his own soda. "I'll be there right after the last bell."

But Scott's stash would *not*.

"You still have what I gave you?" Doug glanced anxiously between Nash and Scott, having caught on to the subject.

"What you *sold* me," Scott corrected.

"Whatever." Doug finally removed his hand from

Emma's thigh and leaned closer to Scott. I chewed, pretending not to listen while Sophie and Emma exchanged rare twin looks of confusion. "I need to buy it back, but I can replace it this weekend."

Scott squirted a mustard packet on his hamburger. "I thought you were gonna have more today?"

Doug shook his head. "Didn't pan out. Sell me yours. I'll pay extra."

"No way." Scott shook his head and picked up his burger. Sophie and Emma weren't even pretending to eat anymore. "But you can have a hit after school with Hudson—" he nodded in Nash's direction "—if you give me your guy's name and number."

Doug's jaw tightened and his eyes narrowed. "I already gave you his name, and there *is* no number. But I'm gonna see him this weekend for sure. I can get you another one then, if you pay up front."

Nash stiffened next to me, and I knew he was thinking what I was thinking. Everett. This weekend. That was our best chance.

"Same as last time?" Scott asked, and my stomach twisted in on itself as Emma glanced at me, brows arched in question.

"Yeah," Doug said, and Sophie rolled her eyes, glossy pink fingernails digging into the skin of her apple.

"I'm bored," she whined. "You guys are like walking sedatives."

"You got something more interesting to talk about?"

Scott snapped, dipping a limp French fry in ketchup. "And don't say the Winter Carnival."

Sophie pouted, gesturing with her apple. "It's on Saturday, and you guys *promised* you'd help with the booths this afternoon." They all had their afternoons free, since football season had ended with a loss to the new Texas state AA champions.

"I'm not feelin' it, Soph." Scott raised one brow and his frown grew into a lecherous grin. "But maybe you could convince me..." He pushed his tray across the table and leaned back, watching her expectantly.

Sophie went from shrew to succubus in less than a second, straddling Scott so boldly that I glanced around, sure there would be a teacher stomping toward us from somewhere, intent on peeling her off.

But no teacher came. The two on duty were busy trying to confiscate a cell phone from some senior rumored to be showing off naked pictures of his girlfriend.

Sophie performed like a trained seal, and I was humiliated for her—because she didn't have the sense to be—but I couldn't look away from my cousin's spectacle. Until Scott's hand inched down from her waist toward the back of her overpriced jeans.

"Sophie, that's enough. Sit down before you get suspended."

The look she shot me could have frozen Satan's crotch, but she slithered off her boyfriend's lap, licking her lips like she could still taste him, while Doug, Scott, and the rest of the team watched her like she'd just danced around a pole. I shot Nash a "why the hell do you hang out with these jackholes" look, but he was unavailable to receive my withering glance. Because he was watching my cousin. But Emma was watching me, *I told you so* written clearly in her expression.

I frowned and elbowed Nash while Sophie reapplied her lipstick with a compact mirror. "So…" She snapped the compact closed and dropped it into her purse. "Any volunteers?"

"I'm in," Scott said, and I understood that Sophie's show was actually a preview of things to come. Was that how she got everything she wanted? "You guys got a couple of hours to spare this afternoon?" Scott glanced around the table for more volunteers.

Nash nodded, but Emma leaned around Doug to answer for us both. "Kaylee and I have to work."

"Oh, well." Sophie shrugged, and the bitch was back. "We'll miss you…" her mouth said, but as usual, her eyes said something entirely different.

When the bell rang, everyone got up to dump their trays, but Nash and I headed into the quad against the flow of smoke-scented traffic into the building, his cold fingers intertwined with mine. When the late bell rang eight minutes later, we sneaked around the outside of the school—the gym side, where there were no windows—and into the parking lot, ducking to run between the cars until we spotted Scott's. Fortunately, he'd parked out of view from the building exit.

The top was up on Scott's shiny, metallic-blue convertible, and through the rear window I saw nothing but a spotless interior; the car was so clean he probably made Sophie take off her shoes before getting in. On the back passenger's side floorboard sat a large green duffel bag. "It's either in there, or in the trunk," I whispered, though there was no one else around to hear us.

Nash dug in his left pocket and pulled out Scott's key. "Then let's get this over with."

He slid the key into the lock—presumably to avoid the telltale thump of the automatic lock disengaging—and glanced toward the building to make sure we were alone.

With the driver's door open, he reached through to unlock the back door, then pulled it open and gestured toward the rear seat. "Be my guest."

Rolling my eyes, I crawled into the backseat and tugged the bag into my lap. My heart thumped as I unzipped it, and I was suddenly sure Scott had put the balloon in his trunk. But there it was, a solid black balloon, next to a football and on top of a pair of green gym shorts, which weren't exactly fresh. I pulled the balloon out with both hands and gasped at the chill that sank immediately through my fingers. The balloon was so cold ice should have glazed its surface, flaking off to melt on my skin.

Yet, other than the temperature and the weighted

black plastic clasp holding it closed, the balloon felt just like any other latex party balloon. It was only half-inflated and I wondered how full it had been, and how much of the contents Scott had already inhaled. When I squeezed it gently, my fingers dimpled the surface and the rubber seemed to grow even colder.

"It's cold," I whispered, without taking my eyes off the balloon. *"Freezing..."*

Nash nodded. "There's a reason they call it frost. Don't you remember what Avari did to that office when he got pissed?"

I did remember. When the hellion had gotten mad, a lacy sheet of ice had spread across the desk beneath him and onto the floor, inching toward our feet, surging faster every time his anger peaked.

"Okay, zip the bag up and let's g—"

"Hudson?" A booming voice called from across the parking lot, and my blood ran as cold as the balloon.

Coach Rundell, the head football coach.

Nash waved his hand downward, inches from my head, and I dropped onto the backseat, bent in half over the balloon. On the way down, I glimpsed the coach between Scott's leather headrests. The middle-aged former jock stomped toward us from the double gym doors, his soft bulk confined by a slick green-and-white workout suit, bulging at the zipper.

"You're not allowed in the parking lot during the school day, Hudson," the coach barked. "You know that."

That ridiculous rule was supposed to stop kids from sneaking cigarettes or making out in backseats, and to prevent the occasional car break-in. Which we were committing, at that very moment.

Panicked now, as the cold from the balloon leached through my shirt and into my stomach, I craned my neck to see Nash digging frantically in his hip pocket. "Sorry, coach. I left my book in here this morning, and I need it for class."

"Isn't that Carter's car?"

Nash shrugged. "He gave me a ride."

Actually, Nash had ridden with me, in my new loaner. But Coach Rundell wasn't going to question his first-string running back. Even if he didn't believe Nash.

"Well, get what you came for and get back to class. You need a pass?"

"Yeah, thanks," Nash said, and I rolled my eyes as he bent into the backseat behind the headrest, where the coach couldn't see him clearly.

That figures. The football player steals a friend's key and breaks into his car, and he winds up with a free hall pass for his trouble. I'd probably be expelled.

Nash pressed Scott's car key into my hand. "Wait until we go in, then lock the balloon in your trunk. Got it?"

I shook my head, pocketing the key reluctantly. "I'm just going to pop it. That way no one else can get ahold of it."

Sudden panic whirled in Nash's irises. "You can't

pop it, Kaylee. What if you accidentally breathe some of it in?"

My pulse raced at the thought, fear chilling me almost as badly as the balloon I was trying not to crush. "Is it…as dangerous to *bean sidhes* as it is to humans?" I whispered.

Nash sighed. "No, but…" He stopped and shook his head sharply, as if to clear it. "I don't know. It's a controlled substance for a reason. It has to be disposed of carefully. I'm going to give it to Tod to take to the disposal facility in the Netherworld. Okay?"

I nodded grudgingly. "Fine."

Nash kissed me quickly on the cheek, then leaned past me to grab the chemistry book I'd brought to lunch. "I'll give it back to you after school." Hopefully the coach wouldn't know Nash was taking physics this year.…

He backed out of the car, held the book up for the coach's benefit, then closed the door, leaving me alone in the quarterback's car, with his stolen key and his stash of a rare, expensive inhalant.

No pressure, Kay.

I peeked between the headrests until Nash and the coach disappeared around the corner of the gym, then I sat up and shoved the frigid black balloon off my lap and onto the floor. I zipped Scott's duffel and put it back exactly where I'd found it, then glanced around the lot again before easing the door open. When I was sure I was alone, I grabbed the balloon, lurched out of the car, and shoved the door closed, then clicked a button on the key to lock it. Then I raced across the lot holding the balloon by its clip, to keep the unnaturally cold latex from touching my skin.

On my way across the asphalt, I slid Scott's key into my back pocket, then dug my own from my hip pocket, holding it ready as I skidded to a stop behind the rental. I jabbed the key into the trunk lock and twisted, relieved when the trunk popped open an inch on the first try. I'd never opened it and, according to Murphy's Law—which they might as well rename after me—it would malfunction when I needed it most.

I dropped the balloon into the carpeted compartment, glad when it sank with the weighted clip. Then I slammed the trunk closed and made myself walk toward the building, concentrating on regulating my breathing and heartbeat with each step.

The last thing I needed was to arrive for class flushed and out of breath.

Although now that I thought of it, that would give me an interesting alibi. Everyone would assume Nash and I had been *occupied,* and had missed the bell.

I smiled at that thought, and the smile stayed in place until I opened the door to my fifth-period English class, where every head in the room swiveled to look at me. And that's when I realized I'd forgotten to stop by my locker for my book.

"Miss Cavanaugh," Mr. Tuttle said, perched on the

edge of his desk with one sockless loafer dangling a foot from the floor. “How nice of you to join us. I don’t suppose you have a late pass? Or a textbook?”

I shook my head mutely and felt myself flush. So much for avoiding rumors…

“Well, now you *do* have detention.”

Naturally. Because detention seems like an appropriate reward for someone trying to save her school from a deadly Netherworld toxin, right?

"DETENTION FOR YOUR FIRST tardy?" Nash looked skeptical as he slammed his locker and tossed his backpack over one shoulder. All around us, other lockers squealed open and clanged closed. The hall was a steady din of white noise—the constant overlap of voices. The final bell had rung three minutes earlier and the entire student body had split into two streams: most of the underclassmen flowing toward the front doors and a line of long yellow buses, and most of the upperclassmen toward the parking lot.

"It was my third," I admitted, turning with Nash as he wrapped his free arm around my waist. "I was late twice last month, since *some*body thought it would be fun to take a private tour of the gym equipment closet while Coach Rundell was out for lunch."

Nash looked pleased with himself, rather than penitent. "Yeah, sorry about that."

"I bet *you* weren't counted tardy for either of those, were you?"

He shrugged. "No one cares if you're late to study hall."

I rolled my eyes. "Not so long as you're wearing a green-and-white jacket."

"You want to borrow it?" He grinned and made a show of pulling one arm from his sleeve. He seemed much more relaxed now that we'd relieved Scott of his Netherworldly burden.

"No thanks. I have too much self-respect."

"For school spirit?" He frowned, but his eyes still sparkled with mischief.

"For being the unmerited exception to the rules the rest of us plebeians have to follow."

"What rules?" Doug Fuller walked toward us with one arm around Emma, his hand splayed over the band of bare hip visible between the hem of her tee and the low waist of her jeans.

I scowled. "My point exactly."

"Hudson, your girlfriend's too serious." Doug dropped his duffel and ran one hand through a wavy mop of thick dark hair, pulling Emma closer.

"She can't help it," a familiar, cold-edged voice said from behind me, and I turned to find Sophie and Laura Bell leaning against the lockers, malice glinting in their eyes like sunlight off the point of a sharp knife. "The staff in the psycho ward *shocked* the fun right out of her."

Simultaneous waves of anger and humiliation surged through me, and for just a minute, I considered letting her take a hit from her boyfriend's balloon. Why was I trying so hard to save someone who would rather see me dead than return the favor?

"Don't look now, Sophie, but your insecurity's showing like the roots on a bad bleach job." Emma smiled sweetly, then glanced pointedly at Sophie's hairline. Then she turned on one wedge-heeled foot and headed down the hall toward the parking lot exit. Laughing, Doug jogged to catch up with her.

Nash and I trailed them while Sophie stood speechless. "You know, she loves it when you let her piss you off."

"Gee, thanks, Dad," I snapped, bending beneath the weight of my own sarcasm. "You think if I just ignore her, she'll go away?"

"No." Nash's hand tightened around mine and I glanced up to find him eyeing me steadily. "I think she's going to be a bitch no matter what you do. But you don't have to make it so easy for her. Make her work for it."

"Yeah." But that was a lot easier for him to suggest than for me to do. "It *kills* me that she has no idea that we saved her life. Or that she'd be just like me, if not for winning the genetic lottery." Sophie's father—my dad's younger brother—was a *bean sidhe,* and because her mother was human, Sophie could have been born like either of her parents. Fate, or luck, or whatever unfair advantage ruled her privileged life, had given her the normal, human genetic sequence, and a snottier-than-thou disposition that seemed to grow more toxic by the day.

"There's nothing you can do about that, Kaylee." Nash pushed open the door into the parking lot and a cold gust of wind blew my hair back as I stepped outside. "And anyway, considering that her mother died and her boyfriend's spending a small fortune to get high off someone else's bad breath, I'd say Sophie's next in line for therapy. At least you know who and what you are," he pointed out with an infuriating rationality. "Sophie knows there's something we're not telling her. Something about her family, and how her own mom died. And she may never find out the truth."

Because Uncle Brendon didn't want her to know that her mother had stolen five innocent lives and souls—including Sophie's, by accident—in exchange for eternal youth.

Nash shrugged. "For me, knowing that I actually feel sorry for her makes it a little easier to put up with the shit she's shoveling."

A warm satisfaction filtered through me at the realization that it *did* help to think of her as an object of pity:

a prospect that would horrify my pampered cousin to no end.

"And Kaylee, I'm sorry about last night. I can wait. You know that, right?"

"I know." He was calmer and happier now. Less intense than he'd been the night before. He'd obviously gotten plenty of sleep and backed off the caffeine.

"Thank you." I stood on my toes for a mint-flavored kiss—a better kiss than what he usually got on school grounds—and only pulled back when shouting from the other end of the parking lot caught our attention.

Scott had just discovered his frost was missing.

"Come on..." Nash took off and I held my backpack strap in place while I raced after him. My boots clomped on the concrete as we tore past my loaner, Doug's loaner, and dozens of other cars still parked in the lot. We had to be there to look surprised by Scott's loss.

Doug and Emma were huddled together in the empty space to the left of Scott's car, hands stuffed into their jacket pockets against the cold. Doug scowled, almost as angry as Scott over the loss. Next to him stood Brant Williams, who'd obviously been promised a sample, too. Other students watched all over the lot, curious but uninvolved.

And suddenly I was really glad we'd taken the balloon, in spite of the risk. This crowd was too big. How were we supposed to protect the entire school?

"Are you sure you brought it?" Doug tugged his duffel

higher on his shoulder and his hand twitched around the strap.

"Hell, *yes,* I'm sure." Scott punched the back of his front seat, which he'd folded forward for more room in the backseat. "I took a hit this morning before I got out of the car, then stuffed it in my gym bag. And now it's gone."

"What happened?" Nash asked as I wandered to the edge of the small crowd to stand with Emma. She tucked a long blond strand of hair behind one pierced ear, then shrugged to say she had no idea what was going on.

"Somebody broke into my car and stole my *shit,*" Scott snapped, and I wasn't the only one surprised by the sharp edge of fury in his voice. Not just anger, or frustration, or disbelief. Scott's words dripped with *rage,* laced with some dark, desperate need no one else seemed to understand. Not even Doug. But as his hand convulsed around the edge of the open car door, *I* understood.

Scott was going into withdrawal. For real. He wasn't just itching for another hit—he was physically, psychologically, maybe even soulfully, addicted. He couldn't function without frost now.

But that couldn't be right. He'd only had one balloon, and it was still half-full. How could this happen so fast?

With that thought, a new fear twisted in my stomach. Had we made everything worse by taking the balloon? Harmony had said withdrawal could be just as deadly as Demon's Breath itself....

But what were we supposed to do, give the balloon back, with our blessings? Let him sink into insanity and brain damage, and possibly drag Sophie along for the ride?

"Dude, calm down," Doug said, sniffling in the frigid wind, and I was relieved by the composed—if stuffy—quality of his voice. Somehow, though he'd been on frost longer than Scott and had taken more of it, he was obviously much less dependent on it. "Unless you want to explain to Coach what you're yelling about."

Scott only scowled and ducked into the backseat again, digging in the green-and-white duffel. But the volume of his anger and denial dropped low enough to avoid notice by the teachers monitoring the parking lot from near the west school entrance.

Nash dropped his bag at my feet, and I was impressed by how steady his cold-reddened hands were as he knelt to examine Scott's driver's side door, concentrating on the seal at the base of the window. "It doesn't look like it was forced, but all that would take is a coat hanger or a slim jim..." He stood and wiped his hands on his jeans, then opened the door wider and fiddled with the automatic lock to demonstrate that it still worked. "There doesn't seem to be any damage...."

But Scott wasn't listening. He was still digging in his bag, anger exaggerating his jerky movements, like he might somehow have overlooked a half-filled black latex balloon among the sweaty sports equipment.

I glanced around the lot for Sophie and found her watching with a couple of her dancer friends, all bundled up as they unloaded several gallons of paint and new brushes from Laura's trunk. Presumably to be used on the booths for the Winter Carnival.

"What's wrong with him?" Emma whispered, still staring at Scott's breakdown. "He's really freaking out."

I shrugged and shoved my frozen hands into my pockets. "I guess frost is pretty hard to come by."

Em huffed, and a white puff of her breath hung on the air. "What is it, anyway? Some kind of inhalant?"

"I don't know." I felt bad about lying to Emma, even if it was for her own good, so I compensated with a little bit of the truth. "But it's not good, Em. Look what it's doing to Scott."

Scott's anger simmered just shy of the boiling point. Fortunately, the small crowd had dispersed—all but the central players—and there weren't many people left to watch as Doug and Nash tried to talk him down. Less than a minute later, their efforts failed.

"Screw this!" Scott threw his bag into the car, where it smacked the passenger's side window, then tumbled to the floorboard. "I can't be here right now." He dropped into the driver's seat and shoved his key into the ignition. Then he slammed the door and gunned his engine before taking off straight across the parking lot. Bright winter sunlight glinted on his rear fender as he raced between two parked cars, sending students scrambling out of his way.

Across the lot, the teachers on duty scowled and crossed their arms over their chests, but there was nothing they could do, except be grateful no one was hit. And possibly recommend that the principal suspend his parking pass.

With Scott gone, and Nash and Doug conferring softly in the space he'd just vacated, my gaze settled on Sophie, who now stood alone in front of her friend's car, a bucket of paint hanging from each clenched fist. Her mouth hung open, her nose red from the cold, and I got a rare glimpse of pain and disappointment before she donned her usual arrogant scowl and marched across the lot in a pair of trendy flats, as if she couldn't care less that her boyfriend had just bailed on his promise to her without a word.

And everyone knew it.

"You sure Scott's okay to drive?" I asked as Nash placed his palms flat against my temporary car, on either side of me. I was trapped, but willingly, *deliciously* so, and when he leaned in for a kiss, I stood on my toes to meet him.

"Yeah, he's fine." Nash's mouth pressed briefly against mine, then he murmured his next sentence against my cheek, near my ear, which lent his words a tantalizing intimacy, in spite of the subject matter. "He's pissed, not high." Another kiss, this one a little longer and a lot deeper. "And I'll check on him when we get done here." He and Doug were going to stay and help the carnival committee, to honor their friend's promise in his time of...withdrawal. "Call me when you get off work?"

I ran my hand up the cold leather sleeve of his jacket. "Yeah. My dad's working late, and I think I might need help with my anatomy."

Nash's brows shot up. "You're not taking anatomy."

I grinned. "I know."

The next kiss was longer, and ended only when Sophie made a rude noise in the back of her throat, wordlessly calling on Nash to help carry the five-gallon buckets of white paint. He waved her off without turning away from me. "Leave them here, and I'll bring them in a minute."

Sophie stomped off, obviously irritated, but silent for once.

"Here, let me get the balloon before you go." Nash glanced around the lot to make sure no one was within hearing range as he unzipped his nearly empty backpack.

"Why don't you just come over and get it tonight?" I said, reaching to open the driver's door.

Nash frowned. "Has your dad checked out the loaner yet?"

"No. He passed out right after dinner last night."

"So what if he gets off early today and decides to take a look? You want him to find that in your car?"

"He's not gonna search the trunk, Nash."

His gaze hardened. "Just give me the balloon, Kaylee," he snapped.

I stepped back, surprised. "What's wrong with you? You're being a dick." And whatever was wrong with him was about more than a couple of strung out friends. It had to be.

Nash sighed and closed his eyes. "I'm sorry. I just don't want you driving around with that in your car. Please let me take care of it, so I won't have to worry about you."

"Fine." It was *not* fine, but I didn't want to argue. Again. "Give me your bag." I rounded the car and opened the trunk, standing ready in case the weighted balloon somehow rose and escaped. It did not. Instead of handing me his bag, Nash leaned into the trunk with it and shoved the balloon inside, then zipped it before anyone could see what he was doing. "Don't get caught with that," I warned. None of the teachers would know what it was, but anyone who'd seen Scott's meltdown might. "And don't forget to put his key back."

He grinned, good mood intact once again. "I'm a big boy."

"I know." But on the drive to work with Emma, all I could think about was Nash walking around with a balloon full of Demon's Breath in his backpack, where anyone might find it.

So after a later-than-expected shift at the Cinemark, I called him as I was getting ready for bed—I wouldn't be able to sleep until I knew he'd safely disposed of the balloon. He assured me he had given it to Tod, and we talked for about half an hour, until my dad knocked on my door and told me to hang up and go to sleep.

Rolling my eyes, I said good-night to Nash and turned off my lamp. But even once I'd curled up with one leg tossed over my extra pillow, I couldn't stop the slideshow playing behind my eyes.

Doug's car smashing into mine.

Scott's fit in the parking lot.

Nash holding the stolen balloon.

We were in deep with the Demon's Breath, and as I lay in my dark room, trying to sleep, something told me that taking Scott's stash was about as helpful as plugging a hole in the Hoover Dam with a chewed-up piece of gum....

"NOOOO!" MY OWN SHOUT echoed in my head like gunfire in a closed room, shocking me into semiawareness in spite of the thick gray haze swirling languidly around my ankles. The haze was like smoke—heavier than air and impossible to see through—except that it carried no heat and no stench of burned debris.

Hesitant to move when I couldn't see my surroundings, I turned in place, then turned again, searching the gray haze desperately for some familiar landmark. Or even an *un*familiar landmark. For anything that could tell me where I was. But I saw nothing but more grayness, as if I'd gone blind, and what lay behind my eyelids now was not the sparking, staticky darkness of closed eyes, but a vast, featureless expanse of gray.

A thing of nightmares.

Okay, Kaylee, think! I demanded silently. *Why were you screaming?*

For one long, terrifying moment, the answer wouldn't come. I didn't *know* why I'd been screaming. Then I sucked in a deep, fog-bitter breath and held it, focusing on how thick and oily the grayness tasted in my mouth. I wanted to spit it out, but I couldn't stop breathing it, because there was no fresh air to be found.

Then the answer came to me, slithering softly into my head like a snake into the solace of a dark pond. Hoping to escape notice.

I'd had a premonition. I'd been screaming because someone was going to die.

Crap! I was in the Netherworld. I had to be, because no place in my world had fog like the thick haze oozing over my jeans to curl around my hands, brushing my fingers like swabs of damp cotton.

Wait, that wasn't right, either. I'd never actually *seen* fog in the Netherworld. I'd only seen it layered over my own reality when I peeked into the Netherworld. So, was I peeking? And if so, why could I now feel the fog, which had always been a simple visual element before?

Something was wrong. I wasn't in the real Netherworld. I was in some stylized version of it as if I were…

Dreaming.

That's it! I was asleep, dreaming about someone's death. Which put me in some dream version of the

Netherworld, the best approximation my subconscious mind could come up with. And even as that truth sank in, the scream welled up in my throat again, greeting the dark, fuzzy form coming toward me out of the fog.

The walking dead.

It was human. Or at least humanlike, with head and shoulders in the proper proportions, and presumably matching pairs of arms and legs. I couldn't tell the figure's gender, though it was only feet from me now, because it was thoroughly obscured by the grayness, which seemed to thicken even as I thought of it.

I clamped my jaws shut against the scream scraping my throat raw and clenched my fists hard enough to draw blood with my nails, hoping to wake myself up. To leave this sleep-version Netherworld before I saw whose demise I was dreaming. Whose death my subconscious was predicting with every bit of stubborn certainty my waking body put into each screech that left my mouth.

But nothing happened. I felt no pain in my palms, saw no blood, and certainly did not wake up. And the figure kept coming.

Five feet away now, and its steps made no sound on the ground. Four feet away, yet there was no brush of fabric or click of heels.

Three feet, and the features started to come into focus through the Nether-smog. A nose. Two shadowy eyes, like the hollows of an unlit jack-o'-lantern. And a mouth like a great, dark void…

My throat hurt so bad I thought it would swell shut. It felt like I'd swallowed rose stems, thorns and all, and someone was trying to pull them back up.

Yet the sound kept coming.

In front of me, as I stood frozen in disharmonic agony, the figure stumbled and went down on one knee. A ghostly hand reached out for me, fingers penetrating the haze for one tortured moment before the hand fell, too, disappearing completely into the fog, along with the body.

But before the haze melted away, before the features came in clearly enough for me to identify, the real scream burst from my throat, slicing through the night—or day?—like a foghorn through the stormy sea.

And still I screamed.

I tried to bring one hand up to cover my mouth, to stop the sound rattling my teeth. But my hand was pinned to my side, though nothing held it there. My limbs were frozen, and with that realization, my panic doubled, dumping a fresh dose of adrenaline on top of the premonition-panic already fueling my wail.

And finally, with nothing left to try, I closed my eyes tight—relieved that they, at least, still seemed to follow my commands—and prepared to ride out the scream.

When the last hoarse note slipped through my mouth like the exhale of a dying man, I licked my lips, then swallowed gingerly. My throat hurt like I'd been gargling shards of glass.

A frigid breeze blew against my bare legs, raising chill bumps the length of my body, and a soft, eerie tinkling sound tickled my ears, a thousand wind chimes all jingling at once.

Wait, *bare legs?* Where did my jeans go?

My eyes flew open and devastating, terrifying comprehension sank through me, anchoring me to the ground where I stood as if I were mired in concrete. But I wasn't. I was mired in razor wheat, and the tinkling hadn't come from wind chimes. It had come from hundreds of tall, olive-colored stalks of grass brushing against one another, as sharp and brittle as blown glass.

I wasn't sure when the dream ended and the real horror began, but I'd woken up at some point, still wailing, and accidentally crossed into the Netherworld. In my tank top and pj shorts. Barefoot and freezing.

Oh, shit!

Gone were my warm bed, fluffy pillows, and worn-thin carpet. Instead, I stood on bare dirt—oddly gray in color—with my big toe pressed against the base of one cold, fragile stalk of razor wheat. Another stalk brushed my elbow as the cold wind blew it toward me, and I froze to keep from shattering it and being pricked by thousands of glasslike slivers.

Harmony had said it wasn't possible. That we couldn't accidentally cross over, because moving from one world into the next required intent, in addition to the *bean sidhe* wail. So what did this mean? That I secretly wanted to cross over?

If so, I'd certainly been keeping that secret well. Even from myself.

But there would be time to figure that out later—hopefully. My immediate concern was getting my defenseless *bean sidhe* butt out of the Netherworld before something predatory came along to eat me. And in the Netherworld, that could be anything. Including the plant life.

I had plenty of intent to cross over when I called forth my wail this time, but nothing came out but a soft, hoarse croak. I'd lost my voice screaming my way *into* the Netherworld, and now had no way out. Nor could I move from the spot where I stood without slicing my bare feet open on every stalk of wheat I shattered.

Then, with panic looming, my hands actually shaking from both the cold and my slim chance of escape, a sudden crashing, furiously chiming sound made me jump. My elbow hit the stalk to my left, and it shattered into tiny needle-sharp shards. Several points scraped my leg as they fell, three or four actually lodging in my skin, but I couldn't bend to examine the damage without breaking more of the wheat. So I stood as still as possible, my mind racing in search of a way out, and I flinched each time the racket from my left grew louder.

The sound was like the tinkling of shattering razor

wheat, only it echoed, and each burst followed a heavy metallic crash.

Desperate now, I held Emma's death in my mind—remembering how she'd looked as she'd collapsed to the gym floor, her eyes empty, her hands uncurling at her sides—as I tried to work up enough saliva to swallow and ease the pain in my throat. Which would hopefully make it possible for me to wail, at least long enough to cross over.

My pulse raced. My palms began to sweat in spite of the cold eating at my skin, echoing the sting of the wheat shards in my flesh. The crashing continued, headed toward me, and I flinched with each new burst of sound.

I swallowed convulsively, wishing I dared to move enough to rub my throat, and wishing even harder that I had something to drink. Something warm and sweet, like the hot tea Harmony always made after I wailed.

Another crash, alarmingly close, and my stomach leaped into my throat. The next was closer still—just yards away now. On my left, stalks of grass swayed to either side in a nearly straight line, like the part between a little girl's pigtails. But the seed clumps at the top of the stalks were eye height on me, so I couldn't see much more than the movement itself.

Drowning in fresh panic, I opened my mouth and forced a sound out, devastated when the croak warbled, then faded.

I swallowed again and clenched my fists at my sides. Then I pictured Emma's pale, dead face in my mind and let loose my wail with everything I had left in me.

A new scream tore free from my throat, just as painful as the last one, but nowhere near as loud. The sound fractured, and I scrambled to pull it back together, closing my eyes in concentration. And when the notes finally steadied, I opened my eyes again to see that the grass around me had gone still. I no longer heard the crashing, but then, I could rarely hear anything over my own wailing. Yet I knew instinctively that the creature in the wheat with me had stopped moving, either scared or surprised by my wail.

The stalks bent in my direction again. I screamed harder. Razor wheat shattered. My pulse raced. My throat ached. My stomach was leading a revolt of my entire body. Then, finally, a familiar gray fog swept in to overlay my vision, heralding my return to my own world.

Just in time.

And as my bedroom began to reform around me—pale walls and furniture oddly overlaid across the still-real olive-tinted field—the crashing creature penetrated the wall of wheat at my side, bursting into view.

I almost laughed out loud.

It wasn't some weird, Netherworld monster, eager to eat me. It was an ordinary trash-can lid. An old-fashioned metal disk, wielded by the handle on the topside.

The suburban knight had used his shield to break the stalks ahead of him, to avoid being sliced to bits by the literal blades of grass.

It was brilliant, really. I wished I'd thought of it.

The improvised shield began to lower, and with the last breath I took in the Netherworld, my gaze landed on a pair of bright brown eyes set into a dark face not much older than my own, crowned by a nest of tight curls and the slightest shadow of a beard.

Then I was back in my room, those eyes fading slowly from the image burned into the backs of my eyelids.

"Well, then, get dressed! Harmony, you have to come *right now!*" my father yelled. Terror echoed in his voice like a shout from a lost cave.

My feet shifted on something soft and springy, and my eyes popped open. I stood in the middle of my bed. My bare toes curled around a fold in my comforter, still smudged with gray Netherworld dirt and dotted with tiny spots of blood from splinters of razor wheat. My father stood at the foot of my bed with his back to me, the home phone pressed to his ear.

"She's crossed over, and I can't get into the Netherworld without you!" he yelled.

"Dad?"

He whirled toward me, eyes going wide even as the line of his jaw softened with relief.

"Never mind, she's back," he whispered into the

phone. Then he hung it up and dropped the receiver on the blankets at my feet. "Kaylee, are you okay?"

"Fine." I whispered, then followed his gaze to the thin shards of razor wheat still protruding from my blood-stained left thigh. "Just scratches," I said, reaching down to pluck the needle-sharp splinters from my skin. I collected them loosely in my other palm, and breathed a sigh of relief that razor wheat—while painful—wasn't poisonous.

"Where the *hell* did you go?" He stomped around the footboard and lifted me from the mattress like a naughty toddler caught jumping on the bed. "I heard you wailing, but by the time I got here you'd crossed over. What were you doing?"

"It was an accident," I muttered, my mouth pressed into his shoulder as he hugged me so tight I couldn't catch my breath. The scruff on his chin scratched my neck, and I felt his heart racing through my nightshirt. "I dreamed someone died, and woke up in the Netherworld."

"What?" He shook his head slowly. "That's not possible." My dad held me at arm's length, searching my eyes for any sign of a lie, but he must have found none, because he didn't get mad. Instead, he got scared. Obviously and truly frightened—a terrifying expression to find on a man who should represent all things strong and safe. "You crossed over in your sleep?"

"Yeah." I set the shards on my nightstand, then sank

onto the edge of my bed, holding my dirty feet away from the mattress. "Please tell me that's never going to happen again. Only say it better than Harmony did, because she said we couldn't cross over accidentally, and she was *wrong.*"

He sank wearily into my desk chair, the golds and browns in his eyes churning fiercely in fear. "I wish I could, Kay, but I've never heard of anything like this. How did this happen? Who were you dreaming about?"

I shrugged, reaching for the clear plastic bottle on my nightstand, wincing as the movement tugged at the fresh cuts on my leg. "I don't know. I'm not sure I even knew in the dream." I gulped lukewarm water, watching my father as he watched me. "What if it happens again?" My voice came out soft with fear, and hoarse because of my raw throat.

"We'll just have to make sure it doesn't." My father's sigh was carried on a breath of determination. "How 'bout some hot chocolate?"

I glanced at my alarm clock, frustrated to see that it was only a quarter to four on Wednesday morning. "Make it coffee, and I'm in." Because I wouldn't be sleeping any more that night. Or any other night until I figured out how to keep from waking up in the Netherworld.

"You drink coffee?" My father frowned as he picked up the phone and followed me into the hall.

"Not if I can help it."

The phone rang in his hand, and he glanced at the display, then handed it to me as we turned into the small galley-style kitchen. "It's Harmony. Tell her you're okay before she and Nash show up with the cavalry."

I answered the phone and assured Harmony—and Nash, by extension—that I was fine, in spite of having crossed over in my sleep. She sounded almost as horrified as I felt, and she promised to see what she could find out about preventing a repeat performance. Then she put Nash on the phone so we could say good-night—or rather, good-morning—and by the time we hung up, the smell of fresh coffee—always better than the taste, in my opinion—was wafting into the kitchen.

Over heavily creamed and sweetened coffee, I told my dad about the field of razor wheat in the Netherworld version of our property and about the trash-can-lid-wielding boy stomping through it. And when we'd exhausted our theories about both the mystery boy and my unscheduled trip, he refilled both of our mugs and started a second pot.

For the next three hours, I sat at the rickety kitchen table with my father, talking about the only thing—other than our species—that we had in common: my mother. He'd always been reluctant to talk about her before; this time he told me everything he could remember about her, probably because, for a few minutes, he'd thought he'd lost me, too. He even answered my questions as I interrupted with them. The only thing we didn't touch on was my death—followed by hers, to save me.

That discussion would have to wait, in spite of the questions I had ready. We were both too tired and distraught from the latest shock to my not-so-human system to handle memories so painful.

But by the time my alarm clock went off, I felt like I truly knew my mother for the first time since my third birthday.

And like I knew my father a little better, too.

NASH'S ARMS WRAPPED around me from behind as I swung my locker door shut, and his voice relaxed me like little else could. "Hey, beautiful," he whispered, dropping a kiss on my neck, just below my ear. "Rough night?"

"Seriously rough. I can't even explain how messed up last night was." I sighed and settled into him, letting the warmth of his chest against my back ease some of the tension left over from my interdimensional field trip. But he couldn't help me fight exhaustion. Fortunately, for that I had two twenty-ounce sodas in my backpack, their condensation probably making a soggy mess out of the chemistry homework I'd forgotten to finish.

"You really crossed over in your sleep?"

I twisted in his arms to face him, laying my cheek

against the thick chenille weave of the white letter *E* on his jacket. "Yeah, it was weird. Scary. I was asleep, dreaming that someone died, and in the dream, I was standing in a bunch of that gray fog you see when you peek into..."

I lifted my head to make sure no one else was close enough to hear. Across the hall, a small cluster of students was gathered around a girl showing off the answers from her algebra homework, but they hadn't even glanced our way. The mohawked junior with the locker next to mine was rifling through his stuff, but his headphones were playing loud enough for me to recognize the bass line of Korn's "Evolution," so there was no way he could hear me.

"...into the *Netherworld,*" I continued, whispering just in case. "I couldn't see who was dying, and I couldn't move. Couldn't do anything but scream."

Nash's arms tightened around me and the greens and browns in his eyes swirled rapidly as he listened.

"And when I woke up, I was screaming for real, and I'd already crossed over. I was standing in a field of razor wheat, barefoot. In my pajamas."

Before Nash could reply, Mohawk man slammed his locker and took off down the hall in the growing stream of early-morning students.

"Damn, Kaylee." Nash sank onto the cold tile floor in front of the lockers and drew me down with him, brushing aside a crumpled piece of notebook paper. "How could that happen?"

I shook my head slowly, almost washed away by the wave of fear that crashed over me at the reminder that I still had none of the answers I needed. "My dad thinks that because I subconsciously repressed so much of my *bean sidhe* heritage for so long—" because no one had told me I wasn't human "—that now it's basically demanding to be recognized." I hesitated, reluctant to mention my father's other theory. "That, or I've somehow developed too strong a connection with the Netherworld." Or with someone—or some*thing*—in it.

Nash paled, which almost sent me into a tailspin of panic. I'd hoped for something more optimistic from him than I'd gotten from my father, as grateful as I was for my dad's honesty. But Nash had no comfort to give. "That's the scariest thing I've ever heard."

I rolled my eyes and pulled my backpack onto my lap. "Thanks, Nash," I snapped. "You're a huge help." I'd just about reached the limit of how much fright and frustration I could take. At least, on so little sleep.

"Sorry." He turned so that I could see him. "You're sure you can't remember who died in your dream?"

I nodded. "I'm not sure I knew even *during* the dream. All I saw was an outline in the fog. I couldn't even tell if it was male or female."

"Do you think it was just a normal dream, or could it

have been part premonition, too? Maybe the way your brain deals with them when you're asleep?"

I shrugged and leaned with my left shoulder against Mohawk man's locker. "I don't see how it could have been a premonition. I've only had them about people I'm physically close to at the time, and there was no one else in the house but my…"

Oh, no… Terror lit my nerve endings, which blazed until it felt like my entire body was on fire. I sat up, and when I looked at Nash, I knew from his expression that my irises were swirling madly.

"What if it's my dad?" I demanded in a horrified whisper. I'd already lost my mother and had just gotten my father back. I couldn't lose him again so quickly. I *couldn't.*

"No." Nash shook his head calmly, running one hand up my arm, over my sleeve. "It can't be. When you have a premonition, someone dies quickly, right?"

I nodded, not yet willing to grasp the branch of hope he held out to me. "Usually within the hour."

"See? And you had that dream in the middle of the night, right?"

I glanced at my watch and counted backward silently. "Almost five hours ago."

"And your dad's still alive, right?" Nash grinned like he'd just discovered the meaning of life, or the root of all evil, or something equally unlikely, but I was already digging in my pocket for my phone. "What are you doing? Didn't you see him right before you left?"

"Yeah. But I have to be sure." I autodialed my father, hoping the school's no-cell-calls policy didn't apply before the first bell.

"Hello?" my dad said into my ear, over the rush of highway traffic, and I let my head fall against the lockers in relief. "Kaylee? What's wrong?"

"Nothing." I could practically hear the smile in my own voice. "I just wanted to make sure you're not asleep at the wheel or anything, since I got you up so early."

"I'm fine." He paused, and I heard his blinker ding faintly. "Thanks for checking, though."

"No problem. I gotta go." I hung up and slid my phone back into my pocket.

"Feel better?" Nash asked, brows raised.

"Marginally." The front doors opened at the end of the hall, admitting a frigid draft, as well as several dozen freshmen and sophomores. The buses had arrived, and class would start in less than ten minutes. "I gotta go finish my chemistry homework," I said, using the lock on the locker below mine to haul myself to my feet.

Nash stood with me. "I'll walk with you."

I wrapped my arms around Nash's chest, content for the moment just to lean against him and breathe him in—until his next words drenched my warm, cozy feeling like a cold wave crashing over a sleeping sunbather.

"Have you seen Carter this morning?"

"No." In fact, I hadn't seen him since he'd torn out of the student lot on Monday afternoon. He'd skipped school on Tuesday—his parents were still out of town, but rumor had it he'd convinced the maid to call him in sick—presumably too ill from withdrawal to deal with the usual school crap. And I hadn't given him a second thought so far today, thanks to my nearly sleepless Tuesday night.

"His car's in the lot," Nash continued, voice low to keep anyone else from overhearing us as the hall filled with students. "But we don't have any classes together till after lunch, and I'm afraid he's—"

"There he is," I interrupted the moment I saw Scott Carter turn the corner from the gym hallway, strutting as confidently as he ever had.

Nash followed my gaze. "He looks happy." Which—assuming he hadn't found a miracle cure for addiction or withdrawal—could only mean one thing. He'd found Doug's supplier and made another purchase.

"Maybe he's just a quick healer," I suggested, determined to be optimistic because the alternative made me want to rip out my own hair.

"We'll know in a minute." Nash held one hand up and called down the hall, "Hey, Carter, where were you yesterday?"

Scott threaded a path through the crowd toward us, greeting guys he knew on the way, and shared a hand slap with Nash, whose face froze the moment they touched.

And if I'd had any doubts before, they were obliterated a second later when Scott's hand brushed mine on its way to his side.

His skin was freezing, and his breath smelled like he'd inhaled a hellion *whole.*

"Sick," Scott said, smiling broadly for no reason I could see. "I could barely get out of bed. Had to get Carlita to call me in sick. Good thing she's picking up some English, right?"

Nash shrugged. "You got a lot of makeup work?"

But Scott wasn't listening. He frowned, eyes narrowed and jaw tense as he stared over my shoulder. I turned to see what he was looking at and found only our own shadows stretched over the lockers, cast by bright light from the office window. But I couldn't help wondering what *he* was seeing.…

"Carter?" Nash repeated, turning to follow my gaze while Scott shook his head, as if to clear it.

"Nah," he said finally, like he'd heard the question on some kind of time delay. "I don't think they'll make me do any of it but that quiz in civics." He stepped back and made a sweeping gesture to encompass his entire body. "I'm Scott Carter, man. Nobody's willing to piss off my dad until the football team gets those new pads and tackling dummies for next season."

"Jeez, you say your name like it should be written in all caps," I mumbled, slapping a smile on at the last minute, hoping they'd think I was joking.

Scott did. Sophie did not.

"It should be," she purred, stopping at Scott's side to run one hand over his shoulder and down his back. "But I guess you usually see *yours* handwritten by some nut job with a half-eaten crayon. Isn't that how they label stuff in the psych ward?"

"Only when *you're* in residence," I snapped. I was too tired to put up with Sophie's crap that morning, and for a moment, awe at my own nerve energized me better than three cups of early-morning coffee had.

Scott laughed while Sophie fumed, cheeks hot enough to spontaneously combust. He slapped Nash on the back, still grinning. "Sounds like your little puss grew some claws! Does she purr when you stroke her? 'Cause this one sure does." He pulled Sophie closer, his hand inching toward the denim pocket curved around her rear.

She smiled and squirmed for his benefit, but when her gaze landed on me, it was cold enough to build a layer of ice in hell.

I rolled my eyes and stepped around my cousin, tugging my backpack higher on my shoulder as I walked briskly toward my first class. Behind me, Scott asked Sophie if she felt like skipping fourth period with him.

I didn't hear her answer—though I was pretty sure it was a yes—because Nash's footsteps pounded rapidly on the tile after me. "Wow. That was…unexpected," he said, slowing to walk beside me.

"Me, or Scott?"

"You." I heard the grin in Nash's voice, but glanced up at him to be sure. "I liked it."

"She had it coming. But Scott..."

"He's just messing around," Nash insisted as we passed his class without slowing. Mine was on the other end of the main hallway.

"I don't care about that." Scott's flirting didn't bother me because it drove Sophie half out of her mind. "But, Nash. He was staring at the lockers behind us like he expected monsters to jump out and drag him off." Which really only happens in the Netherworld. "He's wasted."

"I know."

"We have to do something." I lowered my voice for the next part, leaning closer to him to be heard. "Obviously stealing his stash was a short-term solution."

"I *know,*" Nash whispered as we slowed to a stop several feet from my advanced-math classroom. "He's hallucinating, but I don't think he's hearing things yet, and he's still making sense." Nash shrugged. "As much sense as he ever did, anyway. So I don't think it's too late for him yet."

"What does that mean?" Suddenly I had chill bumps beneath my jacket sleeves. "Why would it be too late?"

Nash's face fell in a mixture of sympathy and surprise, and he tugged me toward the lockers, out of the stream of traffic. "Kaylee, the effects of Demon's Breath on a human are irreversible. If he takes enough to actually sever his tie to reality, cutting off his source may save his life, but it won't fix him. He'll wind up locked in a padded room." He hesitated, searching my face for the truth. "My mom didn't tell you that?"

"No..." I closed my eyes in horror until I had my expression under control. "She didn't know anyone was actually taking it." I pulled my backpack higher on my shoulder, almost fascinated by the irony—the Netherworld had proved to me that I wasn't crazy, but its effect on Doug and Scott would be the opposite.

"How do you know all this?" I glanced at the wall clock over his shoulder to see that we had less than two minutes until the bell. *So much for doing my chemistry homework....*

Nash ran one cool finger down my jaw to the point of my chin. "Most *bean sidhes* don't grow up thinking they're human, Kay." He glanced around at the rapidly emptying hall, then back at me. "Anyway, we have to cut off Carter's access and figure out how to treat him for withdrawal, or..."

"...eventually frost will literally drive him crazy. Or kill him," I finished, leaning against a row of green lockers.

"Yeah, if by 'eventually,' you mean very, very soon," Nash said, a flash of true fear stirring in his eyes. "He's obviously really sensitive to it."

"What do you mean?"

"Scott probably doesn't have any non-human blood in his gene pool. Sophie, for instance, is human, but she'd probably be much less sensitive to the side effects of Demon's Breath—though she could become just as physically addicted to it—because of her dad's non-human blood."

"And by 'non-human'—" my voice dropped even lower and I leaned closer to him "—you mean *bean sidhes?*"

"Yes, us, and anyone else originally native to the Netherworld. There are a few other species that live here in the human world with us. Like harpies, and sirens, and—"

"Whoa..." I felt my eyes widen, and could only hope I didn't look like a complete drooling idiot to the rest of the student body. "You're serious?"

His irises swam in sympathy. "I keep forgetting you grew up in virtual darkness."

"Well, that makes one of us," I mumbled, frustrated all over again by how much I still had to learn about the Netherworld and its non- or part-human elements. Like *me.*

"Anyway, the less human you are, the less susceptible to the effects of Demon's Breath. Though fiends are the obvious exception."

Because those little buggers only existed in one of two states: stoned, and trying to be stoned.

"So, since Doug's addiction isn't progressing as quickly, he probably has some non-human blood in his family somewhere, right?"

"It's possible." Nash glanced over his shoulder to where my math teacher was eyeing us both and tapping her watch. He headed toward the classroom with me. "But it could be way, way back in his family tree, and he probably knows nothing about it."

"Are you joining us today, Ms. Cavanaugh?" my math teacher asked.

I nodded, and Nash squeezed my hand, then he trotted backward down the hall. "See you at lunch...."

I ducked into my classroom, sliding into my seat just as the tardy bell rang, but while my classmates pulled out homework assignments and frantically filled in the blanks they'd forgotten, I couldn't stop thinking about Doug Fuller, and the only thing we had in common, other than Emma.

What I hadn't known about my family nearly got me killed. But what he didn't know about his might just save his life.

"DID SCOTT SAY WHERE he got it?" I asked, bending to dip my paintbrush in white latex paint.

Nash had roped me into helping with the carnival booths after school to keep him company, so I'd pulled the same thing on Emma. Which was how she, Nash, Doug, and I wound up in the school gym at four o'clock on a Wednesday afternoon, slopping white paint and fake snowflakes on booths made of plywood and construction staples. Along with twenty other bright-'n'-shiny cheerleaders, basketball players, and student-council members I'd rarely ever spoken to.

"He said he got it from Fuller again."

I sank to my knees on the canvas drop cloth protecting the gym floor from my subpar artistic efforts and glanced across the basketball court to where Emma and Doug were working on the ice-carving registration booth. And by "working," I mean making out, half-hidden by their booth, with dried-stiff brushes dangling from paint-speckled hands.

"I assume he got it from that same guy? Everett?"

Nash shrugged and used his brush to smooth out a drip on my side of the hot-chocolate stand. "I guess."

"We have to find this guy. Can you get Doug to introduce you? Maybe pretend you want to buy some from him?"

He frowned, critically eyeing the giant marshmallows he was painting on top of a cutout of a mug full of brown liquid. "But then wouldn't I have to sample the product?"

Crap. "Probably. Can't you just fake it?" I sighed, already rethinking my request. Did I want to put Nash in that kind of danger? What if he couldn't fake it and had to take a hit? What if he accidentally inhaled Demon's Breath? Either way, his exposure would be my fault. And I couldn't live with that.

"You know what? Never mind. I'll do it." I stood, trailing my damp brush along the corner of the booth, where I'd evidently left streaks on my first pass. "I'll meet him, and pretend to sample the product, and find out where he gets it. And whether he knows what it really is—"

"No," Nash said. I turned around, and he was so close

onlookers would think he was either challenging me to a dance battle, or staring down my shirt.

"Why? Because I'm a girl?"

His irises churned with...panic? But as I watched, he made them go still—obviously an effort—and there was nothing left to read on his face but the angry line of his jaw. "Because you don't seem to understand that the world isn't yours to save. This isn't a game, Kaylee. You're not an undercover cop. You're just a little girl who's in way over her head, and I'm not going to let you get yourself killed over some stupid hero complex."

I stepped back and my cheeks flamed like I'd been slapped. "I'm not a little girl." And he'd never spoken to me like that. Not ever. "I don't know what your problem is, but unless you pay the rent on my house or wear the black suspenders at the Cinemark, you don't get to tell me what to do."

"Or what? You'll slop paint all over my jacket?" Nash lighthearted grin irritated me.

"Stop smiling. I'm serious," I insisted.

"Yeah. I can see you're fully prepared to deface my letter jacket. Which is exactly why you should let me do this. A Netherworld drug dealer isn't going to be scared of your drippy paintbrush." He tried to take it from me, and when I refused to relinquish the handle, Nash wrapped his hand around both my fingers and the paintbrush and slowly pushed my arm down to my side. "Just let me do this. I don't want you anywhere near

Everett." He let me see truth in his eyes, but that did little to placate me. You don't have to be a jock to know when you're being sidelined.

"What if I don't want you near him, either?"

He shrugged. "I'm bigger than you, and I've been taking hits from guys bigger than me for the past six years."

"Well, that experience should come in handy, so long as you're both wearing football helmets and pads. Assuming Everett's even human."

"So long as he's not a hellion, I can take him if I need to." And hellions couldn't cross over, so the chances of that were good. "And Fuller will be there, too."

Though I had serious doubts that Doug would choose Nash over his dealer if he ever wanted to see another hit of frost.

"Fine," I relented. Nash kissed my nose, then let go of my hand, and I glanced up to find Emma dipping her brush into her paint can, grinning at Doug like he'd invented kissing. My stomach churned at the very real possibility that *he* wasn't what made her feel so good. "Look, they came up for air. This is your shot."

Nash laid his brush carefully across the top of his open paint can. "Be right back." He walked across the gym, exchanging greetings with friends and teammates, and I dipped my brush into the can, wishing I could read lips. I was about to put the finishing touches on the top of our booth when sharp words from the hallway caught my attention through the open doorway several feet to my left.

"Get your ass back in there. Now." It was Sophie, her voice low and unusually soft with anger. I'd never heard her so mad, and she got mad at me a lot. "You are *not* going to bail on us again."

"I'll be right back," Scott snapped, and I knew from the rough edge to his voice that he'd come down from his high. And was getting desperate to regain it. "I have to get something from my football."

"What?" Sophie snapped, and I edged closer to the door, backing along the canvas until I could see Scott, though my cousin remained out of sight.

"I mean my *car.*" Scott rubbed his forehead in frustration. "I can't think with all that noise!" He glared toward the gym, and I ducked out of sight, glancing around the gym at the other volunteers. Yes, everyone was chatting while they worked, but the gym was huge, and it was nowhere near capacity. Nor were we very loud.

Scott was hearing things. Auditory hallucinations? *Not good…*

"I need to get something…" he mumbled, and I risked scooting forward again to see him staring at the wall to his left, as if something were about to burst through it.

"Yeah, and then you won't come back," Sophie spat. "You promised you'd help, and every time you walk out, I look like an idiot in front of my friends."

"Then you need better friends. Or maybe you're not the only one clawing to be crowned Ice Bitch this year."

"It's Snow Queen. And what good would it do me to win if no one's there to escort me?"

Nash had reached Doug and Emma by then, and had drawn Doug closer to the bleachers for their private chat, and it felt weird to be watching them while I eavesdropped on my cousin and her boyfriend.

"I said I'd be there." Scott spoke through gritted teeth that time, and my pulse jumped at the intensity of the anger in his voice.

"You also said you'd help us all week, and this is the first time you've shown up. And now you're ready to bail."

His sneakers squeaked on the tile as he turned and stomped away from her, and her flats clacked after him. "Damn it, Sophie, get *off!*" Then I heard a thud, and a stunned *oof* from Sophie. I whirled back toward the hall to see her sitting on the floor, propped up by both hands, legs splayed in front of her.

"You *ass!*" she hissed, cloth rustling as she picked herself up.

He exhaled slowly, looking both sorry and impatient. "You just…you never know when to quit."

"That sounds like *your* problem," she snapped, and I almost applauded, surprised to find that for once she and I agreed. And I was just as surprised that she'd picked up on his problem. But I shouldn't have been. She was mean, not stupid. "You're acting like more of a freak than Kaylee."

And…there she'd lost me again.

"Whatever." Scott stomped off, his left arm twitching violently, and just before he passed out of my line of sight, he glanced over his shoulder one last time, not at Sophie, but at the row of lockers to his right. As if he saw something that no one else could see.

Sophie straightened her blouse and I hurried back to the hot-chocolate stand as Nash started across the basketball court toward me. An instant later, Sophie clacked into the gym—and stopped short when her gaze met mine.

Her face paled when she realized I'd heard their argument. Then, in true Sophie style, her critical eye took me in from head to toe and a sneer formed on her perfectly made-up mouth. "You're dripping on your shoe," she said, then stomped off to join a group of dancers gathered around the temporary Snow Queen stage with handfuls of fake snow.

"What's wrong with her?" Nash bent to pick up his paintbrush.

"I heard her fighting with Scott. Who just left for another huff from his balloon. I swear, he and Doug are like babies with pacifiers. And Scott's sounding less coherent by the minute."

"Great." Nash's jaw tightened, but then his gaze caught

on the white paint splattered all over my right foot, and he smiled. "You look like you're bleeding milk."

"So I hear." Disgusted, I dropped my brush into my half-empty bucket and knelt to work on my shoe. "What did Doug say?"

Nash sat on the canvas to touch up the bottom of the booth. "He's having a party Friday night, and Everett's going to be there. He said I can buy my own then, but he's not selling any more of his."

I dabbed at the paint on my shoe with a damp rag, but only smeared it. "So, we're going to the party?"

"Looks like." He sighed and glanced around to make sure we weren't being overheard. "But I don't see how that will help. Even if we meet Everett, what are we supposed to do? Haul him out the back door and demand he stop selling in the human world? If he's selling Demon's Breath, he must have a supplier, and there nothing we can do against another hellion." He grabbed the rag I'd dropped to wipe another drip before I could sit in it.

"I know." Or rather, I didn't know. I had no solution. No way of stopping Everett—or the hellion backing him—and no way of knowing that cutting off the supply and sending them into withdrawal would actually help Scott and Doug, rather than hurt them. But we couldn't stand by and watch a couple of incidents turn into the epidemic I'd originally feared. "We're gonna have to bring in someone else."

"Like who?"

"I don't know. My dad? Your mom? Uncle Brendon?" I held my breath in anticipation of Nash's argument.

"Kaylee…"

"Wait, I know how that sounds." I set my brush across the top of the can, like I'd seen him do, and edged closer to him on the canvas so I could lower my voice. "But we wouldn't really be ratting anyone out. No cops, no arrests. Nash, if we don't do something, Scott's going to go insane. Like, talking-to-himself, showing-up-half-dressed, cowering-in-the-shadows *insane.* And that's just the beginning. The same thing will happen to Doug, and everyone he passes a balloon to. And possibly to Emma and Sophie, and anyone else who breathes too deeply near someone who's just inhaled. We have to get rid of Everett and his supply, and we can't do that on our own."

"Okaaay…" Nash frowned. "So what's your dad going to say when he finds out you've known about this for nearly a week and didn't tell him? When he finds out your car was totaled by a guy wasted on Demon's Breath? He'll never let you out of the house again. You want to be grounded for the rest of your life?"

"Of course not. But so what if he does ground me? At least Scott and Doug will still be alive." And hopefully sane. And frankly, being grounded again seemed like a small price to pay in exchange for someone else's life. "Not to mention Emma, and even Sophie. What happens if we don't say anything, and Sophie gets drawn into this? How can I ever look my uncle in the eye, knowing I let his daughter die? Again?"

Nash closed his eyes and breathed deeply, and he didn't look at me until his knuckles were no longer white around the paintbrush he clutched like a lifeline. "Fine. It's not like I can argue with that logic." But he certainly looked like he wanted to. "But let's try it ourselves first, okay? Let's go to the party and meet Everett. Let me see what kind of system he has going before we go tattle. I'm only asking you for two more days. All right?"

I hesitated. I understood Nash's reluctance to rat out his friends, but I did *not* understand his reluctance to keep them alive. "Fine. But if we can't do anything about him, I'm telling my dad. That night. I'm not kidding, Nash. This has already gone too far."

Nash nodded and dropped his paintbrush on the white-splattered canvas. "I agree with you there," he whispered, eyes swirling slowly with frustration and a little fear. "This whole thing has gone way too far."

WEDNESDAY NIGHT WAS hell on earth.

After painting carnival booths until dinnertime, Nash and I grabbed fast-food burgers and ate while I rushed through only the homework that *had* to be done, for the teachers who actually checked. Then I fell asleep on my couch with my head on his lap while he watched old action movies until my dad got home.

When the front door slammed, I woke up and rolled over to find my father staring down at me, looking pissed beyond words. Apparently napping with my nose pressed into my boyfriend's denim-clad crotch was not on the list of approved sleeping arrangements.

Who knew?

But when I broke into tears explaining that I was afraid to sleep alone, in case I woke up in the Netherworld again, my dad's scowl softened into a sympathetic frown, and he suggested we camp out in the living room that night, to put both of our fears to rest. That way, if I started screaming, he could wake me up before I crossed over.

A living-room slumber party with my dad sounded a little juvenile, but I was willing to try anything that might keep me anchored to my own reality.

Unfortunately, his plan worked out better in theory than in practice.

Around midnight, my dad fell asleep in his recliner, head rolled to one side, bottom lip jiggling each time a snore rumbled from his mouth. But I was still awake two hours later, when the *Judge Judy* marathon gave way to an infomercial advertising men's hair-loss products. I couldn't relax. I was *terrified* of waking up in a field of razor wheat, barefoot and hoarse, and unable to move without getting shredded like secret government documents.

So after twenty minutes of watching old men have their hair spray-painted on, I exchanged my pj bottoms and Betty Boop slippers for jeans, a thick pair of socks, and my heaviest pair of boots from the bottom of my closet. After slipping on the black quilted jacket Aunt Val had given me for Christmas the year before, I snuck back into the living room and collapsed on the couch, finally feeling armed for sleep.

That way, if I crossed over, at least I'd be warm, and dressed in defense of razor-sharp, literal blades of grass.

I even considered running outside for the lid to the old trash can we raked leaves into, but in the end decided that would only bring up more questions from my father when the crash of metal woke him up.

Finally prepared for the worst, I managed four hours of light dozing, during which several extra loud commercials broke through my delicate slumber. But by six in the morning, I was awake for good, reading the directions on the back of the coffee grounds, hoping I wouldn't mess up my first pot too badly.

By the time I'd showered and dressed, my father was padding wearily around the kitchen in his bare feet, and the coffee was done. "Not bad." He held up a nearly full mug. "Your first batch?"

Sighing, I sank onto a chair to pull mismatched socks from my feet. "Yeah." I forced an exhausted smile, wondering how I would ever make it through my history review session if I couldn't even find a proper pair of socks from the pile of clean laundry in the basket in my room.

I had to hand it to Aunt Val: she may have been a vain, soul-stealing, interdimensional criminal, but she'd always kept the laundry neatly folded…

"Harmony and Brendon are coming over tonight to discuss your problem. To see if we can't figure out how and why it's happening." My father paused, pouring coffee into another mug for me—this one oversized. "I didn't hear you sing." Which was how male *bean sidhes* heard the female *bean sidhe's* wail. "Does that mean you didn't have any death dreams?"

I shook my head, rubbing my temples. "I had another one. Same as last time, from what I remember. But this time the Geico gecko woke me up before the screaming started."

My dad frowned and crossed the room to set a heavily doctored mug of coffee on the table in front of me. "I could call you in sick, if you want to stay home and rest."

"Thanks, but I better go." I cradled my mug in both hands and blew on the surface before taking the first long, bitter sip. "We're reviewing for midterms today." And as awesome as staying home sounded, I need to be there to watch Scott and Doug for further signs that their sanity was slipping. And Emma and Sophie, for any signs that they'd gotten a contact buzz from breathing near their own boyfriends. "Besides, I could dream about death as easily in the daytime as I can at night, right?"

"I guess so." My father put one hand on the back of my chair, watching me in concern as he brought his own mug to his mouth. "Just be careful, okay? I can't follow you into the Netherworld, and by the time I find someone to take me—" Harmony, presumably "—there's no telling where you'll be."

I nodded and bit my tongue to keep from reminding

coming to Mr. Carter's office at the end of the hall—a space I remembered fondly.

The room was dark, and it took a minute for my eyes to adjust to what little light fell from the cracks in the wooden blinds drawn shut over both windows.

"Close the door!" Scott shouted, and I jumped as he lifted one hand to block the light from the hallway. Nash nudged me farther into the room and pushed the door closed softly, cutting off so much light that I had to wait for my eyes to adjust again.

Scott cowered on the far end of the brown leather couch, and as Nash approached him, Scott began to mumble-chant under his breath.

"No light, no shadow. No light, no shadow..."

Chill bumps popped up all over my arms, in spite of the warm air flowing from the vent overhead.

"What's wrong, Carter?" Nash squatted on the floor in front of his friend, one hand on the arm of the couch for balance. "Does the light hurt your eyes? Does your head hurt?"

Scott didn't answer. He just kept mumbling, eyes squeezed shut.

"I think he's afraid of the shadows," I whispered, remembering Scott's horror when he'd eyed our silhouettes in the cafeteria and his own shadow in the hall the afternoon before.

"Is that right?" Nash asked without looking at me,

his profile tense with fear and concern. "Is something wrong with your shadow?"

"Not mine anymore," Scott whispered, his voice high and reedy, like a scared child's. He punched the sides of his head with both fists at once, as if he could beat down whatever he was seeing and hearing. "Not my shadow."

"Whose shadow is it?" I whispered, fascinated in spite of the cold fingers of terror inching up my back, leaving chills in their wake.

"His. He stole it."

My chest seemed to contract around my heart as a jolt of fear shot through it.

Nash shifted, trying to get comfortable in his squat. "Who stole it?"

"Like Peter Pan. Make Wendy sew my shadow back on…"

I glanced at Nash, and Scott froze with his eyes closed and his head cocked to one side, like a dog listening for a whistle humans can't hear. Then he opened his eyes and looked straight at Nash, from less than a foot away. "Can you get me a soda, Hudson? I don't think I ate lunch." The sudden normalcy of his voice scared me almost as badly as the childlike quality had, and I glanced at Nash in surprise. But he only nodded and stood.

"Just watch him," he whispered, squeezing my hand on his way out the door, which he left ajar a couple of inches.

Uncomfortable staring at Scott in his current state, I glanced around the room, admiring the built-in shelves behind a massive antique desk with scrolled feet and a tall, commanding chair.

"You can go look," Scott said, and I jumped, in spite of my best effort to remain calm.

"What?"

"You like to read, right?" He cocked his head to one side, as if he heard a reply I hadn't made. "Some of them are really old. Several first editions."

I hesitated, but he looked so hopeful, so encouraging, that I rounded the corner of the desk farthest from him, drawn by the spine of an old copy of *Tess of the d'Urbervilles.* It was on the second shelf from the top, and I had to stand on my toes to reach it. To brush my fingers over the gold print on the spine.

The soft click of a door closing shot through the room, as loud as a peal of thunder in my head. I dropped to my heels and whirled to see Scott standing in front of the now-closed door, mumbling something like soft, inarticulate chanting.

My heart thudded in my chest, my own pulse roaring in my ears. "Scott? What's wrong?"

His head snapped up, his fevered gaze focusing on me briefly. Then his mumbling rose in volume, and he seemed to be arguing now, but I couldn't make out the words. He shook his head fiercely, like he had in his car. "Can you hear him?"

I stepped slowly toward the desk between us. "Hear who, Scott? What do you hear?"

"He says you can't hear him," Scott continued, his gaze momentarily holding mine again. Then, "No, no, no, no…"

I tried to sound calm as I inched toward him. "Who do you hear?"

"Him. Can't see him in the dark, but I hear him. *In. My. Head!*" He punctuated each word with a blow to his own temple. "Stole my shadow. But I still hear him…"

Shivers traveled the length of my arms and legs, and my hands shook at my sides. Was Scott actually seeing someone the rest of us couldn't? Hearing something meant only for his ears? Thanks to Tod, I knew better than most how very possible that was.…

But this didn't feel like the work of a reaper. Reapers couldn't steal someone's shadow. Could they?

Scott rolled his eyes from side to side, as if to catch movement on the edge of his vision. My stomach tried to heave itself through my chest and out my throat. I knew that motion. I did the same thing when I peeked into the Netherworld. When I tried to get a clear view of the heard-but-unseen creatures skittering and sliding through the impenetrable gray fog.

Could he see the fog? Could he see the *things?* Was something from the Netherworld talking to him?

No. It's not possible. But my chill bumps were as big as mosquito bites.

"What is he saying?" I was past the desk, four feet from him now, and closing. When Nash came back, I would peek into the Netherworld to rule out that impossibility. To verify that Scott wasn't seeing and hearing something from that other reality. From a world he didn't even know existed.

Because creatures that couldn't cross over couldn't shout across the barrier, either. Right?

Scott looked up and smiled, but it was the kind of smile a cancer patient wears when he's realized chemo isn't worth the pain and nausea. When he's finally decided to give up and let Death claim him. "Take me to him. He'll fix me if you take me to him."

Dread burned like ice in my veins, and I edged back when Scott stepped toward me. "Take you where?"

"There." He rubbed his brow, as if to soothe a bad headache. "Where he is. He says you know how to cross."

Cross. *No.* My eyes closed briefly, and I sucked in a long, devastated breath.

Scott's shadow man wanted me to take him to the Netherworld.

"WHO IS HE, SCOTT?" I shuffled back another step and trailed my fingers over the top of his father's desk, hoping the smooth, cool surface would ground me, in spite of my rapidly thumping heart. I needed to peek into the Netherworld, to see for myself who was talking to him, but I was afraid to take any of my attention from Scott.

"Take me…" he whispered fiercely, matching each of my steps with a larger one of his own. "We have to cross!"

Not gonna happen. I might not have Harmony's experience, or my dad's wisdom and pathological caution, but I was nowhere near naive enough to believe that whoever was tormenting Scott would simply "fix" him if I took him to the Netherworld.

The Netherworld didn't do charity. This shadow man

would claim us both, body and soul, and we'd never see the human world again.

Over Scott's shoulder, the doorknob turned, and relief washed over me as Nash's voice called out. "Kaylee?"

But the door didn't open—it was locked—and I never should have taken my eyes off Scott.

"Nash, he's not having delus—"

Scott grabbed my arm and jerked me forward. He pinned me to his chest and I gasped, more surprised than afraid. Something sharp bit into my throat, just below my jaw, and the shout I'd been about to unleash died on my tongue.

"Take me…" he demanded, and a cold, nauseatingly sweet puff of Demon's Breath wafted over my face.

My breath hitched as I tried not to inhale, and my pulse pounded in my head. I wasn't sure exactly where my jugular ran through my neck, but I was pretty sure accuracy wasn't as important as enthusiasm in the art of throat slashing.

"If you don't take me, I'm gonna die. And you're gonna die with me," Scott whispered, his voice shaky with terror.

His skin was cold, even through both layers of our clothing, and the blade—something small…a paring knife, maybe?—felt warm by comparison. "Scott, you don't want to go there." I had to force the words out, afraid that any movement of my throat would force the metal through my skin. "Trust me."

"Carter, what are you doing?" Nash asked through the door, and I was worried by how composed he sounded—his best friend was about to cut my head off! Not that Nash knew about the knife...

"She won't take me!" Scott hissed, his grip bruising my arm.

"He has a *knife,*" I said as loudly as I dared with the blade still pressed against my skin.

"Take you where?" Nash asked, ignoring my contribution to the exchange. And that's when I realized he was Influencing Scott—trying to talk him down with a little *bean sidhe* push. "Let me in, and we'll talk about this."

"He's not delusional, Nash," I said, struggling to stay calm. "Something wants me to cross over with him. Could you please help me explain why that's not a good idea?"

I needed Nash to do the talking, if there was any chance of his Influence actually working. And I was fighting complete panic at the feel of the blade against my throat.

In theory, if my time was up—if my name was on the list—I would die, and no amount of talking or fighting would stop that.

And if it wasn't my time, so long as I stayed in the human world and avoided Netherworld elements, I wouldn't die, no matter what. That not-death could come about in any number of ways. Scott might turn out to have colossally bad aim with a knife, or Nash might do everything right to stop the bleeding. Or Tod might blink in, then blink me instantly to the hospital. Or we might actually talk Scott out of violence.

Or…Scott could maim me beyond recognition and normal physical function without actually killing me.

But no matter what might happen next, crossing over would be worse. Our expiration dates meant nothing in the Netherworld, which officially made it the scariest place in existence, and the place I was least likely to take Scott.

"You're confused," Nash said to Scott from the other side of the door, and his voice slid over me like a warm breeze. "I can help you. Let me in, and I'll help you."

"No!" Scott shouted, his hand tightening around my arm. "He knows about you. Your voice makes people do things. Shut up or I'll kill her."

My pulse spiked again, and there was only silence from the hallway. Tears filled my eyes, blurring the closed door until I blinked them away and mentally closed the well. Crying would not help me, nor would it help Scott. But there had to be a way out of this.

The light beneath the door flickered, like Nash had stepped closer. "How?" he asked softly, and his normal voice now sounded flat compared to the rich tones that accompanied his Influence.

"How what?" Scott asked, and his grip on my arm loosened slightly.

"How will you cross over if you kill her?" Nash clarified, and I almost smiled, in spite of my predicament. Scott knew about his vocal influence—sort of—so Nash was working without it. He was being smart. If I wanted to live, I'd have to get smart, too.

I closed my eyes, ignoring the hum from the heating vent overhead and the eerie coolness of the body pressed against my back. "Nash can't take you," I whispered, just loud enough for Scott to hear me.

Scott stiffened. "You're lying."

I started to shake my head, then remembered the knife and opened my eyes again. "Nash can't take you, and neither can *he.* If he could, he wouldn't need me, would he?" Scott didn't answer, but he pulled me back a step across the thick, soft carpet. "Ask him. Not Nash. Ask *him.*"

Scott remained silent and rigid against me, and I wondered if whoever he was listening to could hear me, or if Scott had to ask him directly. Silently or otherwise.

Finally Scott seemed to sag against me, though the blade never left my throat. "Take me there. Please take me. Please make it stop," he begged. He was close to his breaking point, which meant that whoever wanted him must be getting desperate.

Scott went quiet again, listening to something we couldn't hear, and I was almost surprised to realize daylight still slipped through the cracks in the closed blinds. It felt like we'd been in that room forever, but it couldn't have been more than a few minutes. Then Scott leaned into me, dragging my thoughts back to the crisis at hand. His mouth brushed my right ear, through my hair. "He says this is all your fault."

What? A wash of confusion diluted my fear. What did any of this have to do with me?

"Scott, if I take you there, he'll kill us both. Or worse."

He stiffened again, and his knife hand twitched. I gasped as the point of the blade pierced my skin with a sharp slice of pain. A warm bead of blood trailed slowly down my neck, and I froze.

"He says I'll die here. You say I'll die there. But if I can't get him out of my head, none of that matters!" He sobbed, then stood straighter, drawing me up with him as the blade pressed more firmly against my broken skin. "Take me there now, or I'll cut your throat wide open."

"Okay…" I said, my heart pounding so hard I could barely hear my own words, much less my thoughts. "I'll take you. Just…put the knife down."

"Kaylee?" Nash demanded from the other side of the door, and something thumped to the floor. He'd dropped the soda.

"No way." Scott shook his head, jostling us both, ignoring Nash completely. "He says you'll run."

I closed my eyes and breathed deeply, trying to slow my racing thoughts. And my racing pulse. Then I opened my eyes to find the doorknob twisting again as Nash tried to force his way into the room.

"If this shadow man is so smart—" my voice wavered with nerves "—he'll know it takes a lot of concentration to cross over. And I can't concentrate with a knife at my throat."

Nash pounded the door. "Kaylee, no…!" he shouted, but he was too upset now to manage much Influence on either of us.

Scott went still behind me, listening to his shadow man again. Then, "Fine. But if you run, he says I should gut you like a goat on an altar."

My heart beat so hard my head hurt, and adrenaline was turning my fight-or-flight instinct into a demand. I knew what I had to do, but had no idea if I could actually pull it off. He was a lot bigger than I was, and a lot stronger and faster. And Nash would be no help from the other side of the door.

Slowly, Scott removed the knife from my neck, and more blood trickled down my throat. A moment later, the blade poked at my back through my jacket and my thin tee. "Yes, that's much more relaxing," I snapped, unable to censor my sarcasm, even with my life in mortal peril.

I stared at the closed door and tried to communicate my intentions to Nash silently, desperately wishing *bean sidhes* were psychic. But that was just another on a long list of really cool abilities I didn't get.

"Okay, this is gonna feel kind of funny," I warned Scott, closing my eyes as I silently wished myself luck. "Your skin will tingle, and it'll feel like you're falling." Which wasn't true in the least. Nash stopped pounding on the door for a moment, as if to listen. He knew I was lying, and had hopefully gathered from that fact that I had no intention of taking Scott to the Netherworld.

But then what I was really planning sank in, and he kicked the door so hard it shook in its frame.

"So, don't freak out if you lose your balance, okay?" I continued for Scott's benefit, doing my best to ignore Nash. "You ready?"

"Yeah." But Scott's voice had gone squeaky, and his grip on my arm was cutting off my circulation. He was terrified.

Good. So was I.

I took another deep breath. Then I spun away from the knife and twisted my arm from Scott's grip. He shouted. The knife arced toward me. I threw my arm up to shield my face. Pain sliced across the fleshy part of my forearm. I screamed and kicked him. My boot hit his hip, and Scott stumbled toward the desk. He tripped over his own foot and went down like a felled tree.

I whirled around before he landed and fumbled with the lock, twisting the knob twice before it would turn. I pulled the door open and Nash shoved me behind him even as he charged into the room, armed with nothing but his own outrage.

Scott lay motionless on the floor, the knife clutched loosely in his fist.

For a moment, I thought he was dead. That his shadow man had been right—he'd died because he hadn't crossed over. Then I saw his chest rise and fall, and realized he was unconscious. He'd hit his head on the desk when he fell.

Nash dug his phone from his pocket and was dialing before I'd even processed what happened. Distantly, I heard him answer the 9-1-1 operator's questions, telling her that his best friend, Scott Carter, had gone crazy. That he'd attacked me with a knife, then fell and hit his head on a desk and knocked himself out.

The operator said help would be there soon. She was right.

Nash was still wrapping my bleeding arm with a kitchen towel when the sirens screamed down the street. "Just go along with whatever I say," he insisted as flashing red lights drew to stop in front of the house, easily visible through the glass front door. He pushed me gently onto a couch in the living room. "Everyone at school will back us up. They all saw him acting crazy."

My eyes watered and the room blurred. "You're going to get him committed…" I whispered, unsure whether or not I meant it as a question.

"There's no other choice," Nash insisted, walking backward toward the front door to let the EMTs in. "There's nothing we can do for him now, and the only way to keep him from hurting anyone else is to lock him up."

"This is our fault, Nash," I sobbed, wiping scalding tears from my cheek with the back of my good arm. "We should have done something sooner."

"I know." His eyes swirled with grief, and guilt, and regret. Then he turned his back on me and opened the front door.

"TELL ME AGAIN WHY you left school?" the police officer said, scooting his chair closer to the E.R. gurney I sat on, my legs crossed beneath me like a kindergartner. Only he wasn't just an officer. He was a detective. Because attempted murder—or manslaughter, or whatever they would wind up calling it—was a felony, and even though Scott was strapped to a bed in the same mental health ward I'd once spent a week in, he couldn't officially plead his mental defect until his parents called in their fancy, overpriced attorney to replace the court-appointed rookie currently shaking in his loafers upstairs.

And if anyone deserved to get off on temporary insanity, if was Scott Carter. He hadn't really meant to kill me. Well, maybe he had, but he would never have done it if he weren't in withdrawal from Demon's Breath and under the manipulation of an as-yet-unidentified Netherworld monster. Both circumstances I was convinced Nash and I could have prevented, if we'd acted sooner. Called in reinforcements.

"Kaitlyn? Kaitlyn, are you okay?" the cop asked, and Nash squeezed my good hand until I glanced up, surprised to find everyone staring at me.

"It's Kaylee…" I mumbled, staring at the neat row of stitches on the arm I held stiffly in front of me, awaiting a sterile bandage. "My name is Kaylee." I was grateful for the local anesthetic, and a bit surprised that it seemed to have numbed my mind, as well as my arm.

Or maybe that was shock.

"I'm sorry. Kaylee," the detective corrected himself, shifting uncomfortably in his chair. I'd insisted he sit, because I didn't like him towering over me. He made me nervous, probably because I felt guilty, though he didn't seem to suspect me of anything. "Kaylee, please tell me again why you followed Mr. Carter from the school parking lot."

Behind him, the thin blue curtain slid back on its metal track and an elderly nurse appeared, nearly swallowed by her purple scrubs. She carried several small, sealed packages, and I eyed them suspiciously.

"Because he was acting…crazy." *There. Maybe I could help with Scott's defense….* "He wasn't making any sense, and we didn't think he should be driving. So we followed to make sure he was okay."

"And he went straight home?"

I glanced at Nash, who nodded. "Yeah. The front door was open, so we went in. He was in his dad's office."

The nurse ripped open a package of sterile bandages and I flinched, startled.

"And he just attacked you with a knife?" The detective was still scribbling in his notebook, not even watching me as I nodded. "Did he say anything?"

"Um… He wanted me to take him somewhere."

Finally the cop looked up, surprised. "Where?"

"He didn't say." Which was true, technically. "He just said he'd kill me if I didn't take him. I told him I'd take him wherever he wanted to go if he'd put the knife down. So he moved it from my throat to my back, and when I tried to get away, he slashed me." I held up my injured arm for emphasis, foiling the nurse's attempt to bandage it.

"Okay, thank you, Kaylee." The detective stood and flipped his notebook closed, then slid it into the right pocket of his long coat. "Your dad's on his way—" I hadn't been able to stop them from calling him and scaring him to death "—and it looks like you're in good hands until he gets here." The cop smiled first at Nash, who didn't even seem to notice him, then at the nurse, whose cold hands shook as they pressed the bandage gently on the long line of stitches curving over the bony part of my forearm onto the fleshier underside. "We'll be following up with you soon, when we know more about what happened. Okay?"

I nodded as he headed toward the exit. He already had

one hand on the doorknob when I looked up. "What's going to happen to Scott?"

Nash glanced at me in surprise almost equal to the cop's, but the nurse didn't even pause in her work.

"Well, that all depends on his attorney. But Mr. Carter—Scott's father—has testified in several cases around here and, for a psychiatrist, he knows a fair bit about the law. I wouldn't worry about Scott. He'll get the best legal and mental care available."

I nodded, but only because I didn't know how else to respond. No amount of money or treatment could fix Scott now, and for all I knew, he'd hear that voice in his head—see that shape in the shadows—for the rest of his life. Even if he never again saw the outside of a padded room.

12

"JUST COME STRAIGHT HOME," Harmony said into her cell phone as I sank onto my couch with my bandaged arm in my lap. She pushed the front door closed, cutting off the chill from outside, then marched into the kitchen, already digging through my fridge for something that hadn't started to mold.

On the other end of the line, my father tried to argue, but she interrupted him with the confidence of a woman accustomed to giving orders. "I already picked her up."

My dad worked at a factory in Fort Worth, while Harmony worked in the very hospital they'd taken us to. So even coming from home—she'd worked the third shift—she'd gotten there nearly half an hour earlier than my dad could have made it.

"Because I was closer to the hospital than you were."

And because Nash's Influence had convinced the doc to release me to someone other than my legal guardian.

Harmony held the phone away from her ear while my father blustered, complained, and questioned. "She's fine, physically. We'll talk about it when you get here." With that, she flipped her phone closed and shoved it into her front pocket with a finality that suggested she would *not* answer if he called back.

Wow. I'd never seen anyone handle my dad like that, and I was so impressed I forgot to argue that I was fine mentally, too. I thought I was handling the whole thing pretty well, considering I'd nearly been killed. Again.

"Kaylee, do you believe in déjà vu?" Harmony smiled amiably and pulled a carton of milk from the fridge. "Because the sight of you lying injured on that couch is starting to look awfully familiar."

"I don't go looking for trouble," I insisted, a little miffed.

Nash set the keys to the rental on the half wall between the entry and the living room, then dropped onto the couch next to me with his head thrown back like it weighed a ton. We'd stopped by the Carters' house on the way home so Nash could follow us in the loaner. Scott's parents had been called back from Cancún early, but they wouldn't get in until the next day, so his house was completely dark and looked oddly deserted, even in the middle of a sunny winter day.

It was creepy, to say the least.

Harmony set a tub of margarine on the counter, then pulled half-full bags of flour and sugar from the depths of a cabinet I'd rarely peeked into. "Yet trouble manages to find you, whether you're looking for it or not."

"In this case, I think 'trouble' is a bit of an understatement," I mumbled, twisting carefully to lean on Nash as he wrapped one arm around me. "Don't you want to know what happened?" I asked, watching her through the wide kitchen doorway.

"Not yet." Her voice echoed from inside another cabinet. "You'll have to explain it all over again when your father gets here, so I'll just wait for that."

"Well, *I* won't," Tod snapped, and I glanced up to find him leaning against the kitchen door frame. He'd shown up in my room in the E.R. right after the detective left, demanding answers we couldn't give him while the nurse was still there. Then he'd blinked out to find his mother, only to discover her already on the way to the hospital. One of her fellow nurses had called her when she recognized Nash.

"Yes, you will." Harmony finally stood and faced her older, mostly dead son, a box of baking soda in one hand. "Making her repeat herself won't make her feel any better."

"Not that there's any chance of that, anyway..." My dad was going to go *apocalyptic* when he heard about the Demon's Breath. And I wasn't entirely convinced

Harmony wouldn't join him, once she knew the whole story.

Tod grumbled and dropped into my father's recliner, apparently willing to physically wait with the rest of us for once.

I sat up and shrugged out from under Nash's arm so I could see his face, but he wouldn't look at me. His eyes were closed, one wave of brown hair fallen over his eyebrow. I might have thought he was asleep, if not for the tense lines of his shoulders and jaw. Nash was just as upset as I was, and probably suffering an even heavier burden of guilt, because Scott was his friend.

Metal clanged against the faded Formica as Harmony set our good mixing bowl on the counter.

A labored engine roared down the street out front, then rumbled to a stop in the driveway. My father was home, and considering how quickly he'd arrived, I was surprised not to hear police sirens following him.

Moments later, the front door flew open and smashed against the half wall. My dad's keys dangled from his hand and his chest heaved as if he'd just run all the way from work. His breathing didn't slow until his gaze found mine. "Are you okay?"

I scooted forward on the couch as Nash sat up straight next to me. "Yeah. I'm good." Thanks to twenty-eight stitches and a strong local anesthetic. But I wasn't looking forward to the next hour of my life. The nurse who'd bandaged my arm had given me two Tylenol tablets.

Because once the local anesthetic wore off, she'd said, I'd feel like someone sliced my arm open.

I think that was her idea of a joke.

"What the hell happened?" my dad demanded, still standing in the open doorway as a cold draft swirled across the room, fluttering the opened bills on one end table and raising chill bumps on my legs. "Don't they have teachers at that school? Why wasn't anyone there to stop this?"

Well, crap. I guess there's no way to avoid the whole truancy aspect....

"We weren't actually *at* school." I squeezed my eyes shut, hoping I looked pathetic enough to thwart the bulk of his temper.

The front door slammed and I opened my eyes to see anger and concern warring behind my father's pained expression. "I don't even know where to start, Kaylee. I've only been back for three months, and you've nearly been killed twice. What do I have to do to keep you safe? Are you out *looking* for trouble?"

In spite of the growing pain in my arm and my general state of guilt and grief, I managed a wry grin, trying to lighten the mood. "You missed that part of the discussion." When his worried scowl deepened, the smile died on my face.

My father sighed and pulled his coat off as he clomped across the living room, bringing with him the scents of sweat and metal from the factory where he worked. He'd had to leave early—giving up part of his paycheck—thanks to me. "How's your arm?"

"Fine." I held out my hand when he reached for it, and he studied my arm, as if he could actually see through the long, thick bandage. "The doctor said there's no permanent damage. It's just a few stitches, Dad."

Tod huffed and propped his feet on the footrest of my father's recliner. "Try twenty-eight," he said, and my dad actually jerked in surprise. I was almost amused to realize that, though he could clearly hear the reaper, my father couldn't see him.

"Damn it, Tod!" He glared in the reaper's general direction. "Do not sneak up on me in my own house—I don't care *how* dead you are! Show yourself or get out."

Harmony and I shared a small smile, but my father didn't notice.

The reaper shrugged and grinned at me, then blinked out of the chair and onto the carpet at my father's back, now fully corporeal. "Fine," he said, inches from my dad's ear, and my father nearly jumped out of his shirt. "Your house, your rules."

My dad spun around, his flush deepening until I thought his face would explode. "I changed my mind. Get out!"

Tod shrugged again and a single blond curl fell over his forehead. "I'll get the scoop from Kaylee later. My break's over, anyway." Then he winked silently out of existence, leaving my father still fuming, his fists clenched at his sides in anger that had no outlet.

I looked up at the clock in the kitchen. It was 2:05 p.m. Tod's shift had only started at noon. If he didn't watch it, he was going to get fired.

"Is he really gone?" My dad glanced first at me, then at Harmony, who shrugged, clearly trying to hide a grin as she shoved several fallen ringlets back from her face.

"As far as I can tell."

Tod didn't torment his mother or me much because he couldn't get such a rise out of us. My father and Nash were his favorite targets, because they took themselves so seriously.

My dad closed his eyes and sucked in a long, hopefully calming breath, then refocused his attention on me. "Where were we?"

"I was telling you I'm fine. No permanent damage." No need to mention the twenty-eight stitches again…

"But you could have been killed," he insisted, and I couldn't argue with that, so I kept my mouth shut. "Come in here where I can get a better look at you." He stomped into the kitchen and gestured for me to take a seat at the table, beneath the brightest light in the house.

I sat, and he sank into the chair next to mine, studying my face as if it now held foreign planes and angles. "Who did this?" He took my chin in one hand and carefully turned my head for a better look at the short, shallow cut on my neck, which the nurse had cleaned and left unbandaged. It hadn't even required stitches.

I sighed and pulled away from his gentle grip, already dreading the explanation I was about to launch. "Scott Carter."

"The same kid who trashed your car?"

"No, that was Doug Fuller."

My father twisted in his seat to glare at Nash, who was now hunched over on the couch, his head cradled in both hands, his broad shoulders slumped. "And they're both friends of yours? Teammates?"

Harmony crossed her arms over her chest. "Aiden, Nash had nothing to do with this."

"Oh, really?" My father turned on her, and I hoped she understood that the sharpness in his voice reflected more worry than anger. "So it's just a coincidence that one of his teammates rammed her car through a brick mailbox, and less than a week later another one tries to hack her head off."

Well, at least I know where I get my penchant for exaggeration....

"Scott's kind of been borrowing trouble from Doug," I said, picking at the edge of my bandage. "But Nash has nothing to do with any of it."

I glanced at Nash for confirmation, but he still had his head buried in his hands. He was really taking Scott's breakdown hard, and I couldn't blame him. I'd be devastated if anything happened to Emma. Especially something I could have prevented. Which was why the whole thing had to end now, even if that meant turning the whole mess over to my dad.

"Exactly what kind of trouble are these boys in?" my father demanded softly. "And what does it have to do with you?"

Nash finally looked up, his eyes shiny and rimmed in red. His hands shook, clenched in his lap, and I wanted to sink onto the couch next to him and tell him it would be okay. That none of it was really his fault. He hadn't given his friends the Demon's Breath, and we didn't know for sure that acting earlier would actually have saved Scott. For all we knew, sending him into withdrawal earlier might only have escalated his breakdown.

But I stayed at the table because Nash looked like he wanted to wallow in private misery. I wanted to respect that. To give him some time. But if he so much as looked at me, I'd be across the room in an instant.

I shrugged, meeting my dad's gaze reluctantly. "I don't think it has anything to do with me." Though Scott's shadow man's insistence that the whole thing was my fault was certainly nagging at the back of my mind. I sucked in a deep breath and spat out the rest of it before I could chicken out.

"Scott and Doug are taking Demon's Breath, and it's making them crazy. Literally."

"What?" my father demanded, at the exact moment Harmony dropped an egg on the kitchen floor. She just stood there, her open hand palm up and empty, slimy egg white oozing over the linoleum toward the toe of one worn sneaker.

Then understanding sank in—I saw its progression across her face—and she stepped absently over the busted egg. "That's why you were asking—"

My father turned on her. "You knew about this?"

"No!" Harmony glanced at me, and the hurt in her slowly swirling eyes withered my self-respect. "I thought she was talking about Regan Page! I had no idea there was Demon's Breath in their school!" Then her gaze narrowed on me again. "You didn't take any of it, did you?"

"Of course not!" It killed me that she even had to ask. But then, I had lied to her—if indirectly—in my search for facts. "Don't you think I've spent enough time strapped to a bed?"

My dad flinched and I almost felt guilty for throwing such a low blow. But he wasn't the one who'd had me hospitalized. My aunt and uncle had done that, in a very ill-thought-out attempt to help me "deal" with abilities I neither knew about nor understood. My father's only crime was leaving me with them in the first place.

"Nash and I were just trying to cut off their supply." I shrugged, hating how unsure of myself I sounded. And how juvenile our attempts at intervention must look to a couple of *bean sidhes* with a combined age of more than two centuries. "Dad, these guys have no idea what they're taking, or what it's doing to them. We took Scott's first balloon and gave it to Tod to dispose of, but he got another one, and—"

"You did *what?*" My father's voice was as hard as ice, and about as warm. "Tod knows about this?"

I shrugged and glanced at Nash, who looked like he wanted to disappear as he avoided his mother's look of disbelief and confusion. "We were assuming you wouldn't want us to take the balloon to the Netherworld ourselves…."

"You assumed right." Yet somehow my father didn't look very happy about my display of uncommon sense. "How did two human boys get their hands on Demon's Breath in the first place?"

"They…" I started, but then a sharp shake of Nash's head caught my attention, and I looked up to find him staring at me intently. And suddenly I wasn't sure what to do. We'd agreed to tell our parents about the Demon's Breath, and technically we'd done that. But Nash clearly didn't want them to know about Everett. Or maybe about the party.

My father watched me expectantly, waiting for me to finish my aborted thought. "They bought it from some guy who sells it in party balloons. He calls it frost." Which was true… "We could ask Doug—"

"No!" My father's palm slapped the table and it shook beneath my arm. "Stay away from him, Kaylee.

Harmony, Brendon, and I will take care of this. I don't want you anywhere near that kid. Ever."

I nodded slowly, unsure what else to do. My dad was starting to sound paranoid. I had to go to school, and unless he'd miraculously graduated in the past few hours, so did Doug.

Harmony knelt on the kitchen floor in front of the cracked egg with a dish rag in one hand, but her attention was focused on me. "How bad off are they? Scott and Doug."

"They're both seeing things, but it's obviously affecting Scott a lot worse than Doug," I said, thinking about Nash's conjecture that Doug had a little Netherworld blood somewhere in his genealogy.

"Scott totally lost it today at school," Nash added, and I glanced at him in surprise; he'd hardly spoken since we'd left the hospital. "He was seeing things, and hearing things, and he was literally scared of his own shadow."

"Assuming it really is his shadow..." I said. Nash and I hadn't discussed my theory that Scott wasn't really hallucinating, but I figured if anyone would know for sure about the side effects of Demon's Breath, it would be Harmony.

"What do you mean?" she asked.

But Nash answered before I could. "Kaylee got creeped out by Scott's shadow fixation. He was talking to them, and listening to them, and the whole thing was pretty convincing. Plus, there was the knife." He shrugged and shot me a concerned, almost condescending look of sympathy. "It's no wonder she started to believe him. She was terrified. I was scared, too."

I bristled, glaring at him. "You think I'm imagining this? I was *not* creeped out!" Though I wasn't going to deny being afraid of the knife.

"Kay…" Nash stood and made his way into the kitchen, his voice flowing over me like warm silk. "He was delusional, and you were scared, and bleeding, and in shock. Anyone would have been freaked out, but try not to read too much into anything Scott said or did. He's not playing with a full deck anymore."

I shook my head so hard my brain felt like it was bouncing in my skull, but I couldn't shake the seductive feel of his voice in my mind. The overwhelming urge to nod my head, close my mouth, and let the whole thing play out without me.

I fought it, but struggling was like trying to swim in a huge vat of warm honey, when it would have been so much easier simply to sink into the sweetness. "Stop Influencing me," I whispered, when what I really wanted to do was shout.

"Nash!" Harmony snapped, and his warm mental presence dissipated like fog in bright sunlight.

Furious now, I pushed my chair away from the table, twisting my injured arm in the process. I gasped over the fresh throb and clutched my arm to my chest, but the pain helped clear my head and I rounded on him, fighting angry tears and the sharp sting of betrayal. "I'm not some hysterical kid, and *I am not crazy!*" Even the implication that my logic had been compromised triggered my very worst fears.

And Nash damn well knew that.

"Kay, no one's saying you're crazy." My father stood, too, and when he reached out for me, I let him pull me close. "You've had a traumatic day, and he was just trying to calm you down, though admittedly he's going about it the wrong way." He shot a pointed scowl at Nash, who had the decency to look horrified by what he'd done. So why the hell had he done it?

"I'm sorry, Kaylee." Nash let me see the swirl of regret in his eyes. But I couldn't forgive him. Not for this. Not yet.

"Stay out of my head, Nash." I stepped back when he reached for me, and he looked like I'd punched him in the gut. Some small part of me felt bad about that, but the rest of me was pissed. I had more to say about this, but not in front of our parents.

So I sat at the table again and ground my teeth when he sat in the chair next to mine.

"I assume people noticed Scott acting strange?" my dad asked as he crossed the kitchen, obviously eager to pull the discussion back on track.

"Um, yeah." Nash fought to catch my gaze, and when I refused to look at him, he fingered a crack in the weathered kitchen table. "But they all think he was high on something...normal." He glanced at his mother, who'd just finished cleaning up the egg slime. "Is there anything we can do for him?"

Harmony shook her head slowly. "The damage to his brain is permanent. And withdrawal will be very hard on him in a human hospital, because all they can do is restrain him to keep him from hurting himself. The only medications I know of that can make him feel better come from the Netherworld."

"Can you get him any of those?" I asked. "Assuming they keep him at Arlington Memorial?"

She leaned with one hip on the counter, drying her hands on a damp dishrag. "I don't work in mental health, but I can probably get in to see him once or twice. And if I can't, Tod can."

"What about Doug?" I asked. "He's not as bad off as Scott is, but the night he hit my car, he said he saw someone in his passenger's seat."

"That's easy enough," Nash shrugged, looking optimistic for the first time since we'd left school. "Next time we hang out, I'll just slip whatever weird medication he needs into his drink." He glanced at Harmony again, eyes shining in either hope or desperation. "You can get whatever he needs, right?"

"I think so. But it won't do any good until the Demon's Breath is completely out of his system..."

"And we still don't know how to cut off the supply," I finished.

"You let us worry about that," my father said with a note of finality he'd probably perfected kicking drunks out of his parents' pub in Ireland. "Let's get you something to eat, then I want you to take a nap while I'm here to make sure you wake up in your own bed."

I didn't even try to argue. I was exhausted, and I wouldn't be any help to Emma or Doug until I could think straight.

My dad and Harmony messed around in the kitchen, trying to put together a decent meal and discuss the situation without saying anything that would upset me. Because apparently exhaustion and blood loss had combined to make me look about as sturdy as a blown-glass vase.

After several minutes spent listening to them whisper, I plodded to my room without even a glance in Nash's direction.

He followed me.

I collapsed stomach-down on my bed while he stood in the doorway. "Go away."

He took that as an invitation to sit at my desk.

"I'm sorry."

"You should be." I turned to face the window, fluffing my pillow under one cheek, and my desk chair creaked as he stood. A moment later, he knelt on the opposite side of the bed, inches from my face. "What the hell is wrong with you lately?" I was worried about the frost invasion too, but it hadn't turned me into a controlling bitch.

"Kaylee, please..."

"That was messed up, Nash. That was...slimy." I sat up and scooted back on the bed to put distance between us. "You make me think I want things I don't really want to do, and it's like losing control of myself. It's worse than being strapped to a hospital bed because it's not some stranger who has to let me up when I stop fighting. It's you, and I shouldn't have to fight you." I blinked back tears, almost as mad at myself for crying as I was at him for invading my mind. "I don't want your voice in my head anymore. Not even to help me."

Nash nodded slowly, his eyes churning with too many emotions for me to interpret. "I'm so sorry, Kaylee. I swear it'll never happen again." He swallowed and glanced at his hands, where they gripped the edge of my mattress. "It's just that everything is so messed up, and it's all my fault. Scott could have killed you, and I...I'm just not thinking straight right now."

"I know." I wasn't, either. I was running on caffeine and adrenaline, both of which were fading fast.

But before he could say anything else, my phone dinged, and I leaned to one side to dig it from my front pocket.

There was a text from Emma. R U OK? LB said you narced on Scott.

Crap. I'd forgotten that Laura Bell—LB—had been home sick all day. She'd obviously seen them load me and Scott into ambulances—his under police escort—and had reported her version of the event.

It was probably all over school. And since I couldn't tell anyone the truth, Laura's version—which evidently blamed me for getting the quarterback arrested on drug charges—would stand on the record.

Great.

I tried to text her back, but I couldn't type very well without my right hand, so after two failed attempts, Nash held out his hand for my phone, watching my face closely. Letting him help would mean I'd forgiven him.

I sighed and gave him my phone. "Tell her I'm fine, and I'll explain later," I said, and he nodded, typing almost as fast with two thumbs as I could. "And that I did *not* rat on Scott."

The part about Scott trying to kill me could wait for another day.

EMMA EYED ME in concern when I collapsed into my chair beside her in chemistry on Friday morning. She'd been preoccupied with Doug for most of yesterday and hadn't noticed my exhaustion, but evidently my zombie impersonation was now too obvious to be overlooked.

"Wow, Kaylee, you look like crap," she whispered as the girl in front of me passed a stapled test packet over her shoulder.

"Thanks." I shot Emma a good-humored smile. At least, I hoped it looked good-humored. "I haven't been getting much sleep."

After Nash and Harmony left the night before, I'd collapsed on the couch—again in my homemade protective gear—but got very little rest, because this time my father refused to sleep and I could feel him watching me. I had two death dreams in a four-hour span, and my dad woke me up from both of them the moment the first note of a soul song erupted from my mouth.

Each time, he sat on the coffee table with a spiral-bound notebook, pen ready to go, but I had no new details to offer. Same dark figure. Same falling through the Nether-smog. Same panic welling inside my dream throat. Same featureless face I couldn't identify.

Between the dream-screaming, the butchered forearm, and my near-death experience, peaceful sleep was a fond and somewhat distant memory. Yet, thanks to Scott's absence and Laura Bell's sensational but inaccurate gossip, the last school day of the semester was even worse than the sleepless night it followed.

I could feel them staring at me as I flipped open my test booklet. They'd been watching me all morning. Ogling the bandage my right sleeve wouldn't cover, which made it obvious that something big had gone down the day before, but left the details tantalizingly vague.

I pretended not to hear the whispers in the hall, rumors linking my name with Scott's. Wondering if he and I had been cheating on Nash and Sophie, which was easily the most ridiculous speculation I'd ever heard.

Until I heard someone claim that Nash had cut me—and was the source of whatever mysterious damage Scott had suffered—when he caught the two of us together.

There were other, quieter rumors from people who'd seen Scott's breakdown in class or in the cafeteria. They knew something had been wrong with him before we'd ever left school, but their tales were less exciting and never really caught on. Which left me and Nash to bear the brunt of the rumors and the stares.

And Sophie, of course. Her conspicuous absence only fanned the flames of the rumor bonfire consuming the school, and for the first time, she found herself tied to a stake at the center of the blaze, condemned to burn alongside me.

I couldn't really blame her for skipping school. Especially considering she had no idea what had really happened between me, Scott, and Nash. For all I knew, she'd actually bought the load of crap Laura was shoveling.

"Just ignore them." Emma glared across the room at a couple of juniors whispering and staring at me while they waited for test booklets. "Their own lives aren't interesting enough to warrant gossip," she said, loud enough for the whole class to hear.

Mrs. Knott frowned and cleared her throat, and Emma avoided her eyes as she flipped open her test. But as soon as the teacher turned away, Em kicked my chair softly to regain my attention. "I'm really worried about Doug," she whispered. "He didn't show up for his English midterm this morning." Ever since Scott's freakout at school, she'd been watching Doug closely for signs that he was headed down the same path. "He's hardly eating anything. And this is going to sound stupid, but his hands are always cold."

I tried to smile and calm her down. She couldn't help him, so worrying would do her no good. "I'm sure that doesn't mean anything, Em. Nash's hands are usually freezing, and he's…"

No. I closed my eyes and swallowed thickly. It was a coincidence. Nash wasn't using. He was helping me get rid of frost for good. He knew how dangerous it was, and he was just as repulsed by the thought of sucking hellion breath as I was.

But Doug *was* using, and it *would* kill him.

I hadn't told Emma the truth about the Demon's Breath, even after what happened with Scott, because Dad and Harmony agreed that the less she knew, the safer she'd be from Everett and his Netherworld supplier. But watching her now, forehead wrinkled in concern for the first high school guy she'd shown any interest in, I couldn't help thinking that Dad and Harmony were wrong this time.

I knew better than most that ignorance was neither blissful nor safe, and it didn't seem fair to put Emma through what I'd suffered. Especially considering that Scott had turned out to be dangerous on Demon's Breath.

What if Doug did, too?

"Em, I need to tell you something." Her brows rose,

and she nodded, but then Mrs. Knott walked down the aisle between us and I'd lost my chance to speak. The test had begun. "After class," I mouthed, then turned my attention to my midterm.

Unfortunately, Doug was waiting for Emma after class, and she waved to me apologetically as she wrapped one arm around his waist, promising she'd catch me at lunch.

At first, I was surprised that Doug hadn't asked me what happened to Scott. Until I noticed the half-eaten candy bar in his fist as they walked off. He held it without the wrapper, and despite his tight grip, the chocolate wasn't melting against his skin. He was frosted, and probably not thinking about anything but staying that way.

Tod's hospital shift started at noon, so I'd fully expected him to pop into class during one of my early midterms, demanding to know what he'd missed when I couldn't possibly answer him. But I didn't see him all morning, and I couldn't help wondering why he was never around during his off hours, but would skip out on work to come bug me and Nash.

By eleven-thirty, my morning overdose of caffeine had worn off and I wobbled on my feet, flinching when I caught myself against the wall with my bad arm. I'd survived my first three midterms—though I couldn't swear I'd aced them—and had three still to go. But after only twelve hours of sleep over the past three days, I could barely spell my name right, and passing the remaining tests seemed like a long shot, at best.

So during lunch, Nash and I snuck out of the cafeteria and into the parking lot, where I slept in the reclined seat of my rental car while he devoured a cafeteria cheeseburger and crammed for his physics test, ready to wake me if I so much as hummed in my sleep.

I jolted awake thirty-eight minutes into our forty-five-minute lunch period, sitting straight up in the driver's seat with Nash staring at me like I'd just recited the U.S. presidents in my sleep. An ability which probably would have come in handy during my history test.

"What happened?" I blinked, confused, until I remembered I was still at school, in a car I hadn't completely gotten used to yet. Was that why I felt so… disoriented? But exhaustion couldn't explain why I'd evidently sat up in my sleep.

Nash's eyes churned steadily with fear and with some emotion I couldn't quite identify, and as I watched, his irises began to settle as he got a handle on the scare I'd obviously given him. "You were making weird noises. So I woke you up."

I was? I didn't remember having any dreams at all, much less the horrifying, recurring death dream. But something had obviously happened, and it had clearly scared the crap out of Nash.

In spite of my rude—and odd—awakening, the short nap helped more than I'd thought possible. Or maybe that was the Mountain Dew Nash handed me as we walked back into the building, just in time for fifth period. "Drink fast and work hard," he said, giving me the sweetest, peppermint-scented kiss on the nose. "I'll see you in the gym after school."

He was trying really hard to make up for our fight the day before, and the caffeine fix was good for several bonus points.

But by the time the final bell rang, the Mountain Dew was wearing off and my arm was really starting to throb. I couldn't stand the thought of spending my Friday afternoon painting booths for my cousin's pet project—left-handed, thanks to my injury—while her friends stared and whispered. If Sophie was skipping, we could, too. So I drove Nash home and crashed on his bed while he played Xbox.

Nash shook me awake a couple of hours later, with hands so cold I could feel them through my shirt. I was relieved to discover that I had neither dreamed nor struck any odd positions in my sleep. "You have to get up if we're going to make it to the party," he whispered, soft, warm lips brushing my cheek.

The setting sun cast slanted shadow bars across Nash's room through his half-closed blinds, and I blinked in the crimson glare, trying to fully wake up. The alarm clock on his bedside table said it was almost five-thirty. "Mmmm…" He smelled so good I wanted to bury my face in his shirt and breathe him in. Then go back to sleep.

Who needs food and water? Nash and slumber would be enough to sustain me. Right?

"What party?" I mumbled, pushing myself up on my good arm, in spite of the heavy hand of sleep threatening to pull me back under.

"Fuller's. Remember? We were going to find Everett?"

And that's when reality came crashing in on me, washing away the serenity that waking up next to Nash had lent me.

Doug's party. Everett's balloons. Scott's knife. My sliced-up arm. Suddenly my head hurt and my stomach was churning in dread.

"I can't believe he's still throwing a party, with one of his best friends in the hospital." And charged with a felony.

Nash shrugged. "The crowd will be bigger than ever tonight, everyone hoping to hear what really happened to Carter."

Well, they wouldn't hear it from me. "My dad'll kill me if we go to Doug's." Not that my father's caution had ever stopped me from helping a friend in need before.

Nash rolled his eyes and pressed the power button on his Xbox, then shoved it against the scratched chest of drawers his television sat on. "If we don't go, who's going to watch out for Emma?"

"Tod…?" I started, but the flaw in that plan was immediately obvious. "Well, I assume he has to actually show up for work at some point."

"Let's hope." Nash hesitated as I ran my fingers through long, sleep-tangled hair. "Maybe you can talk her out of going…" he finally suggested. "You two could do something girlie tonight and let me handle Everett."

I shook my head as I stepped into my first sneaker. "I already tried that. After what happened with Scott, she's determined to keep an eye on Doug." I had to sit on the bed to tug the second shoe on, then I met Nash's frustrated gaze with one of my own.

Nash sighed and sat on the edge of his desk, and I sat straighter as a new thought occurred to me. "Maybe we're making this too hard. Why don't we just get him alone at the party, cross over with him, and leave him in the Netherworld?" Which was a virtual death sentence—or worse—for anyone native to the human world. Yet I felt only a fleeting pang of guilt over that thought, after what Everett's little enterprise had done to Scott, and would do to anyone else who sampled his stash. "I mean, he can't *sell* in our world if he can't *get* to our world. Right?"

His brows rose. "You think he can't cross on his own? If that's true, how is he getting Demon's Breath in the first place?"

Crap. My disappointment crested in a wave of embarrassment.

Either Everett could cross over on his own—which meant he couldn't be trapped in the Netherworld—or he was working with someone who could. In which case getting rid of Everett wouldn't stop the distribution of frost into our world.

I grabbed my backpack from the floor and tossed it over one shoulder, squinting against the reddish light peeking through the blinds. "Nash, we have to tell my dad about Everett."

Nash rolled his eyes. "What's your dad going to do that we can't? Other than make sure we're never welcome at another party…"

"I don't know. But what are we supposed to do? Threaten to scream until Everett's ears bleed?"

Nash sighed and grabbed my keys from the desktop, where I'd dropped them when we came in. "Look, if your dad busts up the party, Fuller will wind up hanging out alone with Emma all night. Either high off his new stash, or crazy from withdrawal."

My heart dropped into my stomach. I swear I heard it splash into the Mountain Dew I drank instead of eating lunch.

He was right. My dad could break up the party and possibly even stop Everett from selling to everyone there. At least for one night. But he couldn't save Emma from Doug once they were alone.

That was up to me.

We went to my house first, so I could change and

pack an overnight bag. On the way out, I left a note for my dad on the fridge, telling him I was going out with Nash and that I'd be spending the night with Emma—so she wouldn't have a chance to be alone with Doug—and that he was welcome to call and check up on me. It's not like I'd be sleeping. Ever again, evidently.

Then, because I knew he couldn't answer his cell at work, I called and left a voice mail saying the same thing. He was working late again, to make up for the pay he'd lost the day before thanks to my trip to the hospital, and with any luck he wouldn't get either message until his double shift was over. Around midnight. By which time I hoped to be stretched out on Emma's bedroom floor, halfway through a pint of Death by Chocolate and a B-grade '80s horror flick, safe from the perils of the real world.

Make that *both* worlds.

EMMA'S AFTERNOON SHIFT at the Cinemark didn't end until seven, so she couldn't make it to the party until eight. Nash and I stopped for cheap tacos and still got there by seven-thirty.

Mr. Fuller had taken Doug's twenty-eight-year-old stepmother with him to some professional conference in New York, leaving Doug alone in a house big enough to sleep the whole football team.

Or host the entire senior class.

We parked at the end of the street again, and I felt

marginally more confident in the safety of my car this time, because it wasn't really mine and because Doug wouldn't be driving. He was already home.

The party was in full swing long before we got there—music blasting, drinks flowing, people dancing, and couples ducking out the back door or up the stairs. In the den, a dozen upperclassmen had gathered around two guys with video game controllers, engrossed in some virtual tournament. One room over, two half-dressed couples had found an alternate use for Mr. Fuller's pool table, and in the kitchen, one of the football team's managers was manning a keg someone's big brother had bought.

I waved to Brant Williams across the living room and he smiled back, dark, friendly eyes shining at me over the heads of most of our classmates. As Nash pulled me through the crowd, I spared a moment to hope Brant miraculously decided he needed to be somewhere else before Everett showed up.

People everywhere shouted greetings to Nash, and more than a few of them looked surprised to find me with him. Evidently seeing us together discredited the worst of the rumors about me and Scott. Several guys asked Nash how Scott was doing, and he told them all he hadn't heard anything since yesterday.

He'd called the hospital that afternoon, but they would only release information to family members. We were hoping Tod could give us an update, but neither of us had seen him since he'd disappeared from my living room the afternoon before.

Sophie was a no-show at the party. While I was glad she was staying out of trouble—and out of my way—I was starting to wonder if she'd even show up for the carnival she'd helped organize. I considered calling her, but she wouldn't answer her phone if it showed my number, so I decided to check in with her dad in the morning. Uncle Brendon knew what was going on—much more than Sophie knew, anyway—and had no doubt taken the Netherworld element into consideration when he let her skip school.

I almost felt sorry for her.

We found Doug near the back of the living room, pouring something stronger than beer into a clear plastic cup of soda. "Hey, man, is Em with you?" He handed Nash a can of Coke from a cooler sitting on a thick rug thrown over the hardwood floor.

"She'll be here around eight," I said as Doug rooted through the cooler again. He came up with a Diet Coke and a regular, holding them both up for me to choose from. I pointed to the regular, and he grinned as he dropped the diet back into the cooler.

"Atta girl. Want somethin' extra?" He held up the small bottle of Absolut he'd poured into his own cup.

"No thanks." There was no way I'd handicap my logic or coordination with Everett the Netherworld crack dealer scheduled to make an appearance.

"She has control issues," Nash said, and I could have kicked him into the next time zone.

Doug raised one brow at me, then shot Nash a sympathetic look. "Lucky you."

"I'm driving," I insisted, but the damage was already done.

"Whatever," Doug said, then something behind me caught his attention and he grinned.

"Hey, guys!" Emma threw her arm around my waist. She smelled like vanilla and looked like sex poured into a skirt. Her sister's skirt, if I had to guess.

"I thought you had to work," I said as she let Doug pull her close.

"I got off early." She stood on her toes to kiss Doug as his hand wandered down from her waist, and I had a moment to hope he hadn't yet unsealed a fresh balloon before she grinned at me like she'd been huffing goofy gas. But this high was natural. I could tell because, as I watched, Doug's hand twitched around her hip.

He hadn't had his fix yet. Which meant we hadn't missed our chance.

"I didn't think you'd come after yesterday," Emma said, her smile fading with the memory of what little I'd told her about Scott and his knife.

Nash popped open his Coke. "She needed a little fun."

Emma grinned. "Me, too."

"Well, then, start with this." Doug handed Emma the

cup he'd spiked for himself, and she drained half of it in one gulp.

"Hey, Em, can I crash with you tonight?" I asked, popping the top on my own can.

"Sure. Your dad being a pain?"

I shrugged, letting her draw her own conclusions.

"Hey, Fuller, is your friend here yet?" Nash asked, his hand tightening almost imperceptibly around mine.

But Doug shook his head. "I wish he'd hurry up."

"What friend?" Emma asked, but instead of answering, Doug pushed her cup toward her mouth until she emptied it, then pulled her into the crowd of writhing bodies, already moving to the heavy beat.

With nothing else to do until Everett showed up, Nash and I joined them on the dance floor and I was just starting to relax when a dark smudge on the edge of my vision seemed to freeze my blood in my veins.

I went still while all around me bodies moved in time to the song, oblivious to the danger now walking among them. I couldn't see the door through the crowd, but I couldn't miss the dark shape hovering near the ceiling—a huge black balloon bouquet, like the centerpiece of an over-the-hill birthday party.

Everett had arrived. And he'd brought enough frost to bake the entire senior class.

14

"LOOK!" I SHOUTED into Nash's ear, to be heard over the thumping, blaring music. I clutched his arm, unable to tear my horrified gaze from the balloons floating a couple of feet below Fuller's twelve-foot ceiling. Before Nash had a chance to focus on the problem, I tugged him toward the edge of the crowd, hoping the noise would abate so we could hear each other.

And maybe see more than three feet into the crowd.

Near the edge of the room I let Nash go and nodded toward the foyer, where the bouquet still hovered over the room like a poisonous cloud. What kind of dealer walks right in the front door? But then, I guess it's hard to be discreet carrying that many balloons.

"That's Everett, right?" We couldn't see him, but who

else would bring three dozen black balloons to a high school party?

Nash looked up. Blood drained from his face so quickly I wasn't sure how he remained conscious. He nodded slowly and began making his way through the crowd, still clutching my hand. I tried not to step on too many feet or bump into anyone with my bandaged arm as my heart raced fast enough to leave me light-headed. Everett was here. And we still had no plan.

Nash stopped when we got to the front window and had a clear view into the entryway, and his hand clenched tighter around mine. I followed his swirling gaze to see that the guy holding the balloons wasn't much older than the crowd—twenty, at the outside—and that he was flanked by two of the most beautiful, eerily flawless girls I'd ever seen.

Between them, Everett, who looked human, was tall and too thin, his slight build only exaggerated by an oversize T-shirt and jeans that barely hung from the points of his hips. I couldn't help wondering if he would let go of the balloons to pull his pants up if they fell off, which was a definite possibility. Based on the hazy look in his eyes and his death grip on the collection of strings, I would have bet my life the answer was no.

Everett wasn't just selling; he was using. Though I couldn't imagine how he stayed sane enough to run his business.

"It's about time!" Doug called across the room, and

I looked up to see him shoving his way through the crowd, dragging Emma behind him. "I have a room set up for you in the back." Doug's gaze jumped from the balloons to Everett's face, his hand twitching at his side. He was hurting—bad—and surely we weren't the only ones who could see that.

Emma raised both perfectly arched brows as she wandered toward me. "Who's that?"

"Everett," I said, desperately wishing I'd been able to keep her away from the party. "Doug's supplier."

"Yeah, I puzzled that out on my own. Who are *they?*" She nodded toward the foyer again and I realized she meant the girls. So I took a closer look and finally realized what was bothering me about them. It wasn't their surreal beauty—though, for the record, nothing so perfect should ever really exist.

Nor was it the fact that they were identical—not like twins, but like two copies of the same person. The *exact* same person. Same long, straight, white-blond hair parted on the left, with exactly the same crook halfway down the part. The same black eyes shining like they were lit from within. They had the same brilliant white teeth and exactly the same pale skin with the barest brush of pink on unfreckled cheekbones. And they stood at exactly the same height, with their right legs bent at the knee.

The whole carbon-copy aspect was definitely creepy, but it wasn't what nagged at the back of my mind, like a skeletal finger tapping my shoulder. What bothered me was their stance. The girls flanked Everett not like arm candy, but like bodyguards.

But I had to be imagining that. Right? What could two slim, unarmed girls in identical white-lace minidresses do in defense of a man six inches taller, with feet the size of small boats?

The crowd parted for Doug and his strange entourage, and they passed through the living room and out of sight in seconds.

"I need another drink," I said for Emma's benefit, already moving back into the crowd. Em had figured out who Everett was, but not what he was really selling, and I didn't want her involved in...whatever was about to go down.

"Let's go!" I whispered, tugging on Nash's arm when he made no move to follow me.

Emma shrugged and held up her empty cup. "I could use a refill, too."

I groaned inwardly, trying to catch Nash's eye. He finally met my gaze and nodded. He had a plan. But instead of clueing me in, he walked off toward the kitchen, apparently expecting us to follow.

Irritated, I smiled at Emma and wound my way through the crowd after Nash. Several feet from the kitchen, he turned to walk backward, facing us with a glance at Emma's empty cup. "What are you drink—?"

Nash tripped over his own foot and grabbed the arm

of the girl next to him for balance. She squealed and overcompensated, dumping her beer all over Emma's shirt.

Em screeched and pulled the cold, wet material away from her skin.

"I'm so sorry, Emma!" Nash ducked into the kitchen and grabbed a towel from the counter, then tossed it to her as his eyes met mine, swirling with mischief.

"What if that hadn't worked?" I whispered, reaching around him to pull a strip of paper towels from a wooden rack.

"Then the keg would have had a malfunction." He turned back to Emma, faking a concerned expression that made me want to laugh. Until I heard his next words. "Kaylee, your overnight bag's in the car, right? You have a shirt she can borrow?"

I glared at Nash in a cold wash of comprehension. He wasn't just trying to get Emma out of the way, he was getting rid of me, too! But I wasn't going to be pushed out of danger because of some prehistoric sense of chivalry. Nash couldn't even cross over on his own! He needed me.

My jaw clenched, and I had to force my mouth open to answer the question, as Emma stared at me beseechingly, still holding the front of her drenched top. "Of course." I dug my keys from my pocket, intending to hand them to her when Nash shot me a warning look and stepped close enough to whisper in my ear, though it probably looked like he was going for a much more intimate contact. "Go with her and keep her out there for a few minutes. I don't want her to come back looking for us and walk in on something she shouldn't see or hear. Do you?" he continued, before I could protest.

And I could hardly say no. Keeping Emma out of danger was my idea. I just hadn't planned on overseeing that part of the plan personally....

I nodded grimly and clenched my keys in my fist, glaring straight at Nash so he could see the anger surely churning in my eyes.

But he only shrugged apologetically, then watched me lead her out the door and into the frigid night, headed toward my car and away from the action—and the answers I was desperate for.

"This f-f-figures," Emma said, chattering violently as we clacked down the brick driveway. "I actually remembered to bring a change of clothes to work and I got off early. I should have known something would go wrong." She crossed her arms over her chest in spite of the cold beer probably freezing to her bra at that very moment. "Maybe we should stay at your house tonight, so I can wash the beer out of this shirt before my mom smells it. Or Traci. Traci's going to kill me."

"It's your sister's shirt?" I rubbed my arms, trying to get rid of the chill bumps prickling my skin.

"You think my mom would let me buy something like

this?" She held her arms out to show off the plunging neckline of the clingy, sparkly top.

When I had the car unlocked, Emma crawled into the backseat and pulled her shirt off while I dug in my bag for the one I'd planned to wear in the morning. It was just a T-shirt, but because I was smaller than Emma up top, it would look much better on her. Unfortunately, for that same reason, she'd either have to go braless or stay cold, wet, and smelly. My spare bra wouldn't fit her unless she could time-travel back to age twelve.

"Does this look obscene?" Em asked, and I turned to see her pulling my snug, crimson T-shirt into place over her braless chest.

"Yes."

"Good." She grinned and glanced at the rearview mirror. "Do you have a brush in there?" Em nodded at the bag I still held in my lap.

"I forgot it." I'd packed in a hurry. "But I think Nash keeps a comb in his duffel." I pointed to the right rear floorboard, where Nash had tossed his gym bag after school.

Emma lifted the bag onto the seat with one hand and laughed. "Not planning to do much reading over the holiday, is he?"

"Not if I can help it." I grinned, thinking about two straight weeks with nothing to keep us apart but a few shifts at the Cinemark and what little sleep we couldn't do without. Assuming we ever solved my current sleeping issues.

Emma unzipped the bag. "What's this? It's *cold*." Something red and shapeless took up half of the duffel. Emma pulled it out with one hand, and her brows rose in confusion.

My next words died in my throat. I could barely breathe around them.

She held a bright red balloon, closed by a weighted black plastic clip.

No. My hand clenched around the back of the front passenger's seat as I twisted for a better look.

"I thought Nash wasn't into this." The surprise in Emma's voice was a weak echo of the denial I wanted to shout.

"He's not," I insisted, in spite of the traitorous voice of doubt in my head and the painful pounding of my heart. "Everett's balloons are black." But that didn't mean anything. Regardless of color, why else would Nash have a clipped, weighted party balloon in his gym bag? A very *cold* clipped, weighted party balloon…

It's not his. Maybe he'd confiscated it from another teammate Doug had sold to. After all, I'd never seen Nash talking to his own shadow or twitching from withdrawal. Nor had I ever smelled Demon's Breath on him. In fact, I'd only smelled…

Peppermint. When did Nash start chewing gum?

No. He'd helped me get rid of Scott's first balloon, and…

I sank into the driver's seat, devastated, as the pieces started to fall into place. I hadn't actually seen Nash give the balloon to Tod. I'd just assumed he had because he'd said he would.

The mood swings. Aggression. Cold hands. He'd stopped me from telling my dad about Everett. Then he'd sent me outside with Emma instead of letting me confront the dealer.

Nash was using. Tears burned in my eyes. I'd wondered briefly before, then dismissed my suspicion as paranoia. I hadn't wanted to believe it. But I couldn't deny it now. *How could I be so stupid?*

"Kaylee?" Emma said, one hand on the back of my seat.

"We have to go. Now." I started to shove my key into the ignition, then stopped when I remembered the balloon. I would *not* have that thing in the car with us.

My vision swimming in tears, I twisted and grabbed the balloon from her. "Stay here," I said, then got out and slammed my door, leaving Emma to stare after me in surprise.

I'd only made it ten steps from the car, my nose already freezing and dripping, when Nash stepped out of Doug's house and pulled the front door closed. He jogged down the steps and onto the sidewalk, shoving cold-reddened hands into his pockets, then stopped when he saw me.

I wanted to believe his eyes were swirling with something painful—regret, guilt, shame. But the truth was that it was too dark for me to tell.

"Tell me this isn't yours." Holding the balloon like a bomb, I stopped about eight feet from him—close enough to read his expression, but not to see his irises—and my stomach flip-flopped painfully. I took a deep breath, so cold it burned my lungs. "Tell me the truth, Nash."

He flinched and dropped his gaze. So I tried again. "Tell me this isn't yours."

Nash sucked in a deep breath and met my gaze. His shoulders slumped and his throat worked furiously, like it was trying to stop whatever he intended to say.

"I can't, Kaylee. It's mine."

NASH'S ADMISSION SHATTERED my fragile composure, splintering my thoughts like jagged shards of ice. For a moment, I could only stare at him, in shock so complete my whole body went numb—and not from the cold. Then the truth of his statement sank in. I spun around and stomped toward my car, anger and confusion raging inside me like two storm fronts about to collide.

"Kaylee, wait!" His words weren't what stopped me. It was the anguish in his voice, the crack on the last syllable, that made my feet pause and my hands clench dangerously around the unnaturally cold balloon.

Forcing my grip to relax, I turned slowly, struggling to unclench my jaw so I could speak. "This is what nearly got me killed yesterday, Nash." My voice was low and hoarse from both the winter air and the raw, holding-back-tears ache in my throat. "What can you possibly say to make me feel better about that? To make it okay that you've been taking the same *shit* Doug and Scott are taking, and lying to me about it?"

The bitter wind stung my face, almost as painfully cold as the balloon stiffening my fingers, and when he didn't answer, I turned and headed for my car again. But this time his feet pounded on the sidewalk after me.

"Kaylee, stop!"

Instead, I broke into a jog. Emma started to open her door, but I shook my head, telling her I was fine. And to stay in the car.

"It was an accident, Kay! Give me a chance to explain."

I whirled on him so fast he skidded to a halt, surprised by my sudden, furious stand. "You accidentally took a lethal inhalant native to another reality? How is that even possible, Nash? You just happen to breathe in at the wrong time?"

"Yeah." He shrugged, as if it were that simple, and I could only blink, unsure whether or not to take him seriously. Or if it even mattered. Even if he *had* inhaled unintentionally, what was he doing close enough to a hellion to breathe in its used air? Beyond that, what was he doing in the Netherworld in the first place?

"Can we go somewhere and talk?" Nash's voice was steady now, though his hands trembled visibly, even when he crossed his arms over his chest.

"I'm not leaving Emma alone, with Doug inside replenishing his stock. Are you going to help me get rid of the dealer, or don't you care if the rest of your friends wind up sharing a padded room with Scott?"

Nash flinched, and I almost felt guilty when I recognized the devastating regret etched in every line on his face. "Everett's gone, Kaylee," he said, remorse riding each word. "I told him to get out, or I'd call in a personal favor from a reaper." Nash forced a halfhearted grin, trying to evoke one from me, but I clung to my stony expression. "Let's go in and talk. Please."

I shook my head. "I'm not taking Emma back in there." I'd already seen what withdrawal from frost could do.

"Fine. Let's talk here." Nash shrugged out of his jacket and handed it to me, but I stepped back. I didn't want his coat *or* his borrowed warmth. Not knowing he'd been lying, and that he could be one missed fix away from hearing Scott's shadow man.

"You're shivering. Take the jacket." He shoved it at me again, and this time I gave in. I didn't want to hear his excuses, but I needed to hear everything he knew about Demon's Breath, and I was nearly frozen solid.

Nash reached for the balloon so I could put his jacket on, but I twisted harshly, angling it away from him. "Like I'm going to give this to *you*."

His eyes widened, irises swirling in pain and disappointment. But he had no right to look hurt; I was the one with a grievance.

I jogged back to my car, where Emma still watched us from the back window, and pulled open the front passenger's door.

"Are you gonna dump him?" she asked as I set the balloon on the leather seat.

"I don't know, but I have to talk to him. I need you to stay here until I get back. And don't mess with the balloon, okay? Don't even touch it."

Emma shrugged. "It creeps me out, anyway." She crossed both arms over the thin tee she'd borrowed. "But I need to go back in and check on Doug. He could be in there singing like the Chipmunks by now."

I shook my head and gave her a half smile. "Nash got rid of Everett before he could sell anything."

"Good. I'm going back in." Emma reached for the door handle, but I shook my head again.

"Em, I need you to trust me. The party's not safe anymore."

She hesitated. "Is this *bean sidhe* business?" We'd used that phrase to refer to anything involving the Netherworld that I couldn't fully explain to her. Considering that Nash and I had brought her back from the dead, she was usually pretty willing to let it go at that. For which I was unspeakably grateful.

I nodded and she frowned, but settled back into her seat. I dug in my pocket, then held out the key to the rental. "Here. Start the engine and turn on the heat. I'll be back in ten minutes, then we'll get some ice cream and a DVD."

"Fine. But I get to pick the movie. And the ice cream."

I forced a grin. "Deal."

She leaned over the seat and started the engine as I headed back to Nash, tossing my head toward the small winter garden to the left of Doug's house. I'd seen several thickly bundled couples on lawn chairs around the covered pool out back, but the enclosed side yard was deserted. And thanks to the music still thumping from the house, the chances of us being overheard were minimal.

Nash followed me through the gate and latched it behind us. "You want to sit?" He gestured toward one of the ornate stone benches in front of a line of tall evergreen shrubs.

I sat, and the cold seeped instantly through my jeans and into my skin. "The gum?" I eyed him frankly and was pleased to see him flinch.

"Covers the scent," he admitted, squinting in the harsh glow from a ground level floodlight.

My heart ached in disappointment, though I'd guessed as much, and I shifted on the cold, hard bench. "The chilly hands?" He nodded again, swallowing thickly, and I sucked in a painfully frigid breath before continuing. "And you didn't want to tell our parents…"

"I messed up—"

"You kept Scott's balloon, didn't you?" I demanded, vaguely frightened by the flat, hopeless quality of my own voice. "You weren't trying to help him. You were getting your fix for free."

Nash looked miserable. "Kaylee—"

"*Weren't* you?" I stood, anger pulsing through my veins, scorching my soul with each excruciating beat.

"Yes. But it was a weaker concentration than what I'm—" he shook his head and corrected his phrasing "—what I *was* getting. Mine comes in red balloons, and the black one wasn't really enough to…"

"Enough to do the job?" I could hear disgust in my voice. "How long?" I asked, but he only frowned, confused. "How long have you been lying to me?"

His eyes closed, and the stark shadow cast behind him slumped as his shoulders fell. "A month." He opened his eyes and stepped out of the light to watch me closely, like he was looking for something specific in my expression. "It happened when we crossed over, Kaylee. In a way, you started it."

"What?" We'd actually crossed into the Netherworld several times, but I had no memory of exposing either of us to Demon's Breath. "You're blaming me for this?"

"No." He sighed. "I'm just frustrated by the irony. The balloons were originally your idea. Remember?"

I did remember. I sank onto the bench again and

barely felt the cold this time as shock roared through me like a roll of thunder.

I remembered thinking the balloon idea was a stroke of genius—a simple, innocent storage solution for a toxic, hard-to-transport substance. I remembered feeling like an enabler when we'd brought three balloons full of the Demon's Breath stored in Addy's lungs as payment for information from a desperate fiend. We'd taunted him with them, denying his need until he gave us what we wanted. I'd never felt so slimy in my life.

And then one of the balloons had popped, and…

Oh, *no.* One of the balloons had popped in Nash's face. He'd coughed and choked—because he'd accidentally inhaled.

And I hadn't even noticed.

"Why didn't you tell me?" I heard the sob in my voice, and it seemed to warble in time with the unsteady rhythm of my heart.

Nash sank onto the bench next to me and stared at his hands in his lap. "I didn't realize what had happened at first, and by the time I started feeling it, you were dying from Crimson Creeper venom. What was my stupid contact buzz compared to your life and Addy's soul?" He shrugged again, as if choosing my problem over his was no big deal. "But I couldn't fight it, and by the time you got better, I was hooked. It just snowballed from there."

Stunned, I let my head fall into my hands, my mind

now as numb from shock as my nose was from the cold. How could I not have known? How could I have seen him nearly every day, and not noticed what was going on?

But that was just it. I'd barely seen Nash in the month after he was exposed, other than a few minutes between classes and half an hour at lunch. I'd been grounded on a massive scale, unavailable to him when he'd needed me most. When it was my fault he was exposed in the first place. I'd dragged him to the Netherworld, and I'd made Addy blow up those balloons.

Focus, Kaylee. There would be time to feel guilty later.

"You should have told me," I groaned, staring up at him again. "I could have helped you."

He shrugged, shoving chapped, clenched fists into his jeans pockets. "I thought I could quit on my own, and you'd never have to know."

"I had a right to know!" I swiped the back of one frozen hand across my dripping nose. "I told you every secret I have—even the ones I wish I could forget—because I thought I could trust you." My hands clenched around nothing, as if I could wring the composure I needed from the air. "But you were lying the whole time. Why, Nash?"

"Because I didn't want you to know!" He stood and stomped across the concrete tiles, staring into the hedges before turning to face me, gesturing helplessly with one cold-reddened hand. "I can't fight it, Kaylee. I don't even *want* to fight it." He blinked, and his irises churned with fervor—with desperation for something I couldn't offer—and an ache settled deep into my chest like a bad cold.

"It feels like the whole world is buzzing, and when you come down from it, everything feels flat and colorless, and all you want to do is get that feeling back. Even before the withdrawal sets in, you'll do *anything* to get that feeling back, because as long as it lasts, nothing's wrong. It doesn't matter if you forget something, or lose something. Or if you fail someone. Nothing's wrong and everything feels good, and you never want it to end. Okay? I didn't want you to know that I don't ever want it to end...."

He sank onto the bench across from mine as his last tortured sentence trailed into silence, but for the thumping bass from the house behind me.

I could only stare at him, trying desperately to calm the storm of fear, disappointment, and anger lashing around inside me. "Nothing's wrong when you're on Demon's Breath because nothing's *important*." And I wanted to be important. I wanted so badly to matter to him. To mean more than his next fix.

"Nash, it should matter to you that you let it go this far. That your habit got Scott locked up and nearly got me killed."

"No." Nash shook his head vehemently, his damp

lashes glittering in the glare from the floodlight. "That had nothing to do with me. The guys have never even seen me with a balloon."

I believed him. He was meeting my eyes too boldly to be lying, his irises swirling calmly with sincerity. But the coincidence was too…coincidental. He had to be connected, even if he didn't know it.

I slid my frozen hands into my borrowed jacket pockets, and the right one curled around something cold and hard. I pulled out a weighted, black plastic balloon clip. "So, I'm assuming Everett is your supplier, too?"

Nash sighed. "Yeah. But I swear I had no idea he was selling to humans until Fuller actually said his name."

Again, I believed him. But again, it didn't matter. "He got to them through you. He must have. None of this makes sense otherwise."

"No." Nash shook his head, and I wasn't sure which one of us he was trying to convince. "Everett doesn't know my name, and I never gave him anyone else's."

I shrugged, a thin thread of panic tightening around the base of my spine, sending cold fingers across my flesh from the inside. "So, he followed you. He saw you at school and realized there's an entire untapped market out there. A whole world full of spoiled, careless kids with more money than sense."

"I don't know. Maybe…" Nash finally conceded.

"What's Everett's last name?" I sank onto the bench again and hunched into Nash's jacket, suddenly overwhelmed by the exhaustion I'd been holding back by sheer will and caffeine.

"I don't know," Nash said, and I raised both brows at him. "I swear!" He shrugged defensively.

"Is he human?"

"Half. His mother's a harpy."

I bet that was a weird childhood. And his mixed blood certainly explained how he'd survived addiction long enough to turn a profit.... "What about those girls?"

Nash shrugged again, and dropped wearily onto the bench beside me. "I don't know. I've never seen them before. Junkies, maybe?"

They didn't look like junkies to me. But then, neither did Nash or Doug.

"How did you get hooked up with Everett?" My teeth had begun to chatter, and I had to concentrate to make myself understood. "How does one even find a Netherworld drug dealer?"

Nash exhaled, then stared at the white puff of breath, obviously avoiding my gaze. "I was referred to him."

That sick feeling returned, churning the contents of my stomach mercilessly. "Referred?"

"You have to understand, Kaylee," he began, turning suddenly toward me with a fevered look in his slowly swirling eyes. "You were still sick from the Creeper venom. We hadn't even buried Addy yet, and I started feeling weak, like I had low blood sugar or something. I couldn't concentrate on anything, but I didn't know what was wrong until I started shaking and twitching, like that fiend, when he was desperate for a hit. I didn't know what else to do. So I got Tod to cross over with me."

"*Tod* took you to the Netherworld?" Normally nothing Tod did surprised me. He didn't see things from the normal human perspective—or even the normal *bean sidhe* perspective—and his moral compass always seemed to point just to the left of north. But Tod would never intentionally hurt Nash. Or let him hurt himself.

"He didn't know why," Nash insisted. "He owed me another favor—don't ask," he added when I opened my mouth to do just that. "And I called it in, no questions asked. He crossed me over, then came back for me half an hour later."

"So you, what? Tripped over Everett in the Netherworld?" I wiped my dripping nose on a tissue from Nash's left jacket pocket. "Can half harpies cross over?"

"Not on their own. I don't think Everett's ever been there." Nash glanced down at his lap, where his hands had nearly gone purple from the cold.

It took me a minute to understand. If he hadn't crossed over to find a dealer…

I felt the blood drain from my face and I backed away from him on the bench. "Please tell me you didn't go there looking for a hellion." Sucking Demon's Breath from a balloon was bad enough, but from the *source?*

Nash frowned, conflict written in every line of his face. “I didn’t know what else to do. I was desperate.”

“What hellion?” I demanded, so softly I could barely hear my own words. I only knew of two in the area—or the Netherworld version of our area—and was horrified by the thought of Nash going near either of them.

“I had to, Kaylee.” His voice pleaded with me to understand. “I thought I was dying. You don’t know what it’s like.”

“Nash, who was it?”

“Avari,” he whispered.

My heart dropped into my stomach. A face flashed from my memory, along with a chill that had nothing to do with the seasonal temperature.

Avari was the demon of greed who’d made a bid for my soul when I was dying in the Netherworld. His icy voice haunted my nightmares, promising that he would one day feast from my suffering, even if he had to destroy everyone I loved to get to me.

Evidently he’d started with Nash.

Terror and anger twisted through me like vines dripping poison into my veins. I shot off the bench, and Nash grabbed my arm to stop me from leaving. "Kaylee, please…" he begged, his warm fingers leaching some of the chill from my own. If his skin had been colder than mine—if I'd had any reason to suspect he still had frost in his system—I'd have run all the way to my car without looking back.

But because he was warm, I turned and made myself look at him. "So, how did it work?" I demanded, my voice as cold as the fingers he still gripped. "He blew up a balloon for you? Just like that?"

"Um, no." And I swear I saw Nash flush, in spite of the little available light. "The initial transfer was more… personal."

Eewww! "You kissed Avari?" My own lips went cold at the thought, and I couldn't help being creeped out that a Netherworld hellion and I had indirectly shared intimate contact through my boyfriend.

"It was more like artificial respiration," he insisted, but his rationalization couldn't make the facts sound any better. The thought of kissing a hellion sent me into realms of terror and disgust I hadn't even known existed. "And after that first time, he set things up with Everett, so I wouldn't have to cross over again."

"Well, wasn't that nice of him!" I snapped, jerking my fingers from his grip.

Nash ignored my sarcasm. "I thought so at the time, and I couldn't figure out why he'd go to that much trouble. But the payoff's obvious now." He gestured toward the house, and the party full of teenagers who'd nearly become the client base of an alternate-realm drug dealer.

But the payoff wasn't obvious to me. "What's Avari getting out of this?"

"My guess is that he'll feed from their suffering until they die. Hell, Carter's just become a twenty-four-hour buffet...."

And suddenly my stomach wanted to send those tacos back up. "Do you think he's given up on them?" I waved my hand at the party still in progress.

"Not a chance. But it'll give us some time to think."

Mentally and physically exhausted, I sank back onto

the bench, far from encouraged by the temporary reprieve. "So, you know how to get in touch with Everett, right? You call him when you need…more?" The very thought gave me chills, but if Nash knew how to find him, at least we'd have some valuable information to give my dad. Or whoever was most qualified to deal with a half-harpy Netherworld drug dealer.

Did we even have people like that? A supernatural equivalent of the police? Or was this a neighborhood-watch kind of operation?

I honestly wasn't sure which possibility frightened me more.…

"Not exactly," Nash said, avoiding my eyes again. "I don't know how it works with his human…clients, but in my case, Everett is just the mule. Avari collects the payment personally."

I closed my eyes, trying to sort the facts out in my head. It was physically impossible for hellions to cross into our world, and Nash said he wasn't crossing over, either.… "I don't get it," I said as a new foreboding twisted my guts even tighter. "How does he take payment if neither of you crosses over?"

"It's kind of a long-distance operation." Nash sighed and finally met my gaze before I could show off another confused frown. "There are a few ways for a hellion to interact with the human world, and they all suck."

He shuddered with some horrible memory, and a sudden wave of intuition rolled over me, dropping another piece of the puzzle into place in my head. "Your nightmare... Avari talks to you in your sleep?"

His eyes closed, like he was scrambling for composure—or for control of the telltale swirling in his irises—and when he met my gaze again, his own seemed somehow closed off. Like he'd slammed shut the windows to his soul. "I wouldn't call it talking, but yeah. In my dreams, or through an...intermediary."

"An intermediary?"

Nash sighed. "He can sometimes talk to me through someone in this world—anyone he has a connection with."

"You mean, like, possession?" *That's not creepy or anything...*

"For lack of a better term, yes. And I'm pretty sure he's Carter's shadow man, too. I think you were right about his hallucinations."

Though I hadn't realized who Scott was actually hearing.

"You knew that, didn't you?" I demanded, my voice actually shaking with anger. I scooted back to put distance between us. "You knew Scott was really hearing Avari, but you made me sound like an idiot in front of my dad. Why?"

"I'm sorry." His gaze dropped like an anchor. "I was afraid that if they knew he was hearing a hellion, they'd want to know who that hellion was, and would eventually connect him to me."

"So, you made me look *crazy* to cover your own tracks? How very chivalrous of you," I spat. The Nash I'd met three months earlier had given me strength and confidence. He'd sacrificed his own safety to help protect me. But now he was lying to me, and Influencing me, and covering up information that could have helped save his best friend. Was it all because of the Demon's Breath? Could breathing from Avari actually change him? Was it already rotting his soul?

"I'm so sorry, Kaylee..." Nash started, but I cut him off with a harsh wave of one hand. I was already tired of pointless apologies.

"Is Avari giving me nightmares, too? Are these death dreams because of him?"

Nash shrugged miserably. "I don't think hellions can make you have premonitions if no one's dying, but I honestly don't know."

I didn't realize I'd been grinding my teeth until my jaw began to ache. How could he answer so many questions with so little information? "So, does this mean you don't have Everett's number, or e-mail, or anything?"

Nash shook his head again. "Avari just tells me where and when to meet him. That's why I had to come to the party. Because I can't get in touch with Everett on my own." I started to interrupt, but Nash rushed on. "Neither can Fuller. I already asked him. Everett calls him and sets up a meeting, and his number shows up as *Unidentified*."

Nash scowled and rubbed his hands together for warmth. I was freezing, too, in spite of his jacket, and part of me wanted to slide closer to him for heat. But I wasn't ready to be that close to him yet.

"So, Avari feeds from the suffering he causes and Everett gets the money," I said, scooting farther away from him for good measure. "But you're not suffering like Doug and Scott are." Presumably because he wasn't human. "And you don't have any money. So how does Avari plan to turn a profit on you?"

Nash's gaze fell to where his hands now clenched the edge of the stone bench on either side of his thighs. And suddenly a devastating new understanding crashed over me, threatening to crush me.

"He already is, isn't he?" My pulse roared in my ears, and I wasn't sure I really wanted the answer. But I had to ask. "How do you pay, Nash?"

He shook his head. "Kaylee, you don't want to—"

"Service?" I interrupted, twisting on the bench to pin him with my eyes. "You're not selling for him, are you?" I whispered, because that was all the volume I could muster.

"No!" Nash insisted, rubbing my back through his jacket. "It's not like that."

"Then what is it like?" I shrugged out from under his hand, silently begging him—*daring* him—to tell me the truth. "What are you paying him, Nash?"

He sighed, and his entire body seemed to deflate as his jaw tensed. "Emotions, in the past tense."

"What?" I felt my forehead crinkle. "What does that mean? You're giving him your emotions? So, you can't feel anything?" The horror rising through me had no equivalent. The only thing that even came close was the black scream that built inside me when I felt Death coming.

"No, not my current emotions," Nash insisted, trying to reassure me, but the gloom in his eyes didn't match his tone, so the look was more frightening than comforting. "The emotions in some of my memories."

"He's eating your *memories?*" I couldn't imagine a more personal violation. Nash was giving away the experiences that made him the person he was.

The person I loved.

I ran my hand over the smooth, cold bench, desperate for something real and sturdy to cement me in reality. In a world where food was food, and memories were invulnerable. Untouchable.

"No." He shook his head vehemently and put one warm hand over mine on the bench. Yet somehow, he seemed to steal my waning warmth, rather than fortify it. "Just the feelings from them. When I think about things from my past, I don't feel how I felt when they actually happened. *Past* emotions." He tried to smile reassuringly, but failed. Miserably. "I don't need those, anyway, right?"

My vision went dark and my hearing began to fade as shock and horror sank through me, cutting my ties to the world. Then my senses came roaring back, stronger than ever, the floodlight glaring in my eyes, the cold numbing my skin. "You don't need those? You don't need to revisit feelings from your past?" I snatched my hand from his and jumped from the bench again, and this time he was too slow to catch me.

"In most cases, it's a mercy, Kaylee," he insisted as I backed slowly away from him, wondering if I'd be making things better or worse if I simply walked away. Would I be giving us time to think, and to miss each other? Or time to realize we shouldn't have been together in the first place. After all, I'd dragged him into the Netherworld where he'd been exposed to Demon's Breath. And he'd lied to me and left me alone with Scott, who'd tried to slit my throat.

Maybe we *didn't* belong together....

"It's like mental anesthesia," he continued, pleading with me silently to understand. "The things that used to hurt..." He shrugged. "Now they're just...numb."

"Numbness is a mercy?" What kind of screwed-up perspective was that? "Do you have any idea what I'd give for more memories of my mother, Nash? What I'd give to remember how she lived, and what it felt like when she died? And you're just throwing your past away!"

"It's not like that." He closed his eyes and inhaled

deeply, in spite of the cold, sharp air. "I'm not losing the memories. They're still there."

"What does that matter, if you can't feel them?" I'd never felt so frustrated or disappointed in my entire life. How could he let Avari have such an important part of himself?

Nash sighed again, and the small slip of air through his lips conveyed a devastating weight of hopelessness. Of despair. "It was the only acceptable price, Kaylee. It's all I was willing to part with. And you'd understand if you knew what he really wanted from me."

His soul? His blood? His service? That time I didn't ask. Those were all unacceptable prices for me, but I'd never been in his position. What might I have given to save myself from the Creeper toxin, if we hadn't made it back to the human world in time? Certainly not my soul. But would I have given my memory-emotions in exchange for my life?

Depends on the memories in question…

"What memories, Nash?" I demanded, suddenly afraid that he'd set no limits on what Avari could take. "Potty training? Pulling your first tooth? Your first independent bike ride? What did you lose?"

He shook his head slowly. "The most intense," he admitted finally. "Only the ones with real value to me have value to him."

I took a deep, cold breath and it caught in my throat, stuck behind a sob. *"Us?"* I closed my eyes, blinking back tears when I remembered all the times in the past few days when his irises had abruptly gone still instead of swirling with emotion. Had he been remembering something all those times? Trying to feel what used to be there?

"Do you still feel what you felt when we met? At Taboo?" I stepped closer for a better look at his eyes, testing the most painful theory I'd ever explored. "When you calmed me so I wouldn't scream? When you figured out what I was? That I was like you?"

His eyes swam in tears, but his irises held painfully steady. Not so much as a twitch of color shifting in the browns and greens I'd always loved.

I swallowed thickly. "Kissing me for the first time?"

Nash closed his eyes to keep me from seeing the truth, and a whip of anger coiled tightly around my spine. *No!* How could he give that away? Did my most precious memories mean less to him than his next high?

What else had he sold?

"Your dad dying? Tod dying? Do you feel what you felt when *I* was dying?" I demanded at last, and when he shook his head, tears slipping from closed eyes, I'd had all I could take.

"It's all gone, Kaylee."

And so was I.

I shrugged out of his jacket and dropped it on the brick patio, gasping out loud when the cold hit me full force. The roar of my pulse in my ears drowned out the noise from the party as I ran across the stone path toward the quaint wooden gate.

"Kaylee, please..." Nash's whisper hit my back with a last, desperate surge of Influence, but I stiffened my spine and kept going. I was too devastated by my own loss—the boyfriend who remembered *why* he loved me—to worry about his.

I swiped scalding tears from my frozen cheeks when I stopped to shove the gate open and was jogging again by the time I rounded the front corner of the house, headed for my car. And for my human best friend, who would soothe me with junk food, though she could never understand the source of my pain.

But bleak panic hit the moment I spotted my car, two blocks down the street. The instant I saw the form leaning against my front passenger's side door, that familiar dark terror wound its way around my spine, sending thick, hot fingers toward the base of my throat.

The beam from a streetlight shone on the bright red balloon clasped between two pale hands, but darkness slanted across their owner's broad torso, leaving the face obscured. Why had Emma left the balloon unattended?

"Kaylee, are you okay?" Emma asked, and I whirled to see her close Doug's front door, already jogging down the steps toward me, wearing her jacket now. "Where's Nash?"

I shook my head and clenched my jaw shut, unable to answer her without screaming as the death wail took me over. It wrapped around my throat like a thorn-spiked glove, and I tasted blood on the back of my tongue. This premonition was strong; he would die very, very soon.

I glanced pointedly from Emma to my car, trying to guide her gaze. To speak to her with only my eyes. But she wasn't Nash. She didn't understand.

"What's wrong, Kaylee?"

Frustrated, I turned my back on her and ran for my car, racing toward death for the first time ever, because this time my effort wasn't pointless. Nash had said deaths caused by Netherworld elements were unscripted, so whoever he was, if Demon's Breath was the problem, I could save him—if I got there in time.

I'd just passed the dark, silent house next door when the old wooden gate squealed open again and winter-dead grass crunched under someone's feet. "What's wrong?" Nash called out behind me.

"I don't know!" Emma shouted as his steps pounded after us. "She won't tell me!"

And that was enough for Nash.

"Kaylee, stop!" he yelled, even as he raced after me. "Wait!" But I couldn't stop. I'd let Nash down. I'd let Scott down. But I could save this one.

Thirty feet. My nose dripped, and my throat burned.

"Stay here," Nash ordered Emma, but his footsteps never slowed. "Kaylee, stop!"

Twenty feet. The form against my car came into focus, his features coalescing in the swirling shadows to form a face I recognized. He raised the balloon. The weighted clip hit the ground.

Ten feet. My jaws ached from being clenched. My throat felt like I'd swallowed razors from holding back his soul song. My hands clenched into fists at my sides, pumping as I ran. And now I could hear him.

"Hudson, you've been holdin' out on me!" His smile was joyous. Relieved. Uncomprehending. "I'll pay you back…."

"No!" Nash shouted behind me, but I didn't turn. There was no time. "It's too strong!"

But Doug put the balloon to his mouth, anyway, and drew in a long, deep breath.

He smiled, even as he began to convulse….

"NO!" NASH YELLED AGAIN, and in the next instant, time seemed to shift into fast-forward. My world hurtled through space and time so quickly my head spun and the neighborhood around me swam in and out of focus.

Doug shook violently and fell against the car. Strands of shaggy brown hair flopped into his wide, empty eyes. His hands seized around the balloon. Demon's Breath burst from it in a frosty white vapor. I skidded to a stop two feet from him, one hand over my mouth to hold the scream back. But I was out of breath and couldn't help sucking in air through my nose to satisfy my abused lungs.

Strong hands grabbed my arms from behind, lifting me. The world spun around me as I inhaled. The air I pulled in was clear and cold. And clean. The hands shoved me forward and I stumbled onto the neighbor's yard, my feet barely brushing the ground.

I fell facedown on cold, dead grass, recently sprayed green with fertilizer. My graceless landing jarred my mouth open, and the scream ripped free from my throat, calling out to Doug's soul as it prepared to leave his body.

Doug fell forward, draped across the sidewalk, still convulsing. His shoes slammed into the road. His knuckles scraped the sidewalk. His skull bounced on the grass. Dark, translucent shadows swirled all around him.

The Nether-fog rolled in from nowhere, swallowing my world whole.

Nash grabbed the balloon he'd dropped and tied the opening into a quick knot, trapping what little vapor hadn't escaped into the air. Then he dropped to his knees at Doug's side, two fingers at his throat, feeling for a pulse, uninhibited by the fog he couldn't see.

I saw both layers of reality, and was desperate to separate them. To push the fog back. Yet still I screamed.

"No!" Emma's mouth formed soundless words of denial. She sank into the fog next me, hands covering her ears, hunched over her knees in shock. Dark things scuttled around her, and revulsion skittered up my spine. Tears filled my eyes, then ran over. "No!" she shouted again, though I couldn't hear her over my own screaming.

Nash looked up.

His eyes reflected pain, and regret, and guilt, and horror, swirling as madly now as they'd sat calm moments earlier. He left his friend still seizing in the fog and churning shadows and dropped to his knees beside me. Nash turned me so that I couldn't see Doug. His lips brushed my ear, but I couldn't hear him. He wasn't using his Influence. Because I'd told him not to.

He leaned back and shouted at me, as Emma sobbed, but I couldn't hear either of them. Yet I knew what Nash was saying. *Pull it back. You can do it, Kaylee. You have to let him go....*

It was hard. It was so hard without Nash's help. But I couldn't let him back in my head.

I closed my eyes and slapped both hands over my mouth, but that wasn't enough. I could practically feel the gray haze lapping at my skin. I forced my jaw closed, but the screaming still leaked from my sealed lips, scraping my insides raw. So I swallowed it, fists clenched against the pain, locking the wail inside myself, where it bounced around my throat like a swarm of angry wasps.

When I opened my eyes, the fog was gone. Nash was still watching me. Doug was still convulsing. Em was still crying. Nash glanced from one of us to the other, and finally his anxious gaze settled on me. "Can you drive?" he asked, and I nodded, relieved to be able to hear him. I wasn't sure I really could drive, with Doug's death song consuming me from the inside, but Emma had been drinking.

It was either me or a cab.

"Okay." He left Doug—still convulsing—and hauled Emma up by both arms, as gently as he had time for. "Em, you have to calm down. He's still alive, and I'm going to do what I can for him." We both knew Doug was as good as dead, but maybe Emma didn't know I'd never yet had a false premonition. "But I need you and Kaylee to get out of here before she starts screaming again." He walked with her as he spoke and carefully settled her into the passenger's seat, then closed the door.

"Go straight to her house," he said, circling the car to open my door for me as I held one hand firmly over my mouth. "Drive slowly, just in case. I'll call you later."

I nodded. I would answer his call, even though we'd just had the biggest fight in the history of fights, because things weren't as simple as "break up and make up" between me and Nash.

What we had was life or death. Literally.

He closed the door and I twisted the key in the engine with my free hand. Then I grabbed the wheel and hit the gas. The last thing I saw in the mirror before I turned the corner was Nash kneeling on the ground next to one of his best friends, already pulling his phone from his pocket. No one had come out yet—the whole thing couldn't have taken two minutes, and the music from the party had helped cover my screaming—but it wouldn't be long before someone wandered outside, and the second party in a week would end in disaster.

When I turned the corner—swerving too sharply in haste—the panic began to ebb, and my throat started to relax. The pincushion feeling faded slowly, and two blocks later, I opened my mouth and sucked in a deep breath, grateful when the only sound that escaped was the rasp of air through my throat.

And that's when I realized Emma was still crying.

She sat huddled in one corner of the passenger's seat, knees to her chest, seat belt unbuckled, right temple pressed against the cold window. Her shoulders shook with each soft sob, and as I watched, she raised one arm to wipe her face with her jacket sleeve.

"Are you okay?" I flicked on my blinker for the next turn, then slowed to a stop at the red light.

"No. Is he dead?"

"I don't know." I wished I wasn't driving so I could really look at her. So I'd know how she was handling this. "But if he isn't yet, he will be soon."

Emma twisted toward me, her brown eyes wide. Imploring. "Can't you save him? Like you saved me?" Her voice cracked on the last word, and she reached up to wipe more tears.

I shook my head slowly, sadly, then glanced at her as passing streetlights lit the car, one after another. Would this explanation ever get any easier? "Em, if we'd saved him, someone else would have to die in his place." Because even though we hadn't seen him or her, there was a reaper somewhere nearby waiting to claim Doug's soul, and if we snatched it back, the reaper would simply take another.

At least, that's how it usually worked. I wasn't sure about unscripted cases, but I wasn't gonna risk it. "You, Nash, and I were the only ones there to choose from, and I'm not willing to sacrifice any of us to save someone else." *Not even your boyfriend.* Though I couldn't say that aloud.

"What if it's not really his time to die? It wasn't my time when I died."

Okay, she had a good point. And a very hard question.

I closed my eyes and exhaled softly, then forced my gaze back to the road. I'd wondered the same thing. But ultimately… "It wouldn't really matter." I slowed for the next turn and flicked my blinker on. "You, and those other girls, and Sophie—none of you were supposed to die. But saving you still meant killing someone else. I can't risk that again."

"Wait…*Sophie?*" Emma said, and for a moment, surprise eclipsed the hurt and confusion she wore like a funeral veil. "Sophie died, too?"

Crap. "Yeah. But she doesn't know, so please don't tell her."

"Like I'm gonna go looking for a reason to talk to

Sophie." Emma paused, and curiosity shined through her tears. "What happened?"

I stepped on the gas to make it through a yellow light, then dropped back to the speed limit. Getting pulled over while Emma still had beer on her breath would *not* be a good way to end the most horrible week in the history of...weeks.

"Aunt Val took her place." Making the very same sacrifice for her daughter that my mother had made for me. Except that it was Aunt Val's fault Sophie died in the first place. Which kind of mitigated her sacrifice, in my eyes.

"That's how your aunt died?" Em wiped tear-damp mascara onto her sleeve.

I shrugged. "Sophie thinks she passed out from shock, and when she woke up, her mother was dead. She has no idea why or how it happened, but she knows I was involved and she's decided I'm somehow responsible." Which couldn't have been further from the truth, but no one—including me—wanted to tell my cousin that her mother had tried to trade five innocent souls for her own everlasting youth and beauty.

"No wonder she hates you..."

"Yeah." But the truth was that Sophie had never exactly been warm and fuzzy.

For several minutes, Emma stared out the window, though I had a feeling she wasn't really seeing the dark houses we passed. Then she turned to look at me, and the weight behind her gaze was devastating. "Kaylee, what was in the balloon?"

I blinked at the road and exhaled slowly. "Nothing you want to know much about."

"I saw how Nash pulled you away." Leather creaked as she shifted in her seat. "He didn't even want you to get a whiff of it, so whatever it is, it must be pretty damn scary."

"It is." Yet he hadn't hesitated to kiss me and breathe all over me while he was taking it. How much could I possibly mean to him if he'd risk exposing me?

"I should have done something." Emma groaned. "I knew he was taking too much, and I just let him!" She stomped the floorboard hard enough to rock the whole car, and my heart broke for her.

"Em, you couldn't have stopped him." I was sure of that, yet I was equally sure that Nash and I could have. I'd failed Scott and Doug, but it wasn't too late to help Nash. No matter what he'd done, I couldn't live with myself if I let him turn out like his friends.

"I should be there." Emma sat straighter, oblivious to the turn my thoughts had taken. "Can you take me to the hospital? He might not be gone yet, and I should be there. I know that sounds stupid—it's not like we were in love or anything—but I feel awful for just leaving him."

I shook my head slowly and made the turn onto her street. "It doesn't sound stupid. But Em, they're not going to let you in. You're not family." And Doug's family—just the father and stepmother, as far as I knew—were still in New York on a working vacation. Did that mean Doug would die alone? Surely Nash could Influence his way into the room.… "Besides, Emma, the last place you need to be is in a hospital swarming with cops."

Emma sighed and sank into her seat as I pulled to a stop on the street in front of her mailbox. Her house was dark.

"Where is everybody?" The hum of the engine faded as I pulled the keys from the ignition.

"Traci's working, and Cara's at her sorority's Christmas party," Emma said as I pushed my car door opened. I hadn't really expected either of her sisters to be home on a Friday night, but I was worried about her mom catching Emma before we'd washed her shirt and brushed her teeth. "And Mom has a date, if you can believe that." She shoved her own door open and stepped onto the grass, surprisingly steady.

Evidently death is sobering. No real shock there.

I grabbed my overnight bag—now minus one T-shirt—then swung the door shut and locked the car. Emma was already halfway up the cute stone path, digging in her pocket for her keys before she remembered that I'd taken them. I gave them to her, but her hand shook too badly to slide the key into the lock, so I took it back and opened the door myself.

"I feel so helpless!" Emma dropped onto the overstuffed

couch as I bolted the door behind us. "Worthless. So frustrated and…impotent!" She sat up straight then and punched the arm of her couch so hard I wasn't surprised when her knuckles came away skinned and oozing blood from the rough weave.

I handed her a tissue from a box on the end table. "That's not a phrase you hear very often from girls." I forced a smile, but my joke landed like a brick dropped from a skyscraper.

I knew exactly how she felt.

"I'm serious." She dabbed at her fist, then dropped the tissue on the coffee table. "What's the point of knowing someone's going to die if you can't do anything about it? How can you stand this?" she demanded. "All this death? How can you stand knowing about it before anyone else does?"

I took my shoes off and lined them up with the others in the front closet, then sank onto the couch beside her, leaning my head on her shoulder. "Have you ever known anyone who died?" Her parents had divorced when Em was only four, but I was pretty sure her dad was still alive. Somewhere.

"Just Roger."

"Who's Roger?"

"The hamster we had when I was seven. Does he count?"

"I don't think so." I almost smiled, but held it back

when I realized she might be offended. For all I knew, she and Roger had been very close.

"Then, no." She folded one leg beneath the other and twisted to face me. "And I've certainly never had to *look* at someone, knowing he'd be dead soon. How can you stand this?" she asked again. And in that moment, I came very close to telling her the truth: that I couldn't. Not without Nash.

"It's not easy." I stood and pulled Emma up by both hands. "In fact, it sucks. Do you have ice cream?"

"Yeah." She wiped fresh tears from her face and gestured vaguely toward the kitchen. "Traci's boyfriend dumped her yesterday. Fourth one this year." Which made no sense to me. The Marshall girls were gorgeous beyond all reason. "There's a pint of Phish Food in the freezer."

"Great. Pick out a movie while I get the ice cream."

Emma nodded hesitantly, then crossed the living room toward the rack of DVDs to the left of a slim, simple entertainment center. "Bring two spoons!" she shouted over her shoulder as she knelt to scan the titles.

For the first half hour of the movie—a lighthearted, predictable romantic comedy—Emma shoveled ice cream into her mouth and glanced regularly at my cell lying on her nightstand, obviously willing it to ring with an update from Nash.

But my phone never rang.

By the time the credits rolled, Emma had fallen asleep,

her spoon still dangling from one hand, several drops of chocolate ice cream dotting the front of the shirt she'd borrowed from me. When I got up to turn off the movie, her spoon thumped to the floor, so I rolled carefully off the bed and took both spoons and the empty ice cream container into the kitchen, yawning so hard my jaw ached.

The clock on the microwave read a quarter to one, and I wondered idly how late Ms. Marshall would be out. I had no frame of reference for adult dating.

I grabbed a Coke from the fridge, then padded back to Emma's room, intending to call Nash. But when I reached for my phone from the nightstand on Emma's side of the bed, her eyes popped wide-open, as if some unseen clasp holding them closed had just been released.

Startled, I squealed and jumped back. "Em, you okay?" But even when she finally blinked, her face still pressed into the pillow, her eyes didn't lose that sleep haze, nor did they focus on me. Or on anything else. "Em?"

She snapped upright in a single, eerily stiff motion and blinked at me, then glanced around her room like she'd never seen it before—easily one of the weirdest things I'd seen in my entire life.

In either world.

"Emma?" I backed slowly away from the bed, my phone clenched in my left hand, as a strange, heavy, fluttery feeling settled into my stomach. Like I'd swallowed a swarm of iron butterflies.

"Not exactly..." A low, scratchy, *unfamiliar* voice said as my best friend's mouth moved.

My heart rate exploded and my pulse roared in my ears. "Who, then, exactly?"

"I am Alec. As presented through Emma Dawn Marshall."

As presented...?

Whoa...

"Who are you, and what the hell are you doing *in* my best friend?" I backed farther from the bed, my empty hand stretched behind me to warn me before I bumped into anything. Part of me—most of me, in fact—wanted to make a break for the door. But I couldn't leave Emma alone with...whatever was talking through her. Possessing her. Because that's obviously what this was.

"I apologize for contacting you through an intermediary, but my options are pretty limited at the moment," Emma said with Alec's voice, and the effect was disjointed, like a bad voice-over in a foreign film. Except the actor and the voice were both speaking the same language. "I promise your friend won't remember any of this. She might wake up sleepy and disoriented, but none the worse for wear." He extended his borrowed arms, like he was testing the fit of a new shirt.

My stomach roiled at the casual gesture and the gruesome image that accompanied it, and my mind raced, trying to make sense of what I was seeing and hearing. Without much luck. Emma was speaking to me in *someone else's voice.* She was being used as a human microphone—this "Alec's" intermediary.

And suddenly a horrifying understanding clicked into place in my nearly scrambled brain. The blood seemed to drain from my face, leaving me cold.

Nash had said Avari contacted him through an intermediary—by possessing someone in our world. And several times in the past few weeks I'd fallen asleep with Nash, only to wake up disoriented and unsure where I was, even during his few covert visits while I was grounded. In the past week alone, it had happened on the way to work, then in the school parking lot during my lunchtime nap....

Nooo!

My hands clenched into fists at my sides, and I had to force my grip on my phone to loosen. Anger and fear rolled through me like thunder across the sky, dark, and low, and threatening. And accompanied by a vicious, white-hot bolt of betrayal that singed every nerve in my body.

I'd played intermediary between Nash and Avari. The hellion had used me as his own personal walkie-talkie.

And Nash had let it happen.

"GET OUT!" I GLANCED around Emma's room for a weapon—until I realized I couldn't hurt the hellion without hurting Emma, too. "Get out of her! She has nothing to do with any of this!" Whatever "this" was. "Emma's human, and she knows nothing about hellions, or the Netherworld, or Demon's Breath, or anything else to do with your warped, twisted, toxic hellhole of an alternate dimension."

Keeping Emma in the dark about everything that went bump in the night was supposed to protect her from those bumps. So why was she now speaking to me with a hellion's voice? What kind of "connection" could she possibly have to this Netherworld possessor? For that matter, what connection did I have to Avari?

My best friend's carefully arched brows rose in

surprise. "*My* warped, twisted…?" Then comprehension washed over her face. Alec grinned with Emma's mouth, and I was floored by how unlike Emma that look was, considering that she smiled at me all the time with those same features. He swung both of her denim-clad legs over the edge of the bed. "You think I'm a hellion." It wasn't a question, and Alec sounded every bit as surprised as Emma looked.

He shook her head slowly, and their shared smile faded into a bittersweet melancholy. "I'm human. Only I have the misfortune to be stuck in the Netherworld."

Surprised, I gripped the edge of Emma's desk to anchor myself to the only thing that made sense while I tried to puzzle through Alec's maze of misinformation.

He started to stand in Emma's body, but I threw one hand out, fingers splayed. "Stay there!"

She shrugged and sank back onto the mattress. "If that makes you more comfortable…"

Like comfort was even a possibility.

"You're lying." I forced my other hand to relax around my phone, to keep from bringing it to his attention. "You're not human." He couldn't be, because humans can't survive in the Netherworld with both soul and body intact.

Which meant that Alec was either lying or soulless. Or that there were big things going on in the Netherworld. Things I didn't understand well enough to fully grasp.

Knowing my luck, it was all three.

"Not solely human, no," Alec admitted, tilting Emma's head so that a strand of straight blond hair fell over her shoulder. "But I swear to you that I mean neither of you any harm." I huffed in disbelief and he continued, furrowing the delicate lines of Emma's forehead. "If I wanted to hurt her, I could have already fed her a bottle of pills or made her cut her own throat." Alec drew one of Emma's own long fingernails slowly across her slim neck, and terror crawled over me like an army of spiders marching up my spine. "But that's not why I'm here."

Somehow, I wasn't very comforted.

"What else are you? Other than human?" I wanted both my hands empty, in case I had to defend myself. Or Emma. But I was reluctant to put down the phone—my security blanket and only connection to the rest of the world. The human world, anyway.

Alec crossed Emma's arms beneath her breasts, looking physically comfortable for the first time since he'd claimed her body. Yet her expression spoke of long-term anger and resentment. Of a grudge that had been allowed to fester. "I am a proxy to a hellion in the Netherworld."

"A proxy?"

Alec's frown deepened as his obvious self-loathing swelled. "I'm used as a servant and energy storage unit. Like an assistant you can eat."

"Eat?" I didn't bother to hide my horror, and Alec

nodded, pushing back a strand of Emma's hair when it fell into her eyes.

"Not literally, of course. Well, not like we eat, anyway." Emma's shoulders shrugged within the borrowed shirt. "Many hellions do consume flesh. Fortunately, the one I serve does not. He uses me like a sports bottle," Alec continued. "An emergency drink when there isn't enough human energy bleeding over from your world."

Eewww! No wonder Alec's grudge was festering.

"Sorry about the whole human Gatorade thing," I said, glancing at the alarm clock on the nightstand—1:08 a.m. What were the chances that Ms. Marshall would stay out long enough for me to get rid of Emma's visitor? "But what does that have to do with Emma?"

"Nothing. It has to do with you." He smiled, like I should have been flattered. "Emma was the closest available intermediary."

"She wasn't available!" I snapped, indignation on her behalf bolstering my courage. "She was asleep." But then something new occurred to me, when I remembered passing out as Nash drove me to work on Sunday. "Did you make her fall asleep?"

Alec shook Emma's head somberly. "That's beyond my ability. The most we can do is give someone who's already tired a little *push* toward slumber. During sleep, the mind is more susceptible to sharing space in the body."

"So you pushed Emma out of her body?"

"No." He chuckled. The talking "boost" actually laughed! "She's still in here. I just pushed her over a bit." He shrugged, looking almost as unconcerned by his violation of her free will as Tod was by his regular violation of closed doors. "She was almost asleep, anyway."

My next breath was an exasperated huff. I'd had it with people—and non-people—taking liberties with moral norms! Personal boundaries—whether body, mind, or home—were not up for negotiation!

"Get out of Emma, and don't ever 'push her over' again!" I propped both hands on my hips, hoping to look threatening, though surely he knew I wouldn't hurt my best friend, even to hurt him. "Pick another intermediary. Or better yet, stay out of my friends and away from me!"

Alec's sigh slipped through Emma's lips. "I would gladly use another body—preferably one without breasts..." My best friend glanced down at her own chest as if she didn't know what to do with such generous curves. "Unfortunately, you don't surround yourself with many potential intermediaries." A hint of desperation leaked through onto Emma's features. "But I swear to you, on both my life and my soul, that if you help me—if you let us help each other—my need for an intermediary will soon be a thing of the past."

I blinked at Emma/Alec in disbelief. "You're asking me for a favor?"

Emma's head nodded steadily. "And offering one, as well."

Curiosity overwhelmed me, in spite of my desperation to put Emma back in control of her body. "What could you possibly do for me?"

His smile widened on her face, and Emma's straight white teeth seemed to taunt me. "Return your damaged lover."

My what?

Confusion must have shown clearly on my face, because Emma/Alec raised both brows in a rather masculine look of amusement. "Your boyfriend. Nash. I assume you remember him. Or does the heart forget so soon?"

Terror shot through me in a jolt of white-hot adrenaline, then settled into my gut like lead. My free hand gripped the back of Emma's desk chair and I sank into it, stunned. "What are you talking about?"

Emma's smile faded and her forehead furrowed as he stepped closer, moving stiffly in the unfamiliar body. "My boss has your boyfriend in the Netherworld. I can help you get him back—in exchange for passage into your world."

Vertigo crashed over me and I wobbled on the chair as Alec's claim truly sank in. *"No."* I shook my head so hard Emma's bedroom swam wildly. Nash couldn't be in the Netherworld. I'd left him at the party less than two hours ago.

"No, you won't cross me over, or no, you don't believe me?"

"No, Nash can't be in the Netherworld." Confused and horrified, I stood and spun away from him, my gaze skipping around the room in search of answers Emma's clothes and furniture could never provide. "He can't cross over."

How did Alec know *I* could cross over?

"Oh, he had help," Alec said, ducking Emma's head to catch my gaze.

Help? Not Tod. He would never intentionally do anything that could hurt Nash.

Except take him to the Netherworld to repay a favor, no questions asked…

Tod, if you're involved in this, I'll kill you! Except you can't kill someone who's already dead. But I could get him fired.…

Assuming Alec was telling the truth, which was a big assumption. He could be lying about the whole thing.

Then where was Nash? Why hadn't he called or answered the two text messages I'd sent?

"You actually saw Nash there? Tonight?"

Emma's head nodded, and Alec said, "Not ten minutes ago, my time." Because in the Netherworld, time was not a constant. It sped up at odd intervals, depending on how closely a specific place was tied to its equivalent location in our world.

"What was he wearing?"

Emma's eyes rolled, and she sank onto the bed again. "Jeans and a T-shirt, with a green-and-white jacket. And I have to tell you, jeans have changed since I last bought a pair."

My eyes widened before I could regain control of my expression. *He'd bought jeans?* Unless the Netherworld had recently become active in the retail market, Alec must have been topside at some point. I couldn't help wondering how long ago that had been, considering his odd mix of hellion-formal and human-colloquial language.

But then, on the tail of that momentary surprise, came a more devastating near-certainty. Alec *had* seen Nash that night. Not necessarily in the Netherworld—he could easily have seen Nash in our world, through another hijacked body—but I wasn't willing to take that chance.

If Nash had crossed over, I had to get him back.

"So, all I have to do is cross over and bring you both back? Just like that?" It sounded too easy.

"Well..." Emma hedged with Alec's voice. "It may not be quite that simple."

Aaaand here comes the catch... "Why not?"

"Because Nash is with my boss right now. But once he's alone, I can get to him."

I closed my eyes, trying not to let frustration and the incredibly small chance I had of ever seeing Nash alive again get me down. "Your boss, the hellion? Nash is with *that* boss?"

"That's the one."

"Why?" I demanded, standing so quickly Em's chair thumped against the desk behind me. "Why is he in the Netherworld? What does your boss want with him?"

Alec shrugged, pulling my T-shirt tight across Emma's chest. "I don't know. Another proxy, maybe?"

Nash, as a demon's proxy? "Why does your hellion need two?"

Emma's bright brown eyes rolled, and Alec leaned her back on the mattress, propping her up on one elbow like a life-size doll. "You're asking the wrong man. I don't think he needs any proxies, but he's had as many as eight at a time." She shrugged again. "What can I say? He's a hellion of greed."

Greed? *No…*

I drew in a deep, slow breath, wishing I didn't have to ask. "Your boss? Is his name Avari?"

Emma's eyes widened to anime proportions. "You know him?"

I sighed and dropped onto the chair again. "We've met, but I doubt he'd consider me a friend."

Emma snorted, and I couldn't resist a small smile. That was the first sound Alec had made that truly sounded like my best friend. "Friendship isn't a popular concept here."

No surprise there. Everything in the Netherworld

was food for something else, and no one was safe except those at the top of the food chain: hellions. And in the three short months I'd known about my species and the existence of the Netherworld, I'd managed to piss off two of them.

But they'd pissed me off, too. "How soon can you get Nash alone?"

Alec stared at the comforter he—they—lay on. "That's the hard part. He's Avari's new toy, and the boss won't want to let go for a while." If I'd had any doubt that Emma was not in control of her body, that doubt died when his gaze met mine. My best friend was not the one staring at me with those big brown eyes. "But there's this thing tomorrow night. A sort of party. I can get to him then with no problem."

"Tomorrow night!" I had to suck in deep, calming breaths through my nose. "You want me to leave him there for an entire day?"

Emma's body sat up and her gaze went hard. "You don't have any choice. You can't get to him without me, and I can't get him alone until then. Beyond that, if we miss our chance tomorrow, we may never get another one."

The entire room tilted as I reeled from shock. I had to close my eyes and grip the sides of the chair to regain my balance.

"Do you understand, Kaylee? It's tomorrow, or never."

"I get it." I swallowed thickly. "So, we wait until tomorrow night, and when you say the word, I cross over and haul you both out. Right? That's it?"

"With any luck, yes."

Luck? We were depending on luck?

Nash is so screwed....

"Is there anything else I need to know?" I leaned forward with both elbows propped on my knees. "Anything you're not telling me? Are we expecting an ambush? Or a giant boot to descend from the sky and squish us all?"

Or a trap waiting to be sprung?

As scared as I was for Nash, I couldn't quite buy the coincidence. Two days earlier, Scott's shadow man—who turned out to be Avari—had tried to get me into the Netherworld, and now Alec the proxy was trying the same thing, on behalf of the same hellion. Albeit, this time the bait was much better, but I was far from prepared to trust him.

And frankly, I was proud of myself for remembering to expect the unexpected—a good rule of thumb when traveling to the Netherworld.

Well, that, and "expect to be eaten by *everything*..."

Alec only shrugged. "The only other thing I can tell you is this..." He leaned forward, peering at me earnestly through Emma's eyes, her pouty lips pressed into a firm, pink line. "You're going to cross over into a big celebration. The biggest event I've seen in my time here. The place will be crawling with Netherworlders."

"And your point is..." Though, by then, I was pretty sure I already knew.

"I know you're going to be tempted to bring backup. Someone older and wiser, maybe?"

My father, of course. I hadn't actually decided to bring him in yet, but I'll admit I was considering it. He knew much more about the Netherworld than I did, and Nash's life was on the line.

When I refused to answer, Alec continued. "Kaylee, you may be able to cross back into your world with nothing more than a thought..."

Yeah, like it's that easy!

"...but if you bring anyone who can't cross over on his own, he's as good as dead. You know that, right?"

My stomach flipped and twisted at the thought of getting separated from my father in the Netherworld. If that happened, he'd never make it out.

"And trying to get more than two of us out at a time will slow you down enough to get us all killed. Do you understand? It's not just your life on the line here. Not just mine or Nash's, either. If you bring help, you're as good as slitting his throat. Though I can promise you his actual death will be neither that quick nor painless."

I swallowed the sudden need to vomit and nodded. He was right. But I didn't like it.

The growl of an engine outside broke through the

excruciating silence Alec's last words had woven. Ms. Marshall was home.

But Emma was not.

I spun in the chair, as if I could see through all the walls between me and the driveway. My heart raced, and I turned back to Alec. "You have to go. Now."

He shook her head and stood, foreign panic playing behind Emma's eyes. "We have to make plans. We're only going to get one chance, and we can't afford to mess it up."

"I know. But not now." I glanced toward the hall again as a key turned in the front door. "I need some time to get rid of her mother." *And talk to Tod.*

As badly as I wanted to save Nash, I was not just going to jump into the Netherworld with someone I'd never met—someone whose humanity I couldn't even confirm—without proof that Nash was actually missing.

And I *definitely* wasn't going to do it without backup. Tod could get himself out, and he could take someone with him, if necessary. And if this whole thing turned out to be a trap—an attempt by Avari to regain the soul that got away—I wanted someone I mostly trusted in my corner.

"How long?" Alec asked as the front door swung open across the house.

"Shhhh..." I hissed, my pulse racing. Then, "Two hours. Can you do that, with the time difference?"

Emma nodded. "I think so."

As loath as I was to subject Emma to another possession, I saw no other choice. "Fine. Now go!"

Alec frowned. Then Emma's eyes closed, and she fell over backward on the bed.

"Em, are you home?" Ms. Marshall called, her heels clacking down the hall toward us.

"Mmm?" Emma's eyes fluttered and she rolled over, one hand rising automatically to run through her hair.

"We're back here!" I crossed the room and sank onto the bed next to Emma. "We fell asleep watching a movie."

Ms. Marshall appeared in the doorway, leaning against the frame with one high-heeled foot crossed over the other, the empty ice cream carton in one hand. She lifted the carton and glanced at the DVD case on Emma's dresser. "Wild night?"

You have no idea....

"TOD!" I WHISPERED as I slammed the car door shut, glancing frantically around the dark concrete maze at mostly empty parking spaces. The chances of the reaper being in the parking garage were slim to none, but honestly, Tod was hardly ever where I expected to find him.

When he didn't answer, I clicked the automatic lock on my rented key bauble and headed for the entrance, wishing I'd thought to change clothes before I left Emma's. But since I hadn't, my walk across the dank parking garage was accented by the clunking of my wedge heels against the concrete and the flash of my shiny blouse in the dim industrial lights overhead.

When the glass door closed behind me with a soft air-sucking sound, I glanced around the empty, sterile hallway, desperate for a glimpse of the reaper Nash and I usually couldn't get rid of. "Tod! Get your invisible butt down here!" Or up here, or over here, or whichever way he'd have to travel to get to me.

Regrettably, superhearing was not among a reaper's many awesome abilities, so I'd have to be within normal hearing range to catch his attention. And since I couldn't see him—he considered corporeality at work to be unprofessional, though evidently shouting at the patients to *hurry up and die!* didn't offend his delicate moral fiber—putting myself within that hearing range could prove quite a challenge.

When he didn't show up in the back hallway, I race-walked down the corridor and around the corner, then through the swinging double doors into the emergency room, where Tod spent most of his working hours. If I didn't find him there, I was screwed, because there was no way a teenage girl would go unnoticed wandering around the intensive care unit by herself in the middle of the night.

Unfortunately, even at two in the morning, the emergency room was half-full and most of the patients looked awake enough to notice me calling out to someone who wasn't there.

"Tod!" I whispered, stepping into the vending machine alcove. Stubbornly resisting a bag of Doritos taunting me from behind the glass, I checked both restrooms opposite the water fountain with no luck.

Back in the waiting area, I jogged past the triage

nurse's station and had one palm on the door leading into the bowels of the E.R. when a familiar voice spoke up from behind me. "Is Emma with you?"

Startled, my heart thumping, I whirled around to find Tod standing with his hands shoved deep into the pockets of a faded, baggy pair of jeans. His sleeves were short and his jacket missing, as usual. Evidently the mostly dead don't feel the cold like the rest of us do. Or maybe that was part of his big bad reaper routine.

"No. Why?" I asked, and the triage nurse glanced at me in surprise, clearly unable to see or hear the reaper. I was going to have to start wearing a Bluetooth headset, or talking to Tod was going to get me locked up again.

"Her boyfriend came in by ambulance a few hours ago, and it's getting pretty tense back there," he said, unbothered by the nurse's presence as I smiled at her and subtly led him away from the double doors, hoping none of the staff recognized me from my visit the night before.

In the waiting area again, I raised my brows to tell him to go on, and Tod shrugged. "His dad's some big-shot lawyer. The governor's personal attorney, or some crap like that. He showed up about fifteen minutes ago, straight from the airport, and has been raising hell ever since. He's threatening to sue the hospital for negligence, and the attending physician for malpractice, and the damned *janitor* who mopped the floor he slipped on, even though there was one of those orange 'slippery' signs right next to him when he went down."

"So Doug's still…alive?" I whispered as he followed me into the rear corridor.

"Nah. He was brain-dead but breathing when he got here, and I put him out of his misery about an hour later. The weird thing is that he isn't on the list. Levi sent a runner with this about twenty minutes after Richie Rich came in." Tod pulled an uneven square of yellow paper from his right pocket and handed it to me.

My hands shook as I unfolded it. It was the bottom half torn from a sheet of legal paper. Neat, loopy handwriting slanted across the lines: *Douglas Aaron Fuller 23:47:33.*

"What is this?" I couldn't refold the paper fast enough. I shoved it at Tod, and he slid it back into his pocket.

"It's an addendum. An unscheduled reaping. The job should have gone to whoever works the sector where Em's boyfriend dropped, but our office didn't get word in time. So they sent it to me here."

Exhaustion and shock had taken their toll, and my eyes didn't want to focus. The hallway blurred until I blinked to clear my vision. "So this didn't have to happen…"

Tod shrugged. "It probably *shouldn't* have happened. This is only the second addendum I've seen in two years, and it just happens to be Emma's new boy toy. And she didn't come in with him. What's going on, Kaylee?"

And suddenly Doug's death hit me—not as a *bean*

sidhe, but as a person—grief suffocating me beneath the weight of my own guilt. I tripped over one wedge heel and caught myself against the wall, barely flinching at the pain in my bandaged arm because it was nothing compared to the ache in my heart.

"You okay?" Tod asked, and he sounded like he actually cared.

"No." I pushed myself away from the wall and tugged him down the hall with me, grateful when my fingers didn't sink right through his arm. "Do they know what Doug died of?"

Tod shrugged. "He had some cuts and bruises, but the doc thinks he got them during a seizure. Blood tests show alcohol, but not enough to kill him. Nothing else has come back yet, but Richie, Sr., insists his kid is clean, and if the tests show otherwise, he'll sue the lab. Man, I hope I'm working when *his* name comes up on the list."

I took the next left to put us farther from the E.R., and from Mr. Fuller. "Someday, someplace, karma is waiting to kick your teeth in, Tod."

"I'm dead." He made a sweeping gesture to encompass his entire body—which death had not damaged in the least. "My teeth have already been kicked in."

Well, he had a point there.…

"So, where're Nash and Emma? And aren't you a little overdressed for two-thirty in the morning?"

"Is it that late?" I glanced at my watch and groaned. Talking Emma back to sleep had taken half an hour, and hunting for Tod had taken longer than I'd expected. I now had less than forty-five minutes to be back in Emma's room, waiting for another call on the human telephone.

"It's a long story." Flustered, I ran one hand through my tangled hair, then crossed my arms over my blouse. "And Nash is the reason I'm here. Did he come in with Doug?"

The reaper frowned. "No. Why would he?"

"Because he's the reason Doug died."

Tod's confusion twisted into dark distress, and I could have sworn I saw blood drain from his face. Though I wasn't sure that was even possible for a dead guy. "What the hell are you talking about?"

But before I could answer, the door at the end of the hall opened, admitting a gust of wind and a couple in their mid-forties, whose stress and fatigue showed in every line on their faces.

"I need to sit," I suggested, irritated when the hand I wrapped around his arm went right through his flesh this time. "Cafeteria?" I whispered, shoving my hands into my pockets.

Tod huffed, already heading down the hall. "The coffee tastes like swamp water tonight, but sure." He led me down the long hallway and around two corners, then through the double doors into an outdated but functional cafeteria dotted with old square tables and cheap '70s-style, vinyl-covered chairs. "You know, you're lucky you caught me here. My shift ended at midnight, and if I weren't filling in for a friend, you'd be out of luck."

Yeah, right. I passed by the stack of trays and pulled a bottle of Coke from a refrigerated shelf. After his shift, Tod would have had nothing to do but hang around and spy on either me or Nash. He was almost always around, whether we needed—or wanted—him or not. At least, he had been until Addison died.

But all I said, as I dug a five from my pocket to pay for my soda, was, "You have a friend?"

Tod scowled. "Well, I wouldn't call him a friend according to the traditional definition, but in the sense that he imposes on me constantly and isn't afraid to point out my flaws, I'd say he qualifies."

"Sounds more like a cousin." I picked the table farthest from the food line and sank into a chair against the wall. Tod sat on my left, where he could see the rest of the room.

"Okay, spit it out." His chair squealed against the floor as he scooted toward the table, and I realized that he was now fully corporeal and visible to everyone in the room—and probably had been since we'd come through the doors. "What's Nash caught up in?" His brows were low and his voice was deep, but he didn't sound surprised. He'd known something was wrong. Maybe he'd known longer than I had.

"Demon's Breath," I whispered, to keep from being overheard. "He's been hooked for about a month, but last week a couple of his teammates got mixed up in it without knowing what they were taking. Doug found Nash's red balloon and now he's dead, and Scott's strapped to a bed in the mental health unit. Did you already know about that? And now Nash is stuck in the Netherworld, and it may be a setup, but even if it is, *we have to get him out!*"

"Whoa, take a breath!" Tod reached for my hand across the table, physically unclenching my fingers so he could squeeze them, and I was surprised by his warmth. Weren't dead guys supposed to be cold to the touch? Or was that only in the movies? "Nash is taking Demon's Breath?"

"Yeah, but it gets a lot worse than that."

"So I gathered." His gaze strayed to the bandage forming a lump beneath my sleeve. "But none of the rest of that made any sense."

"I know." I wiped unshed tears from my eyes with the back of my free hand, and lowered my voice when I noticed the custodian staring at me. "It's all messed up, and Alec says we only have one chance to get Nash back, but I'm *not* going to cross over until I know for sure that Nash is there."

Tod's eyes widened, thick blond boy-lashes nearly touching his eyebrows. "Okay, I need you to slow down and start over." He leaned back in his chair and brushed a stray, pale ringlet from his forehead. I nodded, and he forced a smile. "First of all, what does Nash have to do with the Fuller kid's unscheduled reaping?"

I took a deep breath and forced my throat to relax, though it felt hot and sore from holding back tears. "Demon's Breath—the dealer calls it frost—is sold in black party balloons. Except for Nash's. His are red." I clenched my hands together on the cracked, faded table-top and looked into Tod's bright blue eyes, somehow undulled by death. "Doug found Nash's balloon and took a hit, but Nash's concentration is too strong for humans. Or something like that. Then Doug started convulsing, and I started screaming, so Nash put me and Emma in my car—though, actually, it's a rental—and told us to go. He was supposed to call us with an update, but he never did. Then this guy named Alec *possessed* Emma and said his boss has Nash in the Netherworld, and that if I want him back, I have to help him cross back into our world."

"Wait..." Tod held both hands out to slow me down. "You have to help who cross over? Nash or Alec?"

"Alec. Well, both of them, really. But Alec won't help me find Nash unless I promise to bring him back with us."

"Who's Alec?"

"I have no idea." I shrugged helplessly. "He just... showed up tonight, talking through Emma's mouth. He says he's human, but he lives in the Netherworld. But humans don't live in the Netherworld. They can't, right? It doesn't make any sense."

Tod sighed. "It might, if you weren't saying it so fast."

"Sorry. But I have to be back in half an hour." My mouth was so dry I could barely talk, so I opened my soda and drained half of it. I'd definitely need the caffeine, since I obviously wasn't going to get any sleep for the third night in a row. "Alec says he's a proxy for Avari, who's holding Nash in the Netherworld. Have you ever heard of a proxy?"

Tod nodded slowly. Bleakly. "They're like assistants you can snack on. If you're a hellion. But they're rare, because humans don't hold up very well in the Netherworld, and eventually they'll wear out. It sounds like this hellion is looking to upgrade. With Nash."

I shook my head. "I don't think so. Alec didn't sound very worn-out."

"Okay, let's start with Nash." Tod leaned both elbows on the table, which put his eyes almost exactly level with mine. "He's been taking Demon's Breath for how long?"

"About a month."

The reaper's blue eyes went dark like the ocean at night, and his fist thumped on the table. "Why the hell didn't you tell me!"

"Because you weren't around, and I didn't know!" I hissed, glancing around the cafeteria to make sure no one was listening. "And it's your fault he was exposed in the first place! He accidentally inhaled some when we crossed over trying to save your girlfriend! Then *you* took him back to make his first purchase!"

"I never…" But his denial faded into shocked silence when the pieces fell together in his head. "I didn't know what he was doing, and he wouldn't tell me. He just said he was calling in his favor, and that's all I needed to know. And honestly, I didn't even push him for information. I was so messed up then, I wasn't even thinking."

Because Addison had just died without her soul. His absence and absentmindedness had worried me. But I should have been worried about Nash.

"I should have followed him. I could have stopped this before it even started!" Tod ran one hand through his hair, and several curls fell over his forehead. And when he finally looked up, I couldn't decide whether I was more surprised by his admission or by the guilt and anger churning slowly in his eyes.

I almost never saw Tod's eyes swirl.…

"Me, too." I stared at my hands, still clenched tightly on the tabletop. "I should have noticed something was wrong. A pack of gum, and four weeks of school and back, shouldn't have been enough to make me miss something this big."

Tod sighed. "How did he get into the Netherworld this time?"

"You didn't take him?"

"Hell, no, I didn't take him!" Tod said, loud enough to draw several looks our way.

I leaned across the table and lowered my voice. "Then I have no idea. He was supposed to be here with Doug, but you said he wasn't...?"

Tod shook his head in confirmation. "Not that I saw, and I was here when they brought him in. How did he get Nash's...balloon?"

I sighed and took another sip from my bottle. "Emma found it in Nash's bag during the party. I left Em in the car with the balloon. But she had to go to the bathroom." As she'd explained while we watched the movie. "We think Doug went looking for her and found the balloon instead." I sighed and stared at the table. "I wish we'd never gone to Doug's house tonight. But we couldn't let Em go alone." I glanced up at Tod, searching for agreement in his expression. For some sign that this whole catastrophe wasn't solely the result of my poor judgment. "Not with Everett bringing enough balloons to make a house float."

"Everett?" Tod's hand fell from his hair to land on the tabletop with a thud. "The dealer's name is Everett? Are you sure?"

"Yeah. He's tall and kind of angular. Nash says he's half-harpy, which is why we can't figure out how he's getting his supply here from the Netherworld."

"Everett. That damned pointy-looking, son-of-a-*shrew*," Tod snapped. Then he met my gaze again. "I know how he's getting it." He clenched the cheap plastic saltshaker like it held untold secrets of the universe. "I swear I had no idea what I was carrying, but...*I* brought it over."

"WHAT?" QUESTIONS TUMBLED in my head like shoes in the dryer, clanking painfully as they slammed into one another. Tod was ferrying Demon's Breath from the Netherworld for Avari? "Have you and Nash both lost your minds? This is really a very simple concept—one that you taught me! Hellion equals evil. Period!"

Tod's exhale was long, and low, and heavy. "Avari had something I needed, and he doesn't take cash or checks. Not that I have either one, but I could have come up with some money." The reaper shrugged. "But he already knew what he wanted from me. And Kaylee, I swear I had no idea what I was carrying."

The numbness in my brain and body faded, replaced by a scalding anger. "Is that supposed to make it okay? That you didn't care enough to ask what you were hauling?

What did you *think* he was sending up? Fuzzy kittens and care packages for the children's ward?" People were staring at us now, but I was *so* far beyond caring. "Isn't working for a hellion a conflict of interest?" I demanded through gritted teeth, my open-arm gesture taking in the entire hospital, and the job Tod carried out there.

"It would be, if I were selling him poached souls, or something like that. But my business with him has nothing to do with my job, or with my abilities as a reaper."

"Are you serious?" I shoved my chair back and my pitch rose so high on the last word that dogs all over the neighborhood were probably howling in sympathy. Or maybe in pain. "Your reaper skills are what get you to and from the Netherworld. Without them, you wouldn't have interested Avari except as a snack. Another soul to suck. You're *totally* abusing your abilities. And because of what you've done, one kid is dead, one's gone clinically insane, and your own brother is wandering around in the Netherworld like a protein bar with legs!"

People were starting to openly stare, so I looked at the table and counted to ten to get my temper back under control. When I looked up, Tod was wiping both hands over his face, the muscles in his arms bunched with tension.

"I hope it's worth it, whatever he's giving you," I spat as softly as I could. "I hope it's worth the three lives you've ruined." Four, if you counted Emma's, and five if you counted mine, because there was no guarantee

I'd walk away from the Netherworld alive this time. Or at all.

Tod flinched, but didn't break eye contact. "It's Addison," he said, his voice so low and heavy I wasn't sure I'd heard it at all. "I traded my service as a courier for an hour a day with Addy."

Huh?

"Tod, Addison's dead."

He nodded slowly. "Her body is. But her soul is alive and not so well in the Netherworld, and the only way I can help her is to give her an hour a day free from torture and humiliation. To keep her sane. It seemed like the least I could do, considering I failed to get her soul back before she died." Tod's jaw tightened, and he held my gaze, steadily. Unashamed. Yet I saw the flicker of pain and determination in his eyes.

I felt my heart splinter and thought for a moment that I could actually hear the cracks. How was I supposed to stay mad at him now? Tod had been ruining lives with his own postmodern, interdimensional version of chivalry.

Will all the real men please stand up?

"I swear I didn't know what I was carrying…"

I wanted to ask if that would have mattered. If he'd known what he was really agreeing to, would he have considered five ruined lives—and potentially countless more—worth an hour of comfort a day for Addison? But I didn't ask, because I already knew that where Addy was concerned, Tod had no limits. He'd been willing to let me die in the Netherworld to save her soul. There was nothing he wouldn't do for her. To be with her.

Even beyond the grave.

I sighed and rubbed both hands over my face. "Okay, so how does this work? You blink into the Netherworld and he lets you see Addison for an hour, then hands you a balloon bouquet on your way out?"

Tod's brows rose in bitter amusement. "Do I look like a party clown? It's just a canvas duffel bag with a padlock through the zipper. I could have broken it, or cut the bag open, but honestly, considering what Addy and I have to lose, it didn't seem smart to stick my nose into Netherworld business."

"I hate to tell you this, Tod, but you're already up to your eyebrows in it. And thanks to you and Nash, so are Doug, and Scott, and Emma, and me." Not to mention whoever else Doug might have introduced to frost. I couldn't help marveling at the irony of both Hudson brothers playing separate, secret parts in whatever Avari was up to.

He leaned back in his chair and exhaled heavily. "Avari's going to be pissed when he finds out I'm out of the drug-trafficking business, and he'll probably take it out on Addison. But the more immediate problem is Nash. If we don't get him out before I refuse the next shipment, we'll probably never have another shot."

"Alec says our best chance is tomorrow night. They're

having some kind of big party…" And I couldn't help wondering what there was to celebrate in the Netherworld.

The reaper nodded, pale curls bobbing. "Yeah, I've seen them setting up for it. Creepy."

"…and he thinks he can get to Nash during the commotion. He's gonna call me back in about half an hour—" I glanced at my watch "—make that twenty minutes, to make plans." I stood, and Tod stood with me, and we headed for the hall by unspoken agreement.

"There are no cell phone towers in the Netherworld," he whispered. "How's Alec going to call you?"

I swallowed the horror and disgust my answer brought with it as I pushed open the double doors. "Through Emma."

Confusion narrowed Tod's eyes, then sudden comprehension flowed in, chased by a wave of obvious repulsion. "He's using her as an intermediary? That's what you meant by possession?" he hissed, without bothering to check the cold, sterile hall for humans.

I nodded. "It's awful. She still looks like herself, but she sounds like someone else, and she doesn't move, or sit, or laugh like Emma. She's being *worn*. It's creepy."

"Yeah." Tod's scowl deepened as he walked, and I rushed to keep up with him. "I've only seen the show once, but it was one of the ugliest things I've ever seen." Which surely meant something coming from a reaper. "And it's hard on the host, because he subconsciously fights the invasion. It can leave you exhausted for days afterward."

"Tell me about it." No wonder I was so tired all the time. In addition to giving up sleep to avoid waking up in the Netherworld, I'd had my body invaded by an uninvited visitor twice in the past week.

Tod stopped abruptly and his gaze narrowed on me. "What does that mean?"

I sighed and cradled my bandaged arm. "Avari's been using me to communicate with Nash. I didn't realize it until I saw it happen to Emma, but I'm sure that's what's been happening." I shuddered at the sudden clear understanding that I'd been used, both physically and emotionally. That Avari had been in my body, without my knowledge or permission. Could there be a more horrifying, revolting violation?

I'd never seen a stronger look of disgust—or protective *rage*—than the one on Tod's face. His eyes practically blazed with twisting blue flames. "How could Nash let that happen?"

I shrugged, dropping my empty soda bottle in the trash against the wall. "I don't think he had any choice. I sure didn't when Alec took over Emma."

Tod shoved the parking garage door open with both hands, though he could have walked through it. "You didn't know what was going on, and you had to play nice to get your boyfriend back. Nash had a choice. If he'd wanted to get rid of Avari, he would have found a way. But he just let it happen—let that bastard use you—and he didn't even tell you." His mouth snapped shut against the rest of what he wanted to say, but I heard it, anyway.

If I were as important to Nash as his next fix, he would never have let it happen.

"What the hell is wrong with him?"

"He's not the same, Tod," I said, race-walking to keep up with him, though he had no idea where I'd parked. "He's been Influencing me, and he's lying all the time. He said he gave Scott's first balloon to you to get rid of, but I'm guessing you never saw it."

Tod scowled, adjusting his course when I veered toward my rental. "When was that?"

I clicked the button to unlock the car. "Monday, when you were working double shifts with no breaks." Except that Tod had popped into the cafeteria at lunch that day to ask me if Emma was serious about Doug… "You were never in trouble with Levi, were you? No double shifts?"

Tod shook his head, teeth grinding furiously. "To my never-ending dismay and boredom, we only get a few deaths a day in a hospital this size. I wander off during the lulls all the time, and Levi doesn't care, so long as I don't miss an appointment. And Nash damn well knows it."

"I'm such an idiot!" I kicked the front tire, but that

only scuffed my shoe. "Why couldn't I see what he was doing?"

"I didn't see it, either." Tod's footsteps went silent as he circled the car toward the passenger's side, and I knew that no one else could see him. Still, I was grateful that he hadn't simply blinked into Emma's bedroom, leaving me to drive back alone.

"So, you're not going to get in trouble for leaving now?" I asked as I settled into the driver's seat.

He shrugged, unconcerned. "It's a slow night. No one's scheduled to tumble into the abyss for another hour and a half, and if I'm not back by then, I'll get someone else to cover for me."

"What if you get another…addendum?"

His brows rose, but the corners of his cherubic mouth turned down as he sank onto the leather seat. "Then we have bigger worries than my absence."

I buckled up and started the engine, then twisted to watch out the rear windshield as I backed out of the parking space. "We need help, but my dad can't do it. Bringing someone who can't cross over would just be creating more work for ourselves," I said, then rushed on before he could interrupt. "I think we should bring your mom in on this."

"No," Tod said, and I glanced at him as I shifted into Drive, surprised to find his expression completely unreadable. "Absolutely not."

"But she's five times my age, and she can cross over

on her own." I turned left out of the garage and onto the street, trying not to let frustration leak into my voice. "She's the only option that makes sense."

"We are not dragging my mother into the Netherworld. And we can't tell her about Nash, or she'll go on her own and get killed." His hand landed on mine on the gearshift, and again I was surprised by its warmth. "I'm serious, Kaylee. If you want to bring your dad or your uncle, that's your call. But leave my mother out of this. I've already lost my dad and Addison, and now possibly Nash. I will *not* add my mom to the list."

I could only nod, impressed by his fervor and surprised by the brief glimpse into his heart. *Maybe he doesn't think so differently from the living, after all....*

"Fine." I nodded once more, decisively. "No parents."

EMMA WAS STILL ASLEEP when I snuck back into her room at ten minutes after three. Fortunately, her mother was snoring from behind her bedroom door, and both of her sisters were still out. Obviously the best part about college was the lack of a curfew.

In the bedroom, I knelt to check on Emma, half convinced she would show some delayed ill effect from the abuse of her body, but she seemed to be sleeping peacefully. And deeply. Probably because, as I'd discovered, possession is exhausting.

"She looks okay," Tod said, echoing my own thoughts.

"Hopefully one more round won't hurt her. But let's keep this Alec on a short leash, just in case."

I nodded, yawning as I pushed myself to my feet with one hand on the mattress. Considering I'd never actually met Alec, his leash would be no longer than my pinkie finger.

"How much time do we have?" Tod leaned over Emma and ran one finger gently over her lower lip.

I glanced at the clock on Emma's DVD player. "About five minutes. Don't touch her! You'll wake her up."

He huffed softly. "I doubt that. She looks like she could sleep through the end of the world."

"No thanks to you." I shooed him away from the bed, then had to force my eyes open wide when they threatened to close. "I need a Coke." What I *really* needed was a shot of adrenaline straight to the heart, but caffeine would have to do. "I think you should fade out," I said, backing toward the hall. "Alec doesn't want me to bring backup…." Which was one of the main reasons I found him hard to trust. Well, that and the fact that he'd contacted me through the unconscious body of my best friend. "So we should probably keep you a secret."

"No problem." Tod grinned, and though I could see no difference in him, I had no doubt that he no longer existed physically in the room. If he ever had.

I tiptoed into the kitchen in my socks and grabbed another can of Coke from the fridge. I had drained half of it by the time I made it back to Emma's room. "Do you—" I began, intending to ask the reaper if he wanted a soda. Though I couldn't remember ever seeing him consume anything before.

"Shhhh!" Tod hissed the moment I stepped in from the hall. "He's here."

My voice faded into a tense silence as I glanced from the reaper to the girl lying curled up on one side on the bed. Emma hadn't moved since I left the room, but if Tod thought Alec had arrived—a full four minutes early—I wasn't taking any chances.

Sipping from my can as casually as possible, I strolled across the room toward Emma, and this time when her eyes popped open, I was ready. I didn't spill a single drop.

"Do I what?" Alec asked through Emma's mouth as he stared up at me through her deep brown eyes.

"I was going to ask if you wanted a soda."

Emma frowned, then pushed herself upright on the mattress. "How did you know I was here?"

"You went tense when I walked into the room." I shrugged, totally ad-libbing. "So, you want a drink or not?" I asked before he had a chance to think about my answer.

Emma's brows shot up. "Can I do that? Have a drink while I'm in here?" He spread her arms to indicate her entire form.

I shrugged again. "How would I know? I've never been in someone else's body."

The grin was all Alec. “Me, neither—before tonight.”

“Are you serious?” I shot him a legitimate scowl. “You’re new at this? Here, they don’t let new drivers behind the wheel alone, but I bet there’s no one in there with you to slam on the brakes if this thing goes downhill.”

His grin faded. “Trust me, Kaylee, there’s no one else here you’d trust in your friend’s body.”

“No one here, either…” Tod quipped, and it was all I could do not to acknowledge his joke—or his presence.

“So, how ’bout that drink?” Alec swung Emma’s bare feet onto the floor. “Do you have anything stronger than Coke?”

Yeah. Drano. But even if I knew for a fact that he was drawing me into a trap, I couldn’t poison Emma. “She’s had quite enough to drink tonight, thank you.”

“Well, that explains why she was so easy to push toward sleep.” When I showed no sign of relenting, he sighed and shrugged Emma’s shoulders. “A Coke would be great, thanks. I haven’t had one in years.”

Tod followed me to the kitchen, as I’d hoped he would, and I whirled on him the minute we were out of sight from the hallway. “Just shut up and listen in there, or I swear I’ll tell your boss you’re moonlighting as a Netherworld mule,” I hissed. Then I grabbed another can from the fridge and marched back down the hall before he could reply.

In Emma's room, Alec stood with Em's arms crossed beneath her chest, eyeing the collection of pictures on her dresser. "Here. Drink fast and talk faster. This little powwow's over if anyone wakes up or comes home. Got it?"

Alec nodded, then broke one of Emma's nails popping open the tab on his can. She was definitely going to notice that. "Mmm," he said, swallowing his first mouthful of soda. "I'd forgotten how it fizzes on your tongue. It almost hurts. Do you have any idea how long it's been since I had a soda? I can't believe I can feel it through her. Maybe I should just stay here…"

"No, you shouldn't. Don't you want to feel things in your own body?"

Emma shrugged. "Well, one without breasts would be nice. These things get in the way every time I move my arms."

I rolled my eyes and sank into the desk chair. "I wouldn't know. But she should get her period in a couple of days. Unless you want to stick around for that—" and I could tell from the comically horrified look on her face, and from Tod's less-than-subtle snort, that my dart had hit the bull's-eye "—I suggest you start talking. What's the plan?"

"Okay, here goes…" Alec took his can and settled Emma onto the edge of the bed, leaning forward with one elbow on her knee, her legs spread wide. Like a guy would sit. "Tomorrow is the winter solstice, in both worlds, and for the first time in something like sixty years, Avari has the resources to hold a true Liminal Celebration. I've truly never seen anything like the effort they're putting into this."

"What's a Liminal Celebration?" I asked, sipping from my own can, wishing that the caffeine would kick in almost as badly as I wished Alec would get to the part that included the actual plan.

"It's a festival in honor of the liminal times and places. Do you understand liminality?" I shook my head and, to my irritation, he made Emma nod, as if she'd expected as much. "Liminalities are the spaces and moments between."

"Between what?" I asked, exhaustion having used up all my patience.

"Between anything. Dusk and dawn, for example, are the liminal times between daylight and dark. Doorways are the liminal spaces between in and out. Make sense?" he asked, and I nodded slowly, though I was far from sure I actually understood.

"So, noon would be a liminal time between morning and afternoon, right?" I said, sinking into the desk chair.

Emma's head nodded, and her borrowed eyes lit with satisfaction. "Liminalities are very important, because they thin the boundaries between the two worlds and make human energy easier for those in the Netherworld to access. And the summer and winter solstices are the biggest, most important liminalities of all. They represent the points of balance in the year between the shortening of days and the lengthening of days. The winter solstice is like their New Year."

I drained my can and reached back to set it on the desk behind me. "So, you guys are basically throwing a big New Year's Eve party, and you want me to crash it?"

"Sort of." Emma's eyes narrowed in thought. "I think I can take advantage of the distraction to get your boyfriend alone. Then you should be able to cross over and take us both back with you."

Sounded reasonable enough to me—assuming he was telling the truth.

"Where is this big festival?"

Alec sighed through Emma's mouth. "As near as I can figure, not having been on your side of the gray fog in quite a while, it's across the street from the city park. That's where they're setting everything up. And whatever they've built where the old county courthouse stood must be heavily populated, because the building bleeds through almost entirely. Long hallways and room after empty room."

My heart dropped into my stomach. He was talking about the high school. *My* high school. It had been built five years earlier, after the courthouse burned down and the county seat was moved.

"What time does this party start?" I whispered as chill bumps popped up beneath my sleeves.

"Dusk. The last minutes between sunset and full darkness, when you can still make out things around you, but you can also see stars and planets in the sky. It's the perfect liminal moment."

Crap. Of course it started at dusk. Our Winter Carnival opened at 5:30—which was about when the sun went down in mid-winter—the exact time and place as their Liminal Celebration.

There's no way on earth that was a coincidence. Something bad was going on. Something even worse than the frost invasion and Nash being stuck in the Netherworld, though that hardly seemed possible. And according to the clock on Emma's DVD player, I only had about fourteen hours before dusk brought my one chance to bring Nash back to our world.

"So, I'll meet you at five-thirty by the front steps of the—" *high school* "—new building, and we'll go from—"

But Alec interrupted before I could finish that thought.

"Shhhh, he's coming," he hissed. Then, "Yes. Five-thirty, by the steps, no matter what else happens. I have to—" And just like that, Alec was gone.

Only instead of slumping back into sleep, as she'd done the last time Alec vacated her body, Emma stood suddenly stiff and straight as a bedpost. Her head swiveled slowly on her shoulders, steadily taking in the room and its furnishings before her eyes met mine. Then her mouth curled into a slow, taunting smile.

"Well, isn't this interesting...."

Though I hadn't seen him in a month, I'd know that voice anywhere.

Avari.

"MS. CAVANAUGH, how delightful to find you here." The hellion paused, glancing around the room again through Emma's eyes. "Wherever *here* is."

I shuddered beneath a bolt of near-paralyzing terror, then exhaled silently in relief. If he didn't know where he was, he probably didn't know who he was *in*. Which surely meant it would be hard for him to ever take Emma over again.

But then Em's eyes narrowed as Avari stared through them at a framed photo on the dresser: a shot of me and Emma standing in front of my new-to-me car, on the day I'd gotten it. "Well, isn't my proxy clever?" Avari crossed the room in Emma's bare feet, hips swinging in the exaggerated motion of a man who isn't used to wielding them. His gaze flicked to the mirror behind the picture and his eyes widened in lecherous appreciation. "And doesn't he have the most exquisite taste?"

Seeing Avari in her was a thousand times worse than watching Alec interact through Emma's body. I couldn't stand it. How was I ever going to look her in the face again?

"Get out!" I whispered through clenched teeth, my hands curling into powerless fists at my sides. Avari ignored me and reached for the picture with one of Emma's delicate, graceful hands. "Don't touch that!"

His gaze flicked my way in surprise and I choked on my next breath, shocked and disturbed by how unlike Emma her own eyes could look. "What would you rather I touch?" Avari asked, his smooth, sinister words violating her throat just as brutally as his presence desecrated her existence. "This?" The thin hand changed directions and Emma's fingers splayed across her flat stomach, thumb brushing her sternum, pinkie tucking beneath the elastic waistband of her pj pants.

"Or this?" Avari's voice deepened suggestively, and the hand slid up Emma's torso to lift her left breast through the thin cotton of her nightshirt.

My pulse pounded so fast and hard my vision started to go dark. "Get *out* of her, *now!*" When Avari turned back to the mirror, unbothered by my powerless protest, I glanced at Tod for help, but he could only shrug and press one finger against his lips in a "shhhh" gesture, reminding me not to give away his presence. He couldn't control Avari any more than I could, but if the hellion found out the reaper was helping me, he would take his anger out on Nash, and on Addison's soul.

"Oh, nooo…" Avari ran Emma's hand down her side and over the generous curve of her hip, cocking it to one side for a better view in the mirror. "I like this one. Truly lovely. She is definitely worth the effort of exploration."

My jaws ached from being clenched, but I forced my feet to remain still. There was nothing I could do to hurt Avari without hurting Emma, and I wasn't sure what abilities, if any, Avari brought with him to the body he possessed. Knowing my luck, if I tried to throw a punch—not that I even knew how—he'd freeze me where I stood, or do something worse than groping with Emma's borrowed hands.

"How could I not have noticed her before? She feels familiar…." Both of Emma's hands slid around her hips to cup her backside as Avari's gaze traveled down in the mirror. "But not obviously so. How did Alec ever find her…?" Avari blinked, then turned from the mirror to meet my furious gaze through narrowed eyes. "I do *love* a resourceful proxy." But the hard, angry line of Emma's jaw said that wasn't entirely true. Alec had been up to something without Avari's knowledge, and the hellion was pissed. "And Alec has always been exactly that."

"How long have you…had him?" I asked, stalling for

time as my brain whirred almost audibly, grinding in search of some way to get rid of the hellion.

Avari tilted Emma's head to one side, as if surprised by my interest. And suspicious of it. "Oh, two or three decades," he finally said. "And he has proven most useful." Yet that little twitch of irritation was back. "Even when he doesn't intend to." Emma's body stepped closer to me, one hip cocked, one side of her mouth curved up in a lewd grin. "For instance, you are a hard child to get in touch with. Though I must say you aren't particularly difficult to get *inside* of..."

Rage and horror battled within me as Emma's borrowed gaze swept the length of my form before finally returning to my eyes. I had the sudden urge to cover what little flesh my clothes didn't hide, and couldn't help wondering what the hellion had done with my body when he'd occupied it. And how often that had been.

If I actually got Nash back alive, he was going to tell me every single thing that happened while I was literally out of my own mind—or I'd kill him myself. And based on Tod's angry, narrowed eyes, he was thinking something very similar.

Emma stepped forward again, and I answered with another step back, my pulse racing, my jaws clenched so hard I was half-afraid my teeth would crack. "How many times?" I whispered, trying to showcase my anger while hiding my terror.

He took another slinky step toward me, wearing my

best friend's body like a slut wears spandex. And this time when I backed away, my thighs hit the edge of the desk. I had nowhere left to go, unless I was willing to let him follow me through the rest of Emma's house. Which I was not.

"How many times have I been in you?" Avari asked, leering at me with Emma's wide, brown eyes, and I flinched over his phrasing. My skin crawled just thinking about him being on the inside of my flesh, breaching the most sacred of my boundaries: that which defined my soul.

"Several," the hellion answered at last, and his next step put him—put them—less than a foot away. "And I must say it's a genuine pleasure." Emma's body leaned forward and her cheek skimmed mine, my pulse roaring in my ears.

"Each..." Her lips brushed my jaw, and I swallowed thickly.

"...and every..." Her hot, damp breath puffed against my earlobe, and I closed my eyes, trying not to breathe.

"...time." Avari's last word stirred the sensitive hairs on my neck, just below my ear, and I swallowed the whimper caught in my throat.

I opened my eyes, and over Emma's shoulder I saw Tod standing with his fists clenched, his face flushed in fury, jaw bulging as he silently ground his teeth.

Then the hellion stepped back, smiling through

Emma's pouty mouth, and her eyes took on a lecherous glint so disturbing and disorienting that my whole body shuddered. "But as much fun as I've had playing teenage *bean sidhe*—once when your boyfriend didn't even realize you'd stepped out of your body..."

Rage raced through my veins so fast and hot I thought I would combust. What the *hell* had he done! What had he made *me* do? And did Nash really think it was me doing...whatever Avari had done with my body?

"...I have yet to find a good way to communicate with you. Though we came so close with your classmate the other day." Confusion must have shown through my mounting fury, because as Avari turned, running one of Emma's slim fingers over the desktop, he lifted one of her artfully arched brows and continued. "How is your arm, by the way?" Her loaded gaze traveled to the bandaged bulge beneath my right sleeve.

Understanding slammed into me like a hammer to my skull. It all came back to Avari. All of it.

Nash was right. Avari was Scott's shadow man. He was the hallucination Doug had seen in his passenger's seat. He was the hellion selling its breath to Nash. Avari had possession of Addison's soul. He'd bribed Tod and Everett into delivering and disseminating his toxic byproduct. He was holding Nash captive in the Netherworld. And Avari was organizing the Liminal Celebration, which would conveniently coincide with our Winter Carnival.

How could I not have seen it earlier? All roads led back to Avari. And for some reason, he'd been trying to get in touch with me.

"What do you want?" I demanded, suddenly sure I'd finally asked the right question.

Avari wrapped one of Emma's arms around the shoulder-high post at the foot of her bed and swung her around to face me, exposing a smooth strip of skin at her waist. "You." The hellion's voice went deep and dark, and sounded surreal coming from Emma's still-pink mouth. "I want you. And if you cross over right now, you have my word that I will send your boyfriend back to your world."

From my left, near Emma's closet, Tod shook his head frantically, and it was all I could do not to look directly at him and clue Avari in to his presence. But I didn't need to see Tod to know what he was thinking. Avari might send Nash back, but there was no telling when, where, or in what condition he would arrive.

Or in how many pieces.

"Why me?" I asked, ice-cold dread surging through my veins in place of blood. "Don't you have enough proxies, or servants, or snacks running around?"

"There are never enough proxies." *Of course.* I almost forgot I was talking to a hellion of avarice. "But that is not my interest in you." Emma grinned, easily the most genuine expression Avari had twisted her features into yet. "If you want to know more, you'll have to cross over so we can have this conversation in person."

I shook my head firmly and crossed my arms over my chest. "Not going to happen."

"Even to save your boyfriend?"

I swallowed thickly. Crossing over into Avari's hands was not my only chance to get Nash back, but that didn't make it any easier to say what came next. In fact, the words stuck so firmly in my throat that I had to clear it just to speak. "I don't want a boyfriend who cares more about his next fix than about me." The tears in my eyes were authentic, but with any luck, he'd attribute them to the emotional loss of my boyfriend, rather than to the crippling pain born from my knowledge that I was betraying Nash, and maybe damning his soul. "And I certainly don't want one who lets you step into my body without even telling me I'm being worn like a used condom."

Surprise and amusement glittered in Emma's eyes, and Avari almost looked…satisfied. As if he were pleased to discover something he actually respected in me.

Which sent an even stronger chill through me.

"Is that a no?"

I nodded slowly, as if the decision were difficult for me. As if I weren't planning to come later, on my own terms. With backup. "A very firm no."

I had an instant to hope I hadn't just made a very big mistake, then Avari smiled cruelly with Emma's lips. "In that case, I hope you said a very firm goodbye to your boyfriend."

Emma's eyes closed and her legs folded beneath her. She collapsed to the carpet with a single soft, feminine exhale, and I dropped to my knees beside her as her eyes fluttered open once. Then twice. Then they flew open again and stayed open, focusing on me sluggishly.

"Kaylee?" she asked in her own voice, and relief flavored my next breath, as if the very air tasted better now that Avari had left the building. "What happened?"

"I don't know." I shrugged and glanced at Tod, who now knelt on her other side, though she clearly could neither see nor hear him. "I went to the bathroom, and when I got back you were on the floor. Did you roll off the bed?"

And now I'm lying to my best friend…

Emma frowned and propped herself up on both palms. "I don't think so." Then her gaze narrowed on my blouse before trailing to my jeans, and I knew I'd messed up. Em was smart and she knew I had secrets. "You were sleeping in your clothes?"

I sighed and shot her a crooked smile, scrambling to think on my feet. "I was hoping Nash would call and we'd make up."

"You were going to go over there in the middle of the night?" Her own smile snuck up on me, and I was surprised to realize that our fight had bothered her, too.

"Yeah. But he didn't call." And my next trip to see

Nash would involve much more than a mile-and-a-half drive through suburban Texas.

"He will." Emma pushed herself to her feet. Her eyes were already trying to close, and her next words were stretched through a lion-size yawn. "And everything will be okay. Because Nash loves you, and that's all that matters. Right?"

I nodded as Em sank back onto the bed, and I couldn't help wishing that, for once, things really were that simple.

"HEY, DAD," I SAID into my phone, then covered the mouthpiece to thank the waitress pouring ice water into my glass.

"You're up awfully early after a sleepover," my father said, relief obvious in his voice. This time I couldn't blame him for worrying, even though I'd left voice messages several times throughout the night to tell him I was okay. And still in the human world.

"It doesn't count as a sleepover if you don't sleep," I said, stifling a yawn. "But Emma was nice enough to help me stay awake all night." Which was technically true. After seeing her body taken over by two different Netherworld entities, I couldn't have slept if I'd wanted to. "We watched movies and ate ice cream."

Across the table, Tod rolled his eyes, apparently feeling cheated by the lack of slumber party clichés. After all, what were a couple of teenage possessions compared to the half-naked pillow fight he'd hoped for in reward for staying the rest of the night with us—invisibly—just in case I fell asleep. Or Avari reappeared.

Not that my dad needed to know about either the reaper or the hellion. I saw no reason to worry him, since even the noblest of intentions on his part would only get him trapped in the Netherworld. Or worse.

Tod nodded in thanks when the waitress set a glass of orange juice in front of him. I'd refused to talk to him if he didn't go completely corporeal at the restaurant.

Over the line I heard the clink of glass-on-plastic as the coffeepot bumped the rim of my father's travel mug. "I'm about to leave for work." Which he had no choice but to do, even in the middle of a *bean sidhe* crisis, if we wanted to be able to make next month's rent. And honestly, the only thing I could think of worse than being wanted by a hellion was being *homeless* and wanted by a hellion. "I don't want you alone today. You need rest, and it's not safe for you to sleep alone right now."

A very odd statement coming from my father… But I knew what he meant.

"I'm fine, Dad. I'm being careful." Whatever that meant… I was too tired at the moment for much coherence.

"You're not fine, Kaylee." His mug clunked against the countertop. "You can't function on so little sleep, and you're only going to make yourself sick by trying."

"So what do you suggest?" I asked as the waitress set a

plate of chocolate chip pancakes on the table in front of me. Sugar would keep me awake, right? I thanked her, then pushed the melting scoop of butter around with my knife.

My dad sighed. "I don't know. We're still working on it. Can you stay with Nash or Harmony? As little as I trust that boy in some respects, I do trust him to wake you up if you start screaming."

Unfortunately, hanging out with Nash wasn't an option, unless I was willing to cross into the Netherworld and hand over my soul for the privilege. And I couldn't stay with Harmony without having to explain her son's absence. So maybe Emma, once Tod went to work…?

"Yeah," I said around a sweet, chocolaty mouthful. "Don't worry, I won't be alone."

"Okay, I have to go." He paused, and I heard doubt and concern in the short silence. "I'll call to check up on you, so answer your phone when it rings. And I'll see you tonight."

"Count on it," I said, desperately hoping I wasn't jinxing myself with that one.

I hung up my phone and slid it into my front pocket, then looked up to find Tod eyeing my pancakes. "Do you want something? Do reapers even need food?" To my surprise, he was already halfway through his juice, but I couldn't remember ever seeing him actually eat.

"We don't need it, just like we don't need sleep, but all the same pleasure sensors are still there and functioning.

Including taste buds," he clarified when I grinned with one raised brow. "Unfortunately, the reaper gig doesn't pay in human currency, so I'm perpetually low on funds."

Oh. Now *that* I understood.

"Here. This is more than I need, anyway." I pushed my plate to the center of the table, and handed him a napkin-wrapped bundle of silverware. "I can't eat with you drooling like a starving child."

"Thanks." He dug in, and I watched, amused by the thought that Death had a sweet tooth.

"So, I assume I'm not the only one who isn't buying this Winter Carnival/Liminal Celebration coincidence, right?" We hadn't been able to talk it through before, with Emma around—or even dozing.

Tod swallowed his first bite, nodding. "There's no way they're unrelated. My guess is that Avari's planning a big Netherworld feast to take advantage of such a large concentration of human energy when the boundary between the worlds is so thin. They'll be able to soak it all up with minimal effort in the hour surrounding dusk."

I nodded, chewing my own syrup-soaked bite. "But surely that's not all there is to it. I mean, really? A big picnic? That's Avari's master plan? That makes him sound about as dangerous as Yogi Bear."

Tod shrugged. "Yeah. If Yogi were a soul-sucking, body-stealing, boyfriend-snatching, damned-soul-torturing evil demon from another world. Besides, what else could he be planning?"

"I don't know. But the winter solstice happens every year, and Alec said this was their first festival in decades. Why? What's different about this year?" I took another bite, chewing while I waited for an answer neither of us had. "Whatever it is, we need to know before we get there. Are you supposed to see Addison today?"

Tod nodded and dropped his fork on the plate. "Yeah. But if I refuse to take the shipment afterward, Avari's going to know something's up."

I shrugged and cut another bite. "So take it. Just don't deliver it to Everett. We'll figure out how to get rid of it after we've gotten Nash out of there."

Tod frowned, a bite hovering halfway to his mouth. "Kaylee, we don't even know if Alec is going to show up, now that Avari caught E.T. phoning home. For all we know, he'll have his proxy locked up even tighter than Addison, and we'll cross over into this massive chaos swarming with freaks ready to chew our eyeballs and slurp up our intestines."

I felt my brows arch halfway up my forehead. "Eyeballs and intestines? You've been crossing over every day for a month. Has anyone even looked twice at your soft tissues?"

"No, but I was there working for Avari." He leaned closer to whisper over the table. "Or maybe it's because I'm dead, and even most Netherworlders won't eat dead meat. But you're not dead and you don't have permission to be there. So it's *your* soft tissues we should be worrying about." He shrugged when I swallowed thickly, and leaned back in his chair, crossing his arms over the tee stretched across his well-toned chest. "I just thought you should know what you're getting into."

A chill shot down my spine in spite of the hot coffee warming my belly. "Which is why I need you to keep your eyes and ears open while you're with Addison," I said. "We need to know what happened to Alec, and where they're keeping Nash, and what kind of shape he's in, in case Alec isn't there to help us. We also need everything you can find out about this Liminal Celebration And even if you can manage all that, I have a feeling we'll be walking into a very unpleasant surprise tonight."

"Agreed." Tod mopped up a puddle of syrup with the last bite of pancake. "But I'm not making any promises on this spy mission. It's not like I have free rein of the Netherworld."

I hadn't assumed he did, but… "Don't you do half of your job there? I mean, isn't that where you take the souls to be recycled?"

Tod's brows shot up, and I couldn't tell if he was amused or horrified by that thought. "To the Netherworld? No. If I took souls there, they'd be eaten, instead of recycled. Reapers have access to the Netherworld by virtue of being dead, Kaylee. Not as an employee benefit."

Ohhhh… I felt my face flush at my own stupidity. "So, where do you take them?"

"I can't tell you that." And that time, his grin looked genuine. "Company policy. And as for my business in the Netherworld, I pop into Avari's office—the one we were in when Addy died—and he brings her in. We get an hour, most of which I spend talking to her, to keep her mind from slipping under the strain of constant torture and abuse."

"She has a mind?" I couldn't wrap my own mind around that one, though I couldn't imagine why he would visit her if she didn't. "But she's dead."

"So am I." Tod set his fork on my empty, syrup-smeared plate. "You have to stop thinking of death as the end of everything. Yes, in most cases the soul is recycled, but if that doesn't happen, there are a bunch of ways to be dead, with or without a body, a memory, and a soul. Addy has everything but her body, and I'm not even missing that, as you may have noticed." He spread his very corporeal arms for emphasis and almost smacked some poor waitress carrying a huge tray of food.

"I know. But how does Addy have her soul if she sold it to Avari?"

"She and her soul have been reunited in the Netherworld, but he actually owns it. Thus the constant torture."

"Oh." I made a mental note to keep my mouth shut about things I didn't understand. And to let Tod go invisible whenever he wanted—though I would never have believed it, he actually caused less trouble that way. "Just keep your ears open while you're there, okay?"

Tod nodded reluctantly, and I understood his frustration. The only special skills a reaper could use in the Netherworld were his actual soul-harvesting ability and the ability to cross back over, which made sense, now that I knew he didn't work there. He couldn't go invisible, or walk through walls, or project his voice to only select occupants in a room.

He'd be practically human, and he didn't look very pleased by the thought.

"What about you? What are you going to do?" He glanced to the left, at a clock hanging over the door into the commercial kitchen. "We still have nine hours to kill. Eight, if you want to get there early."

Which I did, for obvious reasons.

"I'm going to see if I can crash at Emma's. It's okay to tell her about my sleeping issues, right, since they have nothing to do with the Demon's Breath epidemic or Nash being missing?"

But Tod shook his head slowly. "Kay, I think you should stay away from Emma for a while."

I frowned, my nearly empty mug of heavily doctored coffee hovering in front of my mouth. "Why?" We could keep an eye on each other. Her, for the demons in my dreams, and me for the demons in her body. "I need to know if Avari possesses her again."

Tod leaned forward with his arms crossed on the table, eyeing me intently. "I know, but the truth is that if you're with her, that's much more likely to happen. Emma is a very convenient direct line of communication to you. But if you're not with her, no one can talk to you through her."

So the best way to protect Emma was to stay away from her.

Well, crap. Looks like I'm on my own today.

Tod glanced at the table for a moment before meeting my eyes. "I'll have a little time between visiting Addy and going to work." And he would *have* to work at least a half shift, because an unemployed reaper was a dead reaper, and a dead reaper was no good to anyone. "So I'll pop in then and you can take a nap."

I couldn't stifle the yawn that came at the very thought of sleep. "Thanks." A nap sounded *sooo* good. Assuming I could keep myself in my own world long enough to enjoy it.

22

OVER THE NEXT HOUR and a half, I drank an entire pot of coffee in front of the TV and fielded phone calls from Emma and my dad, while avoiding one call each from Harmony and Sophie. Emma called in tears, and it took me nearly twenty minutes to calm her down. Thanks to his father's position in the community and his threat to sue the hospital, Doug's death was getting a lot of coverage on the local stations. I felt horrible about not being able to comfort her in person, but Tod's warning kept me firmly on my own couch, telling myself over and over again that I was staying away from Emma for her own good.

My dad was just calling to check up on me, and as bad as I felt about having to lie to him, if I'd told him I was alone, he would have left work—and possibly lost his job—to come sit with me while I napped.

Sophie left me a furious voice mail demanding to know why my presence at a party—or anywhere else, for that matter—seemed to usher in disaster. She'd seen the news and one of her friends had told her Nash and I were at the party. Fortunately, Sophie seemed to have no clue that Nash was missing, which meant I wouldn't have to call her back to find out if she'd seen him before he disappeared.

Harmony called the home phone looking for Nash, who wasn't answering his cell. But since she'd just gotten home from work, she didn't know how long he'd been gone, and she didn't sound too worried yet. Though that would no doubt change as the day wore on with no contact from him. Especially once she heard about Doug's death on the news.

At the end of the message, she said she might have found a way to keep me anchored to our world when I slept. As grateful as I was for that little tidbit of hope, I sat on my hands to keep from answering the phone for details, because then I'd have to lie to her, too, and for some reason, lying to Nash's mom made me feel even worse than lying to my own father.

An hour after her phone call, I was sitting on the couch sipping from the last can of Jolt, watching the loudest action movie I could find on one of the cable networks, shivering in a short-sleeved T-shirt and a pair of jeans. I'd turned off the heat and opened all the windows, hoping cold air would help keep me awake. Yet in spite of the caffeine, the temperature, and the noise, my eyes were just starting to close when the home phone startled me upright with its sharp, electronic bleating.

The caller ID read *Unknown,* so I dropped the phone back onto the cradle without answering. But my gaze stayed glued to the phone dock as the answering machine kicked in.

My father's voice filled the room, asking the caller to please leave a message after the tone, then an obnoxious electronic beep skewered my exhausted, overworked brain. For a moment, the machine produced only soft static, and I started to relax, assuming it was a wrong number.

Then a familiar voice called my name, and I whirled around so fast I nearly fell off the couch.

"Kaaayleeeee," Avari said, and the discordance of a hellion's voice on my regular, human-manufactured answering machine was enough to make me dizzy. "I know you're there. Where else would you be without your boyfriend to keep you warm, or your father to keep you safe?"

What?

I scrambled over the couch so fast my knee slammed into the armrest and my bad arm brushed the rough upholstery, but I barely felt the pain in my rush to get to the phone. "What do you know about my dad?" I demanded, before the phone even made it to my ear.

"I know that he's sitting four feet from me, unconscious but breathing. For the moment."

"You're lying!" I shouted, panic thudding in my head with each beat of my heart. "He can't cross over."

Avari laughed, and the sound was like shards of ice shattering on concrete. "Neither can Mr. Hudson, yet here they sit, waiting for you to come save them."

Noooo… He was lying. He had to be. "Prove it."

The hellion laughed again, and the callous racket was sharp enough to scrape the flesh from my bones. "Your father is a large man, but about as frightening as a stuffed bear. And when he cries in his sleep, as he's doing at this moment, he calls you 'Kay-Bear.' He also asks for a woman named Darcy, whom I can only assume was your ill-fated mother."

Anguish crashed over me, and I sank onto the couch. For a moment, I heard nothing but the beating of my own heart and felt nothing but a hopeless, almost pleasant numbness crawling over my entire body.

"What do you want?" I asked when I was capable of speech again, and my voice sounded like it was being whispered from the other end of a long tube.

"I have already answered that question," Avari said. "And my answer hasn't changed. Cross over now, and I will let them go."

*Or…*he'd keep all three of us, and I would officially

qualify as the dumbest girl on the face of the planet. But if I refused to come, would he kill them? Could I bluff him, or stall him somehow?

The room around me swam with my tears. My hand clenched around the phone. My chill bumps now had nothing to do with the cold room.

"Kaylee? What's wrong?" Tod asked, and I looked up to find him standing on the other side of the coffee table, watching me in concern. For once I was too upset to be startled by his sudden appearance. "And why is it colder than *polar bear* piss in here?"

"Shhhh..." I whispered, covering the mouthpiece with one hand while I wiped hot tears from my face with the other.

He waved my warning off. "No one else can hear me. Who is that?"

"He has my dad..." But before I could say any more, the hellion spoke again.

"Time waits for no *bean sidhe,* Ms. Cavanaugh. Are you coming or not?"

"Avari? On the phone?" Tod's jaws bulged with fury, and he spun around like he'd punch something, but there was nothing within reach. "How the hell did he...?" The reaper swung back around to face me, eyes narrowed on me. "Who is he *in?*"

Oh, crap. I hadn't even thought of that.

I covered the mouthpiece again, and the words fell from my lips so quickly even I could hardly understand them, but Tod seemed to have no trouble. "Emma. It has to be. Can you help her?"

He scowled, his fists clenching around air at his sides. "I don't know. I'll be right back." Then Tod was gone, and I was alone in my freezing living room with the very voice of evil.

"How did you get to him?" I demanded, uncovering the receiver. Yes, I was stalling, but I also needed to know how he'd crossed my father over, so I could stop him from doing it again. Otherwise, bargaining for my dad's freedom, or even his life, would be like holding ice in my palm in July; it would only melt away again.

"My resources are vast, Ms. Cavanaugh, and unlike you, I have no moral qualms preventing me from using them to my advantage."

I stood, pacing the length of my living room as I spoke. "Is that your way of saying you have people?"

He chuckled again, sounding genuinely amused that time. "I suppose so. I have many, many people. One more, in fact, than I had an hour ago."

My anger raged again at his implication, but I did my best to contain it. Avari was trying to make me mad. Trying to rush me into a snap decision that would likely get all three of us killed.

Out of the corner of my eye, something moved, and I glanced up to see that Tod had returned. "It's not Emma," he said, breathing hard, as if he'd actually had to exert himself for that piece of information. Or as if he was too furious to breathe properly. "She's having brunch with her mom and one of her sisters. It's not my mom, either. I already checked."

Crap! Who else could it be?

"So what about your people, Ms. Cavanaugh?" Avari asked, blessedly oblivious to the other conversation I was holding. "What are you willing to do to save them?"

I covered the mouthpiece again and sank onto the edge of the coffee table, my head spinning with anger, frustration, and exhaustion. "It could be anyone..." I moaned to Tod, staring up at him in desperation. "What are there now, six billion people on the planet?"

Tod shook his head. "He can't just possess some random sleeping stranger, Kaylee. The host has to be someone with a connection to the Netherworld. Someone who's left a psychic imprint there, either by crossing over or by tasting death in one form or another. Which is how he got Emma. She was technically dead for a couple of minutes back in September, right?"

I nodded, my thoughts as scattered as dandelion fuzz on the breeze. Em had died, and I'd crossed over. Those were our connections. Were we both now fair game for demon possession?

"It probably also has to be someone with a connection to you. Otherwise, how would he get your phone number? It's unlisted right?"

"Kaylee?" Avari's impatience reclaimed my attention,

as Tod's new information began to process in the back of my mind.

"It's not about what I'm willing to risk!" I snapped into the phone, having hit the limit of my own tolerance. "It's about what I stand to gain from that risk. Which is nothing, because we both know you'll never let them go if I cross over." After all, he was a hellion of greed.

"I might not," the hellion agreed, and in my mind, I saw a featureless, borrowed head nodding sagely. "But you'll have to take that chance if you ever want to see your father and boyfriend again."

I covered the mouthpiece and met Tod's eyes. "Someone who's tasted death and has a connection to me. Like Emma…" Oh, no. *No, no, no…* "It's Sophie." My eyes closed in horror, but I knew I was right. "Avari's in Sophie."

Tod frowned, then he was gone again.

"Well?" Avari said into my ear. "Which do you value more—their lives, or your freedom?"

But I had no answer to that because it wasn't a fair question—if I crossed over, I'd be giving up both options. "Give me a gesture of goodwill," I demanded. "A sign that you intend to keep your word."

Avari laughed so hard they probably heard him in the next dimension. "What did you have in mind?" he asked, amusement still ringing loud and clear in his voice. "A pinkie swear?"

I rolled my eyes. Where did he get his cultural references, Hannah Montana? "Send one of them back now," I clarified. "And I'll cross over, then you can release the other." Of course, I had no intention of crossing over, because I didn't believe for a second that he'd actually give back either my father or Nash. So his next question stunned me into speechlessness.

"Which one?"

"What?" I asked when his words finally sank in.

"Which one will you trade yourself for? Which one will you save?"

"Oh, right," I snapped, digging deep to find the courage for a few more words—and desperately hoping my bravado didn't get anyone killed. "Like you're actually going to let one of them go."

Avari chuckled softly, and the sound skittered up my spine like spiders crawling on long-dead bones. "I'm just intrigued enough by your proposition to actually send one of them back. But only because your agony over the decision promises to be a rare and extravagant treat."

As if I would ever let him snack on my pain…

Still, it was a chance to get one of them out alive, immediately, which meant Tod and I would only have to escape the Netherworld with two passengers, instead of three.

"So, which one will it be? The father or the lover? Which do you love more?"

I don't know. My father, who loved me, but abandoned

me to his brother. Or my boyfriend, who loved me, but lied to me, Influenced me, and let a hellion wear my body.

There were no guarantees that I'd make it out of the Netherworld alive with whichever one I left in Avari's… care. So the only one whose safety was guaranteed—assuming the hellion's *people* couldn't get to him again—was whichever one he sent over immediately.

And I couldn't choose.

"This offer expires in two minutes, Kaylee…" Avari's intimate whisper made me feel dirty, and promised much worse things to come when we met in his territory. Things that may have already happened to my father and Nash. And I couldn't decide which of them to rescue….

Fortunately, before I could squeak out a desperate, impulsive answer, I heard a dull thud over the line, then the smack of something hitting the floor.

An instant later, Tod's voice spoke to me over the line. "You were right. It was Sophie."

"What did you do?" I demanded. My momentary relief was eclipsed by concern for my cousin, who hadn't exactly volunteered her body for hostile occupation. Even if her own occupation of it was usually hostile.

Tod chuckled. "You can't possess someone who doesn't have control over his or her own body. That's like stealing a horse without grabbing the reins—how are you supposed to control the animal?"

Had he just compared my pampered cousin to a beast of burden? *I shouldn't like the comparison, but I do....*

Still... "So what did you do?" I repeated.

"I hit Sophie on the back of the head with a universal remote. This thing is huge. It's like a cell phone from the '90s."

"You were supposed to get rid of Avari without hurting the host!"

"Yeah, I didn't get that memo. Maybe next time you should be a little more specific when you boss me around while I'm saving your ass. Though, frankly, this whiny little shrew is lucky she only has one bump, 'cause she's had this coming for a while."

Well, I couldn't argue with him there. "Is she still breathing?"

"It was a remote, not a sledgehammer. Anyway, it's not her time. She'll be fine."

"She better be." I sighed and sank onto the couch again, desperately hoping I hadn't just signed my father's death warrant. Or Nash's. "But the real question is how can we keep it from happening again? What's to stop Avari from taking over everyone I know?"

"Other than the qualifications for an intermediary? I mean, how many people do you know who have a connection to the Netherworld?"

Not many, fortunately. Not that I knew of, anyway. But there were a few—Emma, Sophie, Uncle Brendon, and Harmony—none of whom I wanted to see hurt. Especially because of me.

"Besides," Tod continued, suddenly appearing in the middle of my living room floor, still holding Sophie's home phone. "I think the key to keeping Avari out of your friends and family is right in front of us."

"It is?" I dropped my phone back into its cradle as Tod nodded solemnly, ignoring the static bleeding from the receiver in his grip.

"Alec."

"The proxy?" Finally wide-awake, I made my way toward the open kitchen window.

"Yeah." The reaper's gaze followed me, but in true Tod fashion, he made no move to help as I used most of my weight to force the first heavy pane of glass closed. "Possession takes an enormous amount of energy, and most hellions can only do it every now and then, and only for short periods of time. A few minutes, at the most. But Avari's been possessing you regularly for a month now, right?"

I latched the kitchen window, then moved on to the two in the living room. "As near as I can tell." I felt sick just thinking about it. How could Nash let Avari possess me? Had he even *tried* to evict the body snatcher? Even once I forgave Nash for lying about the Demon's Breath—after all, he'd been exposed while helping me—I wasn't sure I could forgive him for letting Avari inside me. And even if I could forgive, I could never forget....

"And he's been able to do it twice in two days, since he got his hands on Nash and your dad," Tod continued, dragging my thoughts back on topic. "Which suggests that he's using them as additional energy supplements—logical for a hellion of greed, don't you think?" The reaper raised one brow for emphasis.

"Yeah." And that also supported my theory that Avari had no intention of returning them, no matter what I did. Especially now that I'd blown the "one now" deal.

"But without proxies to boost his energy level, Avari won't have the power to possess his own wardrobe, much less the entire cast of the Kaylee Cavanaugh show."

"Okay, that makes sense..." I nodded slowly as I reached into the fridge for another Coke. "But won't he just get more proxies?"

The sides of Tod's mouth lifted in the first true smile I'd seen from him in a very long time. "He'll try. But we're banking on the fact that proxies like he has now are few and far between."

"Wait, Dad and Nash are *bean sidhes*—I get that. But Avari was possessing me way before he had either of them, back when Alec was his only walking snack. And Alec is human, right? He called himself a human proxy."

The reaper shook his head slowly. "I don't know exactly what this Alec is, but I'd bet my afterlife that he isn't only human. If he were, there's no way he could have possessed Emma for so long. Or twice in one night."

So Tod was right. The key to disabling Avari's human-telephone mode was to get Alec away from him. Not to mention my father and Nash. But since he'd just been physically expelled from my cousin's body by an unknown third party, the hellion would probably guess that not only would I be coming for my men, but I'd have backup.

Something told me that getting us all out of the Netherworld would *not* be as easy as Alec seemed to think....

TOD HAD TO REPORT to work at noon, but before he popped out of my living room at three minutes 'til, he swore he'd be back by five o'clock. That he would find someone to cover his shift, even though he'd already burned most of those bridges with his previous absences. Then he disappeared from my reality, leaving me alone with thoughts of my missing father and boyfriend.

Well, with those, and with Sophie's phone.

Great.

With a frustrated sigh, I grabbed her phone and my keys, then shrugged into my coat on the way out the door. All the way to Sophie's house, I tried out different explanations for how I'd gotten her phone, and why she'd woken up on her living-room floor with a big bump on the back of her head. But my efforts turned out to be unnecessary—she was still unconscious when I got there.

My old house key still worked, and when I pushed the front door open, I found Sophie lying facedown on the living-room floor, her cheek against the carpet, her eyes closed.

She looked so fragile without her figurative fangs bared at me, or her eyes flashing in bitter triumph over the advantages her life had over mine. Unconscious, she looked frail and tragically human, and it was easier than usual to remind myself that she hadn't chosen her own path in life any more than I had chosen mine. And she certainly hadn't chosen to have her body hijacked by a nefarious Netherworld entity she didn't even know existed.

Even if she had deserved the whack on the head. *Speaking of which…*

I knelt on the spotless white carpet next to the huge remote control and gently prodded the lump on the back of my cousin's skull. Sophie didn't even flinch. How hard had Tod hit her?

Resigned, I sat on the coffee table and slid my cell from my front pocket, dialing my uncle's cell number from my contacts list. He answered on the second ring.

"Kaylee? What's wrong?"

Jeez, what isn't wrong? I honestly had no idea where to start, without completely freaking him out. "Okay, Uncle Brendon, I have to tell you something, but first I need you to promise you won't tell Harmony. I swore to Tod that we'd keep his mother out of this, no matter what."

Something clicked, and background music died, leaving only highway noise and the sound of his engine. He was in the car. Hopefully on the way home. "Did something happen to Nash?"

I sighed. "Just promise, or I can't tell you until it's over."

"Kaylee, you're scaring me..."

"Then promise."

He exhaled heavily. "I promise."

"Thank you." I sucked in a deep breath, then spit the whole story out, as coherently as I could, considering my current state of exhaustion, stress, and fear. "Avari the hellion of greed is holding Nash and my dad in the Netherworld, and after he took them, he possessed Sophie so he could call me and try to talk me into trading myself for them. But I know he's not really going to send them back. So Tod hit Sophie on the back of the head with your universal remote to kick Avari out of her body. It worked, but now Sophie's unconscious on the living-room floor with a big bump on her head. Could you come home and take a look at her? And maybe let me nap on your couch for a couple of hours?"

For a moment, there was only silence on the other end of the line. Then my uncle released the breath he'd been holding. "I'll be right there." The phone went dead in my hand, and I smiled, more relieved than I could express that he and my father were two completely different people.

Twenty-five minutes later, my uncle walked through his own front door, and he seemed almost as relieved to find me still there as he was upset to find Sophie still unconscious. "I think part of it is exhaustion from being possessed," I said as he knelt beside me. "Emma slept for a long time afterward, too."

"Emma Marshall?" he asked, gently turning his daughter over. "This hellion possessed her, too?"

I nodded solemnly. "Tod said that so long as they're sleeping, he can get anyone with a connection to the Netherworld. Which Em and Sophie both have, since they've both been technically dead."

"Yes, but that takes an enormous amount of energy from a hellion. He shouldn't be able to do it very frequently or for very long." He brushed Sophie's hair back from her face and pulled back her eyelids to check her dilation. "Otherwise, you'd hear about people committing crimes in their 'sleep' all the time."

I shrugged and perched on the end of the coffee table. "Well, he has a proxy, and Tod thinks he's feeding off my dad and Nash, now that he has them."

Uncle Brendon's expression went as hard as I've ever seen it. "I'll kill him." Presumably Avari, not Tod. Tod was already dead. But was Avari actually living?

"That'd be great, except we don't think you can kill a hellion, and you can't cross over on your own."

"Take me." He stood in one fluid motion, lifting his daughter like a sleeping toddler.

"No way." I shook my head. "You have to stay here and watch Sophie, to make sure Avari doesn't take her over again." *And because you can neither defend yourself in nor escape from the Netherworld…* "Don't leave her vulnerable just because you want revenge, Uncle Brendon."

"I don't just want revenge." My uncle stomped down the hall and into Sophie's room so quickly I had to jog to keep up. "I want my brother back. And Harmony's lost enough already. We can't let her lose Nash."

"I want them back, too." I crossed my arms over my chest and sat on the edge of my cousin's desk. "And we're going to get them tonight. But you have to stay here, and you already promised not to tell Harmony. If you do, she'll run out after Nash and get herself killed. Or worse. And it'll be your fault."

Uncle Brendon frowned at me like I'd lost my mind. Again. "The same could happen to you, Kaylee. What am I supposed to tell your father then?"

I raised both brows at him as he lowered his daughter gently onto her bed. "If I don't make it back, there won't be any father to tell."

My uncle sighed so deeply I thought his entire body would deflate. "One hour." He stood straight and scowled at me, and I knew that was the best we'd get, and only because we'd given him no other choice. "You and Tod have one hour in the Netherworld, then Harmony and I are coming after you. Do you understand?"

I nodded. "But we can't cross over till five. Can I sleep here until then?"

He pulled the desk chair closer to the bed and sank into it, folding his daughter's limp hand into his own. "You know you're always welcome here, Kaylee."

Yeah. So long as Sophie was unconscious. "Great. It'll be like old times." Except that now there was a Netherworld demon out for my soul and my cousin's body.

SOMETHING HARD POKED my elbow, and I struggled to rise from the mire of sleep that had swallowed me like a sinkhole. A warm, soft, peaceful sinkhole…

The poke came again, hard enough to jar my injured arm that time. "Why are you passed out on our couch? This is not a park bench."

Sophie.

I opened my eyes to find her glaring at me in full beauty-pageant makeup, both hands propped on her bony hips. But my relief at seeing her alive and well was dampened a bit by the contempt shining in her eyes.

"Did your dad finally kick you out?" Sophie sneered, then her expression tightened into a mask of dread and irritation. "You're not moving back in, are you?"

I pushed myself upright with my good arm, rolling my head on my neck to alleviate the stiffness that had set in. I wasn't dumb enough to expect a thank-you for helping save her from demon possession, or for calling her dad when she was hurt, but a little courtesy would have been nice. Or even just a little quiet while I slept.

Of course, I wasn't sure what Uncle Brendon had told her, but I doubted it referenced much of the truth, or my part in it. As usual.

"I was just taking a nap," I said, leaning forward to fish my shoes from under the end table.

"Well, nap somewhere else. I have to get ready for the carnival, and I don't need you hanging around, sucking all the normal out of the room."

The Winter Carnival. *Crap.*

Sophie started toward her room and the pageant dress hanging over her door, pausing halfway to glance back at me over one shoulder. "Laura thinks we should cancel the whole thing, because of what happened to Doug, but I don't think Doug would want his tragic death to take food out of the mouths of impoverished children, right? And anyway, we're gonna open with a moment of silence, and there's that whole memorial service next week."

I shot her a blank stare. Untimely and tragic as his death may be considered in certain social circles, I seriously doubted Doug Fuller had ever given much thought to mouths that didn't belong to hot, willing teenage girls. But if Sophie wanted to rationalize a way to preserve her party—despite the death of a friend and the mental breakdown of her own boyfriend—nothing I said would change her mind. And without the Winter Carnival, there would be no reason for Netherworlders to gather, and no way for us to get a fair shot at stealing back Nash and my dad.

I hopped into the kitchen on one foot while wedging my shoe onto the other. The clock over the stove read four fifty-five. I was running late.

"Where's Uncle Brendon?" I shoved one arm into my coat sleeve on my way to the front door.

"Testing Christmas lights in the garage." Sophie smoothed a wrinkle from the skirt of her hanging gown without even glancing my way. "I have a massive headache, and the blinking was making it worse."

I raised one brow and tried not to smirk as I dug my keys from my jacket pocket, then hesitated with my hand on the doorknob, twisting to eye my cousin critically. "How do you feel?"

The sudden flush in her cheeks was hard to miss. "Dad told you I fell?" Her mouth stretched into a long, hard line. "I swear, Kaylee, if you tell anyone I was sleepwalking, I'll make sure—"

"Sleepwalking?" I laughed. I couldn't help it. Of all the ridiculous explanations Uncle Brendon had fed her to cover past *bean sidhe* activity, he was really pushing the credibility envelope with that one. "You sleepwalk?"

Sophie's gaze hardened. "I never have before. But it figures that you'd show up the first time it happens." Her frown deepened. "Somehow, you're always there whenever anything really weird goes down. You're like a walking bad luck charm."

"Have fun at your carnival, Sophie," I said, pulling open the front door. "I'm sure you're a shoo-in for the Ice Bitch crown." I slammed the door before she could reply.

I was halfway down the driveway when Tod materialized in front of me, wearing his usual loose jeans and dark tee. "You okay?"

"I overslept. Sophie's fine, too, by the way."

The reaper shrugged. "Like I'm going to pass up an opportunity to smack your cousin."

I grinned, half hoping that next time she was possessed, I'd be there to do the honors. "You ready?"

"As ready as I'm gonna be." He strode past me toward the car, sneakers squeaking on the concrete.

"You think Alec will make it?"

"Addy said she'd do her best. They won't let her near Nash or your dad, but she thinks she can get to Alec. She'll pay for it later, though." Tod's jaw bulged and he stuffed tightly clenched fists into his pockets. "We shouldn't have involved her."

"That's her call, Tod. If she wants to help, she has every right. And we're kind of screwed if she can't get to Alec."

"I know." Conflict was clear on his face as he stepped through the passenger's-side door and settled onto the seat with that weird, selective corporeality reapers typically flaunted. It must have been hell having to choose between the girl he loved and his own brother. Maybe as hard as it was for me to choose between Nash and my dad. Only Tod hadn't gotten out of making his decision.

The school parking lot was already half-full when we got there, the pink-and-purple sunset reflecting broad streaks of color on row after row of windshields. Once the carnival actually began, cars would line the street in both directions. Fortunately, the park across the street was still mostly empty, and thanks to the frigid temperature, no one sat in front of the fountain. In our reality, anyway.

I parked as close as I could, then hunched into the fading warmth my coat held as Tod and I made our way toward the fountain. It was a simple scalloped circle of brick with a smooth concrete ledge, surrounding a single broad jet of water, still spraying in spite of the near-freezing temperature. We were hoping that since we were half an hour early, the crowd in the Netherworld would be as sparse as the one in our world.

"You want me to check first?" Tod asked, after one look at the terror which must have been churning in my eyes.

"That'd be great." What I really wanted was for him to find out where Nash and my dad were being held, so we could cross over right next to them, then escape before anyone noticed we'd arrived. Unfortunately, they were probably being held in the Netherworld version of some building I didn't have access to in our world.

Which was why we needed Alec.

"I'll be right back," Tod said. "And if for some reason I'm not, do *not* cross over alone. Okay?"

I nodded, but we both knew I was lying. If he didn't come back, there would be no one left to go with me, and I wasn't going to leave Nash and my father to die in the Netherworld. Or worse.

Tod shot me his lopsided, cherubic grin, then blinked out of existence.

I sat on the edge of the fountain, just out of reach of the frigid spray, prepared to wait as long as it took. Which turned out to be about fifteen seconds.

"This isn't gonna work," Tod said, and I heard the first word almost before he materialized in front of me. "They're everywhere. It's like that big Halloween party they have downtown, only the costumes are real. And everybody looks hungry."

Great. My pulse swooshed rapidly in my ears, and my heart began to ache from beating so hard. "Did anyone see you?"

He shrugged. "I don't know, but I don't think it matters. Reapers aren't very appetizing. You're the one we have to worry about."

"Okay, so what do you suggest? A costume?" I asked, thinking about the furry werewolf mask in a box at the top of my closet.

Tod frowned. "No costume you could possibly own would make you look like an actual monster. Some of them don't look all that different from us, anyway..." His voice trailed off, and I saw the idea the moment it sparkled in his eyes. "But everyone is all dressed up for the festival, so if you had a fancy dress or something, you might pass for one of the harpies, or a visiting siren. I could pop into a store and try to find you something." He stepped back and eyed me critically. "What size do you wear?"

"No need..." I said as movement from the school lot caught my eye. If I hadn't known her all my life, I might never have recognized my cousin from such a distance, but there was no mistaking that slim build, or easy, rhythmic sway of nonexistent hips as she walked down the sidewalk with a skinny friend who could only be Laura Bell. And if Sophie had arrived, so had her pageant gown. "Come on. I think I know where we can get one."

Assuming I could squeeze my normal-size body into her skeleton-size dress.

We found Laura's car in the third row, and when we were sure we were alone in the lot, Tod stepped through the door and sat in the driver's seat with one leg hanging out as he popped the trunk from the inside. I pulled up the trunk lid when it bounced open, then lifted the long, white dress box from inside, hoping the gown would be long enough to cover my sneakers. Because even if I managed to squeeze myself into Sophie's dress, I could never wear her size-five heels, and running around the Netherworld barefoot was not an option. Not after I'd nearly died when a Crimson Creeper vine had lashed itself around my ankle.

I changed into the dress from the semiprivacy of my own backseat, but had to emerge and suck in a deep breath so Tod could force the zipper past my hips. And finally I understood why pageant contestants had such good posture: they had no choice. I couldn't breathe in the stupid dress, much less slouch.

"Wow." Tod stepped back for a better look, and I had to glance down to see why he was staring. Sophie's dress was too small for me, which meant that my meager assets were heaped above the strapless, gold-embroidered bodice, and my waist cinched by the torturous ribbing. The skirt flared with several gathered layers of material, and only barely brushed the ground around my shoes. It would have been longer on Sophie, but I wasn't going to complain about the length of a stolen dress.

"You really think I'm going to blend in wearing this thing?" I eyed him skeptically, suddenly certain the reaper was playing a horrible, ill-timed joke.

He grinned. "Actually, now I'm pretty sure you're gonna stand out, but in a good way."

"But I still look human." Especially with chill bumps popping up all over my exposed arms and shoulders.

"So do sirens. And anyway, they'll probably assume there's a tail or a third leg under your skirt."

"How very comforting..." I mumbled, slamming the front door. Then I took a step forward and realized I'd closed Sophie's skirt in the car. Frustrated, I opened the door and pulled the material free, wincing at the grease stain obvious on the white beaded satin, even in the rapidly fading daylight. Sophie was going to *kill* me. "Let's get this over with."

With any luck, I could reclaim my men and return Sophie's dress before she discovered it missing. And under the circumstances, I'd be happy to let her wonder about the unexplained stain for the rest of her life.

"Okay, now try to walk around like you belong there, but don't make eye contact with anyone," Tod said, taking my hand as he half led, half tugged me across the street. "And if it looks like it's going to go bad at any time, I want you to cross back over. You won't do anyone any good if you get caught."

"The same goes for you," I pointed out, then clenched my jaw to stop my teeth from chattering as we came to a stop in front of the still-spraying fountain.

"Acknowledged." Tod grinned again, but this time his smile felt forced. "You ready?"

"Not even a little bit." But I bid a silent farewell to the human world, anyway, and closed my eyes as his hand tightened around mine. Tod was going to cross me over, so I could save my voice for the return trip.

Since they didn't have to conjure up a death song, reapers crossed almost instantly, and I found the process disorienting, compared to my own routine.

While my eyes were still closed, the air around me

took on a different quality as it brushed my bare arms and shoulders. It was every bit as cold as the December chill in the human world, but felt somehow sharper. More dangerous.

The sounds from my reality faded rapidly. Gone were the growl of a distant engine and the Christmas music tinkling faintly from inside the school gym. The park lights no longer buzzed overhead, nor did the wind rattle the skeletal branches of the trees all around us.

Instead, a constant hum of strange conversation filtered into my ears, and even the familiar words were spoken with an unfamiliar lilt, or pitch, or syllabic stress. Even the light pitter sound of the fountain had changed, as if something thicker than water now splashed onto the brick ledge to my left.

I opened my eyes and gasped. I now stood beside the stone park fountain in Sophie's white Snow Queen dress, both of which had bled through from one reality to the other without so much as an atom out of place. Except that now the fountain shot a thin stream of blood high into the air, to splatter into the gruesome crimson pool at its base.

I really should have seen that coming.

But the fountain was just the beginning. Unlike the park in our world, on this side of the gray fog, Tod and I were no longer alone.

Not by a long shot.

24

"YOU OKAY?" TOD WHISPERED, leaning so close I could feel his breath on my ear, warm in contrast to the bone-deep chill of the Netherworld.

"Mmm-hmm," I mumbled, afraid to speak for fear of somehow giving away my species. His hand squeezed mine, reassuring me with the physical presence he couldn't avoid in the Netherworld.

All around us bodies milled, clustered in restless groups or walking aimlessly around the grassless park. Some whispered words as thin and wispy as the wind, while others thundered in deep, round tones. Everywhere I turned, sparkling, flowing gowns were decked with large multilobed feathers from birds I couldn't identify. Long swaths of crystalline material draped forms whose gender I couldn't determine.

Several people wore masks, and as I watched, a man with three legs and a tail lowered a visage painted with four glittering lilac eyes to reveal a smooth, featureless expanse of chalk-white flesh where his face should have been. I gasped, and Tod squeezed my hand, then pulled me swiftly through the crowd.

He stopped at a tree with a massive, twisting trunk in varying shades of a deep, earthy gold and tugged me beneath branches bowed with thick, spiky, rust-colored foliage. "If you want to blend in—" he whispered "—it might help *not* to flinch and gasp every time you see a Netherworlder. I hear they're pretty common around here."

"I know. I'm sorry." But the featureless face was new to me. As were the short, thick creatures with wickedly curved claws instead of fingers, and long, sharp beaks where their noses should have been. "Do you see Alec?"

"I don't know. What does he looks like?"

"You've never seen him?" Frustrated, I reached up to brush a spiky, orange-ish plant pod from my hair, then stopped myself just in time. For all I knew, the tree we stood under was just as poisonous as the Crimson Creeper that had nearly killed me a month earlier.

"When would I have seen Avari's proxy? You think he parades his staff in front of me every time I visit Addison?"

Lovely. "Well, we know he's human." I shrugged.

"Or at least he thinks he's human." But then again, so had I.

Tod stared out at the crowd. "Okay, so we're looking for someone who probably stands out almost as badly as we do. How hard can that be?"

It turned out to be pretty damn hard. People were everywhere—"people" defined as beings able to move under their own power—and while the vast majority of them looked terrifying to my humanoid-accustomed eyes, sprinkled throughout the array of extra limbs, missing extremities, backward joints, wings, horns, claws, and the odd tentacle were the occasional normal-looking beings with the proper proportions and standard number of appendages.

Some of these creatures, upon closer examination, were very definitely *not* human. One normal-looking woman turned out to have perfectly round, anime eyes with bright teal irises, surrounded by rich, deep rings of lavender. Another man's flesh, when I saw it up close, was covered in shallow but pervasive wrinkles, like a Sphinx kitten, and for several seconds, I battled a horrifying impulse to tug on a flap of the skin drooping from his arm to see how far it would stretch.

Yet others could easily have been kids in my third-period class, or the parents who picked them up after school. The variety of shapes, sizes, and colors was truly astounding and almost too disorienting for me to process, with shock and fear still racing through my veins.

So when my gaze finally settled on a familiar profile in the crowd, it was all I could do not to shout her name across the multitude, which would surely have gotten us all killed.

Instead, I grabbed Tod's arm, trying to guide his gaze with my own. "Addison..." I whispered, standing on my toes to get as close as I could to his ear.

As if she heard me, Addy suddenly turned, and my breath caught in my throat, trapped by horror so profound it had no expression. Addison's profile was just as I remembered it, bright blue eye, heavily lashed lid, and a flawless cheek and nose. But the other side of her face was a ruined mass of oozing red wounds and black crusted flesh, stretching from her scalp—where most of her beautiful blond hair had been burned off—to below her collarbone, where her skin disappeared beneath her shirt.

My hand tightened around Tod's arm, but he only pried my fingers loose and squeezed them, then let me go.

I forced my gaze away from Addy to glance at Tod, who betrayed neither horror nor shock. He exhaled in relief, then headed for Addison with quick, determined strides.

Gathering Sophie's stupid long skirt in both hands, I rushed after him and caught up as he sidestepped a tall, skeletal woman with dark eyes and cheeks hollow enough to cradle a pool ball. "What happened to her?" I whispered as we walked, my horror on Addison's behalf almost eclipsing my terror of the creatures all around us.

"It looks like he lit her on fire today."

"Today?"

Tod nodded grimly as Addy's gaze found him, and her half-scarred mouth struggled into a gruesome smile. "What part of 'eternal torture' don't you understand? Yesterday he peeled her flesh off while she screamed, and you could see her teeth through her cheek. He always leaves one side perfect, though, so she can mourn her own beauty. Her room is walled-in mirrors, and the damage goes all the way down her body."

I couldn't voice my horror; I had neither the words nor the nerve. Questions were all I could manage, and my voice croaked as I forced it into the bone-cold air. "How does she even have a body? We buried her. I saw her in the coffin."

"Avari gave it back to her."

I dodged a man with a suspicious lump roiling beneath his broad white shirt, lowering my gaze at the last second to avoid his. "But is it real?"

Tod's jaw tightened. "Real enough to feel every second of agony."

By then we'd reached Addison, and I forced my mouth closed, unwilling to embarrass either of us with my ignorance. Tod slid one arm around her waist and, though Addy winced, she didn't shrug out of his grip. Without a word, he led us back toward that same weird tree, and only once we were hidden by the heavy branches did he exhale, and even Addison seemed to relax.

"Kaylee, you look beautiful!" She reached out with one mutilated hand—fingers fixed into a clawlike position by her fresh, puckered scars—to touch Sophie's pristine white satin dress.

"Thanks." I wished I could say the same to her, but the most I could manage was a small smile to cover my horror. "It's my cousin's."

It's not your fault, I thought for at least the twelfth time as I stared at my skirt to avoid looking at her wounds. I hadn't done this to Addison; she'd done it to herself when she sold her soul. All I'd done was fail to save her…

"Did you find him?" Tod said, rescuing me from my own guilt and denial.

Addy nodded eagerly, then winced when the skin on the right half of her face stretched. "I let him out. He's supposed to meet us here when he finds your brother. And your dad," she added, glancing at me in sympathy. "Hey, there he is!"

I twisted to peer between two low-hanging branches, and my eyes nearly fell out of my skull. Walking briskly toward us from the edge of the crowd was the trash-can-lid-wielding boy I'd seen in the field of razor wheat when I'd woken up in the Netherworld.

"You!" I said as he ducked beneath the limbs into our private powwow.

"You, too," the boy said, in a voice I'd last heard from Emma's mouth.

"You know each other?" Tod's eyes narrowed as he glanced back and forth between us. But I couldn't tear my gaze from Avari's proxy.

"You're Alec?"

"Since the day I was born." He shrugged, dark eyes watching me closely. "Though the name's about all I have left from that existence."

"I saw you in the razor wheat on Wednesday."

Alec nodded. "I was looking for you, and your house seemed like a good place to start."

Great. A *sarcastic* demon proxy.

"But I have to say you look better in formal wear than pajamas," he continued, eyeing Sophie's dress—and me in it—appreciatively. Suddenly I wanted a coat, to cope with more than just the cold.

"Wait, why were you looking for her on Wednesday?" Tod asked. "Nash didn't go missing until yesterday."

"Yes, but I wanted out of here two and a half decades ago, and she seemed like my best shot in years."

I propped both hands on my hips. As badly as I wanted to know who he was and how he'd known I could get him out, I had more important things to worry about at the moment. "I'm not taking you anywhere until you take me to Nash and my father."

"Are they at Prime Life?" Tod asked. The Netherworld version of Prime Life, one of the largest life insurance companies in the country, was Avari's home base when he was in town.

Addison shook her head in stiff, obviously painful motions. "Not that I could find. And I looked everywhere I had access."

"They're in there." Alec pointed off into the throng and I followed his finger toward the building rising over the heads of the crowd gathered in front of it. Eastlake High.

Or the Netherworld version of it, anyway.

"Why are they in the school?" I asked, dread clenching around my stomach with an iron grip.

"Avari's planning something big, and I think he wants them both nearby to boost his energy," the proxy said, and Addison nodded.

"He wants them near?" I repeated, glancing again at the second floor of the school, which was all I could see over the crowd. "Does that mean they're not actually with him?"

"They don't have to be in the same room, no," Alec said. "They just have to be close enough to draw power from."

I shrugged, a thin pulse of hope threading through me. "So, we can just go get them, right?"

"In theory..." Addison started, and that was enough for me.

"Let's go." Human-looking people were rare enough in the Netherworld that four of us together might be noticed, so Addy and Alec each started off on their own, one veering to the left and one to the right. Tod and I stayed together for strength in numbers, since neither of us belonged there or had any defensive abilities. We headed down the middle, hoping to avoid notice at the edge of the throng, where the crowd was least dense.

The multitude swallowed us whole, and I let it, breathing deeply through my mouth as we walked, trying to calm my racing pulse in case any of the predators could hear it. Sophie's skirt swished around my ankles, brushing other pieces of clothing made of rich, iridescent materials I didn't recognize, several of which seemed to move independently of their wearers.

A tail brushed my hand and I shivered. A soft, warm breeze caressed my face and exposed cleavage, and as it passed, I both heard and felt the words it whispered into my ears, though I couldn't understand a bit of what was said.

I clung to Tod's hand as we crossed the crowded street, grateful for how very *there* he felt in the Netherworld, though no doubt his physical vulnerability made him feel exposed and defenseless. And finally, when we stepped past the edge of the crowd onto the sidewalk in front of the school, I exhaled. We were still alive, and we were almost there.

"Ready?" Addison appeared at Tod's side and took his hand, just as Alec emerged on my right.

We both nodded. Then the double front doors of the school opened, and my gaze was drawn toward the literally dazzling figure that emerged.

"Who's that?" I stared at the girl, who looked completely human except that she glowed with a beautiful, intense inner light. As if she were lit from within, like a human candle, shining so brightly it hurt my eyes to look at her.

Her eyes were dark pinpoints in a face so brilliant I couldn't make out her actual features, and though her short, fitted dress was a pristine white, it was dull in comparison to flesh that gleamed and glittered like sunlight on the ocean. In one glowing hand, she carried a slim, dark cylinder I couldn't identify from that distance.

"That's Lana. She's one of the lampades," Alec whispered as the girl sank onto the top step, like a school kid waiting for a ride. "She's one of Avari's favorite pets in decades. This whole celebration is for the lampades. *About* them. And Avari has two of them for the first time in living memory. Lana, and her sister, Luci. They just got here yesterday."

"What are they?" I asked, unable to drag my focus from the girl glowing like a living jack-o'-lantern, even though the light hurt my eyes.

"Lampades are the only creatures I know of that

exist in both worlds at once, in the exact same time and place." Alec headed slowly away from the crowd and we followed him, the cold Netherworld wind seeming to push us along. "If you were to cross over, you'd see her sitting there in your world just like she is here. Lampades are walking liminalities. You see how Lana's glowing like someone shoved a lightbulb up her butt?" Alec asked, and I nodded, amused by the visual in spite of the circumstances. "That's liminal light, and it runs through her like blood runs through us. A concentration of that light can temporarily merge corresponding sections of the Netherworld and your world if she shines it at a liminal space, like a window, or a threshold."

Sudden brutal understanding uncoiled like a whip inside me, snapping tight around my brain. "Can someone go through that…merged space? Like a doorway?" I whispered, dreading the answer even as I asked the question.

"Maybe…" Alec began, and I recognized comprehension as it swept over Tod, and the reaper met my gaze. "But he'd have to move fast. Shining her light is like bleeding for a lampade, and she'll bleed to death if she's not careful."

"But you said there are two of them, right?" I asked, and the proxy nodded, dark curls almost blending with the shadow of the building. "So if they worked together…"

"…they'd only have to bleed half as much," Alec

finished, and the deep furrows in his forehead said he was starting to understand.

"That's how he got them," Tod said, and I nodded. "These lampades took Nash and your dad."

My eyes closed in sudden cruel certainty. "And I could have stopped them."

"How?" Addison asked, stepping from the sidewalk onto the umber-colored grass on one side of the school's front lawn.

I gestured toward the steps, where Lana now sat with her hands clasped over her knees. "I think I met both of them last night. They came to Doug Fuller's party with Everett. Nash ran them off, but they must have come back after Em and I left. After Doug died."

"What?" Tod's eyes flashed in anger, and I knew exactly how he felt.

"These lampades? I'd bet my life they were the arm candy hovering over Everett last night at the party. Only they didn't glow then."

Alec rubbed one hand over his forehead, like he was fending off a headache. "They only glow here. In your world, they'd look like normal people."

I rolled my eyes. "Yeah, except they're identical, and flawlessly gorgeous." More than enough to give a regular girl an inferiority complex, without adding evil to the mix. "I'm going to cross over and make sure I'm right."

"Want me to come with you?" Tod asked, but I shook my head.

"Stay here with them." I knew he didn't want to leave Addy, and I needed him to keep an eye on Alec, whom I had no intention of bringing with me until we found Nash and my father. "I'll be right back."

I rounded the corner of the building quickly to cross over without being seen in either world, and my silent scream came fairly easily that time, which scared me almost as much as the necessity of using it. I faded into my own world near the back corner of the parking lot, then hugged the wall of the building all the way to the front of the school, to keep from being seen. Sophie's satin gown whispered against the rough bricks, and twice I had to tug the material free when it snagged. My cousin was going to *kill* me.

Assuming I survived long enough to be murdered.

At the edge of the building, I peeked around the corner to see Lana—definitely one of the girls I'd seen with Everett—sitting on the front step, exactly where she'd been in the Netherworld. Only now she held an ornately decorated metal flashlight. It was unlit—for the moment.

I crossed back over and rejoined the group without bothering to lift the hem of Sophie's skirt when I walked. "It's her," I said, shivering from the cold. "The lampades are the girls from the party."

"What are they doing here?" Addison asked as the

front door of the school opened and Luci joined her sister on the top step, holding an identical unlit flashlight. "Waiting to be celebrated?"

"They're obviously waiting for something," I said, and no sooner had the last word fallen from my lips than the girls twisted in unison to glance at the sky to the east of the school, where the sun was just starting to sink below the horizon, a mirror image to the sunset in the human world, but for the bruised green-and-purple of the Netherworld sky.

"Uh-oh..." A heavy new dread anchored my sneakered feet to the sidewalk.

"What?" Tod asked, but my gaze found Alec—the man with the answers.

"What effect would other liminalities have on this doorway a lampade can create? Big liminalities. Like, once-a-year events." Such as the winter solstice.

Alec's eyes closed in alarm as the reaper tensed visibly. "They would amplify the power of the liminal light."

"And would that make this doorway any bigger? Or hold it open any longer?"

The proxy nodded, because words were no longer necessary. We finally understood the purpose of Avari's Liminal Celebration. "He's using the solstice to bridge the gap, when the veil between the two worlds is thinnest," I whispered, terror rendering my voice a hoarse echo of itself.

Even as I spoke, the lampade sisters stood and took

up positions on either side of the double front doors, facing each other. And that's when the last piece of the puzzle fell into place. "Crap!" I whispered fiercely, grabbing Addison's scarred hand without thinking. "They're about to start."

"Start what?" she asked, pulling her blistered hand firmly out of my grip.

"Don't you get it? Avari's planned the whole thing out! The school, a carnival full of high schoolers, the solstice… Dusk is a liminal time, the lampades are liminal creatures, the front door is a liminal place, and teenagers are at a liminal age in life. Lana and Luci will shine their light across the threshold at dusk. And when the carnival opens, instead of heading into the front hall, a couple of hundred teenagers will cross directly into the Netherworld, like lambs to the slaughter."

25

My head throbbed in time with the stitched gash on my right arm, and my heart ached like never before. Of all the trouble I'd walked into since finding out I was a *bean sidhe,* nothing compared to this. To the abduction of a couple hundred teenagers right through the front door of our own school. Disappearances the human authorities would never be able to understand, much less solve.

And we were the only ones who could stop it.

"If he's planning some kind of forced migration, why bother bringing Nash and your dad over?" Addison asked as Tod guided us subtly toward the right edge of the crowd. Suddenly, standing directly in front of the lampades didn't seem like such a good idea.

"For more power." Alec rubbed his arms, fighting chills from the bitterly cold breeze. "I thought he was just being greedy, which makes sense, and is probably half-true. But he needs every bit of power he can get—as well as what he'd hoped to get from Kaylee. He'll have to pour energy into Lana and Luci to keep them alive while they hold the doorway open."

"Would Nash and my dad survive that?" I asked, rubbing my own chill bump–covered arms.

"No. And neither will they." Alec nodded toward the lampades. "Though I doubt they know that."

"So, how do we stop it?" I asked. "Take away their flashlights?"

Alec shook his head. "The flashlights are just focal points—decoys to fool the humans. The lampades shed their own light, and you can't extinguish it without killing them."

Which I wasn't ready to do yet, no matter how much of a threat to humanity they represented. Because despite everything they'd done, Lana and Luci were being used by Avari just like Nash and my father were, and death seemed like an unfair penalty for that. Especially considering they'd probably die, anyway, if Avari got what he wanted.

"What if we take the girls?" I asked, still looking for an alternative to murder.

"Take them where?" Tod ground his teeth in frustration, his fingers linked through those on Addy's good hand. "It's not like you can just cross over with them. They're in both places at once."

"Can't we just…chase them away from the doorway? And maybe separate them?" I propped both hands on the waist of Sophie's gown, wishing I weren't dressed like a china doll during what might turn out to be the last moments of my life. "If they're not together—and at the threshold—they won't be able to open this door, right?"

"Well, not the big door Avari's counting on," Alec agreed. "So that might work, at least long enough to get Nash and your dad out of here. Which will rob Avari of the power he needs to make this work."

"If we're gonna do it, we better do it now," Tod whispered as the buzz of the crowd around us faded into an eerie quiet. Almost as one, the audience turned toward the school doors, clearly readying themselves for the main attraction—a building full of food, ready to be harvested. "Because we're about to lose our chance."

We turned, too, to avoid standing out, as badly as it nauseated me to be standing among the wolves, waiting for the sheep to be slaughtered. Or eaten. Or slurped up. Or whatever.

"We should do this from our world," I said, so softly I could barely hear myself. "To keep Avari from interfering."

"I'm on it." Tod squeezed Addy's good hand again, then met my gaze, speaking softly through one corner of his mouth. "I'm gonna grab one of the walking Lite-

Brites, then I'll be back to help with Nash and your dad. Will you be okay here?"

I nodded, careful not to let my uncertainty show. "Yeah. I'm good. But work fast."

An instant later, Tod was gone.

A moment after that, one of the lampades let out a piercing scream, and Lana was suddenly pulled off her feet by…nothing we could see. The effect was bizarre, and reminded me of a scene in an old slasher movie, where a teenager stuck in a nightmare is hauled up her bedroom wall by an invisible evil force.

Lana fell backward, smashing the front door open, then disappeared from sight.

The crowd around us roared in surprise and outrage, shouts varying from high-pitched squeals to rumbles low enough to reverberate deep within my bones. There were even several protests I seemed to hear in my head, rather than through my ears.

A minute later, as several dozen representatives from the mob raced toward the stunned and abandoned Luci, Tod reappeared at my side, wearing the biggest Cheshire cat grin I'd ever seen outside of *Alice in Wonderland*.

And what a bizarre wonderland we'd fallen into…

"Where is she?" I stood on my toes to yell into his ear as the shouts around us reached a brain-numbing crescendo.

"In the utility closet by the art room. I had to knock her out, but that should hold her for a while. Let's find

Nash and your dad, then get the hell out of here before Avari puts Humpty Dumpty back together again." Then his gaze met Addison's and regret took over his face. He took her hand as if to apologize for leaving her, but she only smiled and shook her head.

"Go find your brother. We knew this would end sooner or later, and I'm grateful for the time we had. The time you gave me."

Tod nodded, then squeezed her hand and turned to follow me and Alec as we raced toward the other side of the school, hidden in plain sight among the outraged crowd. Alec was fast, and as the proxy's head disappeared into the crowd ahead of me, my foot came down on something thick and lumpy. I lost my balance when whatever I'd stepped on was jerked out from under me, and a horrific, bleating roar trumpeted over my head. My right foot snagged in the hem of Sophie's dress and one hand went automatically to my ear to protect my hearing, while the other flew out in front of me to keep my face from hitting the asphalt.

But before my palm could hit the ground, someone hauled me to my feet, tearing the dress with a dull thread-popping sound. Tod pulled me back, pressing me into his own chest as the creature on our right drew himself up to a terrifying height. Gray, leathery wings beat at his back, stirring the heavy skirt of Sophie's dress as his tail—which I'd obviously stepped on—whipped around his legs to lash my ankles.

"I'm so sorry!" I cried as Tod backed us swiftly away from the beast whose grayish cheekbones were literally sharp enough to slice the flesh from his face. The creature roared again and knelt like a bull about to charge. But then his massive right wing clipped the shoulder of the hairy fellow at his back, and both Netherworlders exploded into sudden violence like two giant cats with claws bared.

Tod and I raced away, thrilled to realize we didn't represent a big enough threat to keep the beast's attention.

Ahead, Alec's brown curls bobbed through the crowd, and we followed him, Tod occasionally pulling me out of the path of another stampeding monster. We didn't stop to catch our breath until we rounded the corner of the building. The empty span of gray grass—representing the quad in my version of the school—was still unoccupied and relatively peaceful, at least until the Netherworld residents discovered that the building had more than one entrance.

I led Tod and Alec to the cafeteria door, and we frantically searched every classroom, peering in through the windows of the locked doors and ducking around corners whenever footsteps headed our way, be they heavy, lumbering thuds or sharp, quick scuttles.

The first floor was deserted, except for the closet where Tod had stashed the unconscious lampade, so we ran up the wide staircase and repeated the search again, racing from room to room. And finally, through the rectangular window in the last door on the right, I spotted my father, slumped over a warped and dented metal teacher's desk, still in the flannel shirt he'd worn to work.

My heart leaped into my throat and I struggled to breathe around it as I twisted the knob desperately. But it wouldn't turn, nor would the door budge. "Dad!" I shouted, begging him frantically to wake up and let us in. To help us help him. But he didn't move, and only once I'd forced myself to go still and concentrate could I see that he was still breathing.

"Here, let me try." Tod pushed me aside with one outstretched arm, and I remembered that he couldn't walk through walls in the Netherworld. Alec and I stepped back, and the reaper exploded into motion. His foot flew, connecting with the door just beneath the knob with an echoing crack of wood. But the door didn't open, so Tod backed up and tried again, this time letting loose a heartfelt grunt as his leg shot out.

That time more wood splintered and the door swung open with the metallic groan of little-used hinges. I rushed past Tod and dropped onto my knees on the floor next to my father. "Dad?" I ran one hand down his ruddy, stubbly cheek. His eyes didn't open, but he moaned, and his head fell to one side. "I think he's okay." I glanced up at Tod and laid one hand on my father's shoulder. "I'm going to cross over with him, but I'll be right back."

"Take me, too." Alec's voice trembled, and for the

first time I saw true fear shining in his greenish eyes. "Please. You don't need me anymore."

"You're not going anywhere until we find Nash," I insisted, folding my hand around my father's. I almost felt guilty, knowing that if we left Alec, he'd probably be punished like Addy had, or worse, for his part in my father's escape. But as callous as it sounded, even after everything he'd done, Nash meant more to me than any stranger. Even a stranger who'd helped me find my father. "I'll be right back."

Before either the proxy or the reaper could protest, I closed my eyes and called forth my wail with practiced speed, trying not to think about the fact that the more often I crossed over, the harder it would be to stop myself from doing that very thing by accident. As my recent dream-shrieking had shown me.

The odd cacophony from outside faded into a more familiar, benign, excited buzz. I opened my eyes to find myself standing in one of the Spanish classrooms, surrounded by empty desks and travel posters from Spain, Mexico, and South America. My father sat beside me, and as soon as I was sure he was still breathing, I stood and dug my cell phone from my pocket, only mildly relieved to be in the relative safety of my native reality.

I dialed by memory, and the familiar electronic tone rang in my ear. "Kaylee?" Uncle Brendon said, his voice thick with tension. "Are you okay? Did you get them back?"

"I got my dad, and I need you to come get him out of here. He's in the last classroom on the right, on the second floor. The door's open."

"You're at the school?"

I rushed across the room and twisted the lock to open the door. "Yeah, and I have to go back for Nash and Alec, or Avari's going to use the lampades to open a big doorway into the Netherworld, and everyone here's going to walk right through it."

"No, that's impossible. Kaylee, Sophie's there."

"I know. I'm wearing her dress."

"What?" Over the line, I heard a door slam, then an engine purred to life. My uncle was already on his way. "Kaylee, you have to get her out of there."

"I can't, Uncle Brendon. I have to go back for Nash and Alec. Call Sophie and tell her to go home. And tell her I'm sorry about her dress."

"Wait, Kaylee, who's Alec—?"

But I hung up without answering, then kissed my unconscious father on the cheek and summoned my wail to cross over one more time.

In the Netherworld classroom, Alec had his hands curled around clumps of dark curls on either side of his skull, as if he were about to rip them out. Tod stood in the doorway, staring down the hall in case anyone else showed up. "Okay, let's go find Nash," I said, and both heads whipped in my direction.

"You came back..." Alec said, relief and disbelief warring for control of his wavering voice.

"Of course I came back. You think I'd leave Nash here?" The proxy frowned, and I couldn't help but smile. "Or you? Let's go!"

But we'd only made it halfway down the hall when a sudden unanimous roar of triumph from outside made my blood run cold in my veins. I grabbed two thick handfuls of white satin skirt and ran into the nearest classroom and over to the row of windows set into the outside wall, which—thanks to the H-shaped footprint of the school—looked out over the broad front lawn.

I yanked on the dusty pull-cord dangling in front of my face and the aluminum blinds ratcheted up, shining the dying, anemic light from outside into the dark classroom. The crowd gathered in front of the school had nearly doubled since we'd come inside. And every single bizarre, misshapen face was turned toward the broad front porch, where three familiar figures now stood.

In the center was a tall, darkly elegant male form who could only have been Avari, the host of the night's twisted jamboree. And on either side of him stood a glowing, white-clad female figure.

Avari had found the missing lampade, and the night's festivities were back on schedule.

As if to punctuate that fact, Alec suddenly doubled over, arms wrapped around his middle like his guts were being twisted from within. "He's drawing power from me. It's too much, too fast, without a supplement from your dad." The proxy gasped, and struggled to stand in spite of obvious pain. "He's feeding them, and it's going to kill me. And your boyfriend."

"Tod, do something!" I insisted, panicked, unable to tear my gaze from the spectacle outside. "Whatever it takes to stop them from opening that doorway."

The reaper glanced from my desperate, earnest expression to the spectacle outside, to the now-pallid proxy, then back to me. "I'm not leaving you here, Kaylee."

"I'll be fine. I have Alec, right?" I insisted, and the proxy nodded halfheartedly, his face now waxy with pain. "We'll cross over as soon as I find Nash. Now go, or none of us will get that chance!"

After another moment's hesitation, Tod nodded, then disappeared from the Netherworld just as a sudden swell of bright light from the ground drew an eerie "Ahhh..." from the crowd below, and a low groan from Alec. And while all eyes were focused on the light shining from the front of the school, a sudden, darker movement in the opposite direction caught my gaze.

Something was moving in the crowd. Something headed steadily away from the lampades, while everyone else was easing gradually toward them.

I squinted against the painful glare of living light and finally made out Addison's long, half-head-full of straight blond hair, the other half of which had been singed from her scarred, pink skull. And just behind her, being pulled along by her good hand, was a form I would have recognized anywhere, in any reality, even hunched over in obvious pain.

Nash.

"There he is!" I cried, my voice approaching dog-whistle pitch. I pointed with one finger pressed to the cold window glass, and Alec's pained gaze followed mine as he clutched the windowsill for balance. "See? Heading for the tree at the back of the crowd?" The one we'd huddled beneath only a quarter of an hour earlier.

Alec nodded and stifled a moan. "I see him."

Unfortunately, while Addison was pulling him away from the Netherworld crowd and Avari's new pets, she was also pulling him away from us, and I wasn't sure we could get to them in time. Not without being noticed.

But we had to try.

"Come on!" I hiked up Sophie's dirt-smudged skirt and pulled Alec out of the room and down the hall, fervently hoping he wouldn't trip, or collapse entirely. At the top of the staircase, I paused and glanced back at him with one finger pressed to my lips in the international—and hopefully cross-reality—symbol for "shhhh." Then I took the stairs as softly as I could in sneakers, my hand tight around his.

From the bottom step, I could see Avari and the brightly glowing lampades clearly through the glass front doors, and my pulse raced as I paused to stare for a moment, desperately hoping they couldn't hear my heart pounding in my chest louder than a jackhammer through concrete.

"What are you doing?" Alec whispered pulling me weakly away from the front entrance. "Is there another way out of here?"

I blinked as tears filled my eyes to defend them from the bright light still forming red circles behind my eyelids. "Yeah. The gym." One arm around his waist now, I led the way down the hall and through the double doors into the gym. I half carried him across the deserted wooden floor—absent of any basketball court makings—and paused at the closest exit while I crossed my mental fingers.

Then I pushed the door open slowly, just enough to peer outside.

The excited mass mumblings from the crowd swelled immediately, but there wasn't a single creature in sight on this side of the building. Glancing back, I nodded at Alec, then pushed the door open far enough for us to slip through—snagging the hem of Sophie's dress on something sharp once again. I tugged the material free and held the door open for Alec, then let it close gently.

Now came the hard part; we had to sneak across the school yard, around and behind the crowd, just like Addison had, without getting caught. And it might have worked—except that all hell broke loose at that very moment.

Suddenly the powerful shine from the front door

dimmed into a dull glow, and the crowd's excited mumblings shifted into fresh cries of outrage. Tod had done his job. Unfortunately, he was now hauling Luci away from the school and around the human-world version of the crowd toward us, drawing all eyes our way.

"Come on!" I shouted, and took off toward the tree, pulling Alec behind me. Fortunately, with the hellion no longer feeding his pets, the proxy grew steadily stronger until he was running on his own.

We were ten feet from the tree when Avari stepped out from under the branches, one hand wrapped cruelly around Addison's scorched arm, the other around Nash's. My heart nearly burst through my chest in terror and surprise.

Stupid hellion powers!

To my horror, Nash didn't seem to know who held him. Or even where he was. I'd never seen him like that before. His eyes were focused on nothing, and as I watched, they actually rolled back into his head. He was as high as the international space station. Nash would be no help in his own rescue.

"I knew you'd show up eventually," Avari said, and a soft crackling drew my gaze to the ground at his feet, where a thin, delicate layer of ice was now spreading toward us over the gray grass.

"It's too late," I said, drawing my gaze back up to his. "You're missing a lampade, and you can't open a doorway of any size without both of them."

"Not yet." The hellion nodded formally in concession, and the layer of ice thickened, obscuring the gray ground it covered. "But the summer equinox is only six short months away, and I'm sure we can find some way to amuse ourselves until then. Since we'll all be here together…"

Alec squeezed my hand and tugged me backward, his cold fingers trembling in mine. "Cross over!" he hissed, without taking his eyes from the hellion.

Avari shook his head slowly, confidently, wrinkling the collar of his starched white shirt. "She won't go without this one." He jerked ruthlessly on Nash's arm, hauling him upright hard enough to make me flinch. "Loyalty is her weakness. It renders her predictable and tells me just where to aim. If only the rest of your world were so feeble… Ahhh, but then where would be the fun?"

"Kaylee, *cross!*" Alec begged, tugging on my arm, but I shook my head again.

"I won't leave him here!"

"You won't have to," Addison said. And before I could register her intent, she jerked her arm free from the hellion and spun around behind him, screaming in pain when the sudden movement split her crusted skin. Blood streamed down her torn flesh, and when Avari reached for her, his fingers slipped in the crimson streaks. Addison's screams hit all new notes as more raw skin tore when she tried to run.

As the hellion's hand closed around the charred

remains of her hair, she shoved Nash with an agonized grunt. He stumbled forward. Alec and I raced toward him. Nash fell to his knees, and we knelt beside him.

"Take him!" Addy screeched. I expected to find her trying to pull Avari away from us. But instead, she clung to him, her fingers barely clasped around his torso, and as I watched, as his fury grew, a thin, bluish film of ice traveled over her, freezing the blood that flowed from her new wounds. "Now!" she screamed.

Avari gave a mighty snarl and threw his arms away from his body, literally breaking her hold. Her scarred forearm shattered and fell to the ground in several gruesome, frozen chunks.

Addison screamed again, holding her severed arm up as her broken body thudded to the ground. I'd seen all I could stand.

My heart pounding, I grabbed both Nash and Alec, then closed my eyes. My wail that time was for Addison, whose pain had only begun at her death, and who would endure it for eternity, or until Avari died. Neither of which seemed imminent.

As my throat began to sting and burn, the imprisoned cry scraping my flesh raw, Avari's roar of fury faded from my ears, and the unnatural cold of the Netherworld became a benign December wind, stinging my bare arms and shoulders above the ruined pageant gown.

On my left, Alec dropped onto the frozen grass and burst into tears of relief. He knelt on his hands and knees, sucking in breath after frigid breath as if he'd never tasted anything sweeter than normal, everyday air.

Nash sagged on his feet, his stare as heartbreakingly vacant in the human world as it had been in the Netherworld. He didn't seem to know we'd crossed over at all.

Harmony would know what to do for him. Surely she'd know how to bring back the Nash who'd first asked me to dance three months earlier, even if he never again remembered how that moment felt.

Exhausted, I sank onto the freezing ground next to him and lay on my back in Sophie's dress. I barely felt the cold on my bare shoulders, or the grass that tangled in my hair. All I could think was that I was alive. We all were. Except for Addison, and though it bruised my soul to admit it, there was nothing else I could do for her.

The tree branches overhead were skeletal in the human world, devoid of weird spiky pods, and beyond, I saw a vast, clear sky full of blessedly familiar constellations. We were alone on our side of the gray fog, because the human crowd had gathered on the front lawn of the school, kids and adults alike waiting in a long line to enter the building.

I propped myself up on one elbow to see that the front doors had opened. And not one of the carnival-goers was disappearing into a painfully bright void. Tod had done his job. Sort of.

A sudden commotion from our left drew my attention,

and I glanced up to find the reaper running toward us, fully corporeal, dragging Luci the lampade—in her human guise—across the frozen ground. Two school security guards ran several feet behind them, overweight and panting, their cheeks flushed by the cold. Tod stopped beneath the tree branches and abruptly dropped Luci's arm, his eyes swirling with both relief and pain at having left Addy. Then he shot one worried look at Nash and blinked out of existence, hopefully having returned to the hospital to finish his aborted shift.

Assuming he had a job to return to.

"Where'd he go?" The security guard stumbled to a stop in front me. He was bent in half, wheezing with both hands propped on his knees.

I stood, brushing my hands on the ruined skirt of Sophie's dress. "Where'd who go?" I asked, my eyes wide in innocence as the astonished lampade gaped at me.

The guard scowled, thick forehead furrowed. "The… boy. Who was pulling her…"

"There's no one here but us," Alec said, wiping tears of joy on his sleeve. He looked like he'd almost laughed himself to death.

"Are you okay?" the other guard asked Luci, and she could only nod, no doubt stunned by events on both sides of the gray fog, which she could see simultaneously.

"I'm f-fine," she stuttered, her voice high and clear. "Thank you."

"Let us know if he shows up again," the first guard

said, then the pair waddled off toward the carnival again, shaking their heads in confusion. When they were gone, the motley members of our odd gathering could only eye one another warily, *bean sidhe,* former proxy, and lampade each equally stunned by our near capture.

"He'll send us after them again," Luci said finally, glancing briefly at Nash as if he held no interest to her at all. As if she didn't care one way or another which world he occupied.

"Yeah, but if you take Nash and my father back to Avari—if you give him anyone else strong enough to power his little human generator—you may as well put a gun in your mouth. And your sister's, too."

Luci frowned, and I realized I had truly captured her attention for the first time. "What does that mean?"

"He would have killed you both," I said as I pulled Nash closer with one arm. He came willingly, but made no move on his own. "Avari was going to bleed you both until you died powering his pedestrian bridge to nowhere. And he still will, if you give him a chance." I held Nash tight as he began to chatter, his freezing skin leaching the warmth from my own.

Luci only blinked at me, her stunned expression edged by distrust. "You're lying."

I shrugged. "Fine. Believe what you want. But we both know Tod could have killed you if he'd wanted to. Twice. And I'm sure he was tempted, considering you kidnapped his brother. But he didn't so much as bruise your arm dragging you away from certain death. What does that tell you about who means you harm and who doesn't?"

Luci's frown deepened, and true fear flitted across her face. But she hadn't so much as glanced at Nash in regret, and had yet to ask about my father.

"Look, I don't care where you go or what you do, so long as you stay away from us. And if you want to live, you should get your sister and stay away from Avari, too."

And finally, Luci nodded. She was still nodding when Alec and I walked off with Nash wobbling between us.

"Kaylee Cavanaugh, you bitch!" A shrill voice called as I pulled open the front door of my rental car minutes later. "That's a *six-hundred-dollar* gown, and you ruined it! What the hell are you doing in my dress?" Sophie demanded, flanked by two other Snow Queen contestants in long formal gowns, while she still wore jeans and an angora sweater beneath a pink quilted down jacket.

"Saving the day," I said, closing Nash's door as Alec settled himself into the backseat. I crossed in front of the car and sank into my own seat, tucking the voluminous, ruined skirt in around my legs. "You're welcome."

Then I slammed my door and drove off, leaving Sophie and her friends to stare after us in astonishment.

26

MY HAND SHOOK as I turned off the car and pulled the key from the ignition. Nash's front porch light shone through the windshield, highlighting his face, but all I could think about was how he'd kept me in the dark, fighting an evil he'd already embraced. He leaned against the passenger's-side window, staring at his unlit house. His mother was out, and hopefully blissfully ignorant of what we'd gone through. That wouldn't last long; we'd have to tell her everything soon, because if we didn't, my father would.

But for the moment, this private, temporary reprieve from chaos was too valuable to waste.

For lack of any place else to take him, I'd left Alec at my house with my dad and my uncle when I'd gone in to change clothes. My dad was worried about me, furious with Nash, and understandably scared by the whole thing, though he covered it with almost believable bravado.

Uncle Brendon was relieved that everyone had survived and that Sophie hadn't been sucked into the Netherworld. And he didn't give a damn about the ruined pageant gown. He'd promised to work on calming down my dad while I took Nash home.

But taking him home was as far ahead as I'd planned.

When I dropped the keys in my lap, Nash twisted in his seat to face me. "What now?" His skin was pale and damp with sweat, in spite of the temperature, but his eyes were clear. He was coherent, and withdrawal hadn't set in yet. If we were going to talk, this was the time.

"I don't know." I fiddled with the key bauble, trying to bring my scattered thoughts into focus. But they didn't want to focus. They wanted to remain mercifully blurry, so I wouldn't have to come to terms with what I'd almost lost. What I might still have to give up.

"Kaylee..."

"Inside." I shoved open my car door without looking at him. "I don't want to do this here." In the driveway. Within sight of any neighbors who happened to peek out the window.

I locked the car while he unlocked the house. He held his front door open, then closed it behind me after I brushed past him into the living room. I followed him down the hall and into his room—we both knew the way, even in the dark—then closed the door at my back. I didn't think Harmony would mind this time, even if she'd been home. My plans for the evening included neither Nash's hands, nor his bed.

Nash kicked his shoes into the corner, then pulled his shirt over his head and dropped it on the floor. He collapsed onto the bed, leaning against his headboard, but for once I wasn't tempted by the display. Nash looked like hell.

Avari had nearly drained him.

I pulled out his desk chair and sat, swiveling to face him. Without taking off my coat. "Nash, I don't know where to st—"

"I'm sorry. Kaylee, I'm so sorry." He looked like he wanted to touch me, but knew better than to try. "I don't even know how to tell you how sorry I am." He watched me, studying my reaction, but I could only stare at my hands in my lap, blinking away unshed tears. "But that's not enough, is it?"

Two months earlier, it would have been. Nash had been the sun lighting up the horizon of my life, outshining everything else in my world. I'd thought once that he was too good to be true.

Turns out I was right.

"Kaylee?" he asked, and his voice was like thin, brittle glass. One heavy word from me, and he would shatter.

"I don't know." I made myself look at him, though

the pain and regret swirling in his eyes bruised me, deep inside. I didn't want to be the cause of so much suffering. But I didn't want to feel it, either, and he wasn't the only one hurting. "You lied to me."

"I know. I lied to everyone." His voice echoed with shame, but it wasn't enough. Regret couldn't fix what he'd broken. Apologies couldn't bring back what he'd lost. What *we'd* lost.

"But you lied to *me,* Nash." I swallowed more tears and cleared my throat. "You said you loved me. Then you lied to me, you Influenced me, you tried to make me sound crazy in front of my dad, and you let Avari possess me and do—I can't even imagine what—with my body."

"Kaylee, I'm…"

I sat straighter, anger overwhelming everything else for the moment. "Don't say you're sorry. That won't fix this." I wasn't sure *anything* could fix this—now.

But if I'd been paying more attention… If I'd thought more about Nash and less about being grounded, I'd have seen what was happening before it got so bad. If I'd watched him as closely as I'd watched his loser friends, who'd started using of their own free will… If I'd told my dad earlier… If I'd never taken those stupid balloons to the Netherworld in the first place…

There were a million what-ifs that could have stopped the whole thing. A million things I wished I'd done differently. But in the end, I was left with what actually happened. With my mistakes and his.

And with the question of which mistakes I could live with.

"How many times?" I demanded, so soft I barely heard my own words. I picked at my cuticles because I couldn't stand to watch him struggle for an answer. "How many times did you let him…use me?"

Nash sighed, and the bed creaked as he moved closer, but I didn't look up. "I don't know. I wasn't counting. I was trying to forget."

You should have been trying to stop him. "Make a guess." I rolled away from the bed until the chair back hit the desktop.

"I didn't see you very often when you were grounded. So…maybe once a week. Until the last week of school."

"Twice that week?" I asked, and Nash nodded miserably. "So, six times?"

He shrugged. "I guess so."

"What did I do?" I demanded, far from sure I really wanted the answer.

"Kaylee, you don't want to—"

"No, *you* don't want to," I snapped. Because the guilt was killing him. I could see that. But I needed to know. "Tell me."

"Most of the time, he just talked through you. Told me where and when to meet Everett. Made me remember things, so he could take his payment." A concept which horrified me to no end.

"But it was more than that once, right?" Unless Avari was lying. Please, please let him be lying…

Nash closed his eyes and let his skull thump into the headboard. "The first time." He opened his eyes and met my gaze so I could see the earnest colors swirling in his irises. The brutal honesty. "I didn't know what was going on, Kaylee. I swear, I had no idea. I didn't even know it was possible."

"What happened?"

"Your dad was at work, and I came over with a movie. You fell asleep on the couch, and I was gonna let you sleep. But then you woke up, and we started…kissing."

"That's it?" I could tell that wasn't it. The thought of Avari kissing him with my mouth was revolting, but it wasn't bad enough to account for the crimson flush of shame in his cheeks.

"No. You… *He* let me…touch you. He took your shirt off. I should have known it wasn't you, but I—"

"Yeah, you should have!" My head was a maelstrom of rage and humiliation, spinning fast and hard enough to make me dizzy. I pulled my jacket closed over my shirt, as if that could somehow block what he'd already seen. What he'd touched. But I couldn't undo it. It was done when I couldn't stop it, and he *didn't* stop it.

I stood, breathing too fast. Terrified by the thought

that I could have been so out of control of my own body. *I can't do this.* It was too much.

I whirled on him, anger burning deep inside me. "You can't remember what our real firsts felt like, and I wasn't even *there* for this one. How am I supposed to deal with that?" I scrubbed both hands over my face. "I'm lost, Nash. What happened while I wasn't here—what you thought you were doing with me—may have been no big deal to you, but it would have been special to me. Something *I* was supposed to give to you, but someone else gave it to you instead, and now it's ruined. And I want it back, but you can't give it back to me..." I blinked away more tears, struggling to cling to anger instead.

Nash stood, too, but gave me space. "Kaylee, I swear I had no idea what was going on."

"You didn't want to know! You saw what you wanted and took it, and it didn't occur to you that something wasn't right until..." I stopped, my focus narrowing on him as my stomach pitched with a sudden horrifying certainty. "When did you know? Did you stop on your own? Did you figure it out, or did he tell you?"

Nash dropped his gaze. His hands curled into fists, and he shoved them into his jeans pockets. "We were... He said something, and it wasn't your voice."

The churning in my stomach grew into full-fledged nausea. "So he stopped you, probably only because cluing you in would be more fun. How far would you have gone if he hadn't? Would you have stopped at all?"

Had Nash Hudson ever waited three months for anyone to give it up before? Could he even be expected to have that kind of willpower, when I wasn't saying no?

Nash read the fear on my face. "Kaylee, no. I would have figured it out." He stepped forward, and I backed up until my spine hit the wall, and I had nowhere else to go. He stopped, begging me silently to listen. To try to understand. "I know your limits. I know *you*. I would have figured it out. I would have stopped."

"Why should I believe you?" I felt used. I felt cheated and dirty, and though I knew that wasn't entirely Nash's fault, I couldn't help hating him a little bit, for letting it happen. "You called me a tease. You said anyone else would have walked away already. But would you have, if I seemed willing? You've already tried to Influence me out of my clothes."

"Kaylee, that's not fair. I wasn't thinking. I was…"

"High?" I raised both brows, and he nodded miserably. "Yeah. You were. And you're right—it wasn't fair. So why should I believe you now?"

"Because he never fooled me again." Nash made eye contact and held it, letting me see the truth. "I know you. I love you, Kaylee. I know you probably can't forgive me—hell, I don't think I can forgive myself—but I swear on my life that it'll never happen again. Any of it.

No more frost. No more lies. No more Influence. Please, just give me a chance to prove it. Will you give me one more chance?"

"I…"

But before I could come up with an answer, Tod appeared in the desk chair, where I'd sat minutes earlier. "Hey. Am I interrupting something?"

"Yes," Nash said. "Get out."

But Tod was watching me, and I could tell from the angry line of his jaw that he'd been listening long before he showed himself. He'd heard what Avari had done to me. What Nash had let him do.

"You want me to go?" Tod asked me, his back to his brother.

Nash implored me silently to say yes. Tod waited patiently.

"No," I said, looking right at Nash. He scowled, and his shoulders sagged.

"Good." Tod stood and kicked the rolling chair out of his way. "I just checked on your friend in the straitjacket. But first…" The reaper swung before either of us realized what he intended to do.

Tod's very solid fist slammed into Nash's jaw. Nash's head snapped back. He stumbled into the wall. Tod shook his hand like it hurt. "That's for what you let him do to Kaylee."

Nash shoved himself away from the wall, swinging at his brother. But his fist went right through the reaper's incorporeal head, and Tod only frowned, turning back to me while his brother seethed.

I gaped at them both, surprised beyond speech.

Tod pushed the rolling chair toward me, and I sat. Nash sank onto his bed, glaring at his brother and rubbing his jaw. "How's Scott?" I asked, still trying to absorb the abbreviated fistfight and avoid answering Nash's last question. "Still hearing voices?"

"Just that one voice,"

Tod said. "According to the chatter at the nurses' station he's been much worse tonight. I figure Avari's been throwing fits ever since we crossed over."

And if Avari was taking his rage out on Scott, I didn't want to know what he was doing to Addy.

"How does he look?" Nash asked, staring at the floor rather than look at his brother.

"Crazy." Tod shrugged. "He stares at the walls like they're going to swallow him, and they're keeping the room lit from all four sides to eliminate shadows. Even at night. Otherwise, he screams until they have to sedate him." The very thought of which triggered memories of my own time strapped to a bed. "They seem to think his fear of shadows is part of his neurosis."

But we knew the truth: the shadows really *were* out to get Scott Carter.

Because Avari was in the shadows.

"Mom says they're connected now. Because Scott inhaled so much of his breath, Avari has a permanent, hardwired connection to his brain. The bastard's playing with the shadows, and probably planting thoughts directly in his head."

I swallowed true horror.

"That won't happen to me," Nash insisted, obviously having read the fear on my face. Or in my eyes. "If Avari could have spoken to me directly, he would have." But he couldn't. Avari's serial possession of me was proof of that.

I nodded. Nash seemed to be immune to the connected-consciousness thing by virtue of being a *bean sidhe.*

"So…you talked to Mom?" Nash frowned at his brother.

"Yeah. I didn't tell her everything, but I had to tell her you crossed over. She's on her way here." Tod raised one brow at his brother. "Consider this your heads-up."

"Thanks for the warning." Nash stood to show Tod that his presence was no longer required. He was still pissed over being punched, but obviously realized that fighting the reaper would do no more good than trying to argue with him.

Tod glanced at me in question.

I sighed and nodded. I couldn't avoid Nash's question forever. "Thanks, Tod," I said. Then, acting on impulse, I stood and gave him a hug before he could blink out. I wasn't sure whether I was thanking him for helping save Nash and my dad, or for watching over Scott, or for giving a damn what happened to me. Maybe it was all three.

But more than any of that, I was thankful for the possibility he'd shown me: that a man really could love a woman enough that he'd do anything to protect her. That's how much Tod loved Addy.

That's how much I wanted Nash to love me.

When I let him go, Tod held my gaze for a long moment, searching my eyes. Then he blinked out of sight without a word.

I turned to face Nash slowly, my pulse racing. I stared at the floor as I weighed my options, the possibilities, and my own heart.

"Kaylee?" Nash whispered, and I looked up to find him watching me. Still waiting for my answer, as if Tod had never interrupted. "I know it doesn't do any good for me to make promises, because you don't trust me right now. But I swear, I'll spend every day earning your trust back. Let me prove it. Give us one more shot, Kaylee." He stood, and his eyes were shiny with tears. "Please. I need you."

I didn't know what to say. Needing me wasn't enough. Not after what he'd done. Love should have meant more than getting high. *I* should have meant more…

Nash did love me. I could see the truth of that in his eyes and I desperately wanted it to be enough. But Avari would never die, and even though he was clean now, Nash would always be addicted to him. And what if he started using again?

I'd already lost classmates, and free will, and trust, and I'd almost lost both my father and Nash. How much more could I afford to lose if he gell off the wagon?

"I can't, Nash. Not yet. I'm sorry." My eyes watered, but I blinked away the tears and opened the door.

"Kaylee, wait." He pulled my hand from the doorknob and held it, and I saw that his eyes were damp, too. "What do you want? Tell me, and I'll do it. Please."

My next breath was painful, but I held it for several seconds, swallowing tears I refused to let fall. Then I looked into his eyes, trying not to see the honest pain and regret in them.

"I want to take it all back. I want to save Doug, and heal Scott, and protect Emma. I want to fix your memories, so you can remember what this felt like the first time." I stood on my toes and kissed him, long and slow, and hot tears rolled down my cheeks, because I knew that—at least for now—I was kissing him goodbye. Then I leaned against his chest, listening to his heartbeat. Already missing it.

"Nash, I want you to get better, so I can have you back."

I tugged my hand from his grip and stepped into the hall, pulling the door closed behind me. Then I ran for my car.

And cried all the way home.

★★★★★

Can Nash regain Kaylee's trust?
Or could a new rival change their
relationship forever?

Turn the page for a sneak peek at

My Soul to Steal

the spine-tingling fourth instalment in the
Soul Screamers series.

"So, did you see the new girl?" Emma asked, making a valiant attempt to change the subject as she tore the crust from her triangle of pizza.

"What new girl?" I didn't really care, but the switch in topic gave me a chance to think—or at least talk—about something other than me and Nash, and the fact that there was currently no me and Nash.

"Don't remember her name." Emma dipped her crust into a paper condiment cup full of French dressing. "But she's a senior. Can you imagine? Switching schools the last semester of your senior year?"

"Yeah, that would suck," I agreed, staring at my tray, pretending I didn't notice Nash staring at me. Was it going to be like this from now on? Us sitting across from each other, watching—or pointedly not watching—each other? Sitting in silence or talking about nothing anyone really cared about? *Maybe I should have stayed in the cafeteria. This isn't gonna work…*

"She's in my English class. She looked pretty lonely, so I invited her to sit with us." Emma bit into her crust and chewed while I glanced up at her in surprise.

First of all, Em didn't have other girl friends. Most girls didn't like Emma for the same reason guys couldn't stay away from her. It had been just the two of us since the seventh grade, when her mouth and her brand new C-cups intimidated the entire female half of the student body.

Second of all…

“Why is there a senior in your junior English class?” Nash said it before I could.

Emma shrugged while she chewed, then swallowed and dipped her crust again. “She got behind somehow, and they’re letting her take two English classes at once, so she can graduate on time. I mean, would you want to be here for a whole ’nother year, just to take one class?”

“No.” Nash stabbed another green bean he probably wasn’t going to eat. “But I wouldn’t want to read *Macbeth* and *To Kill a Mockingbird* at the same time either.”

“Better her than me.” Em bit into her crust again, then twisted on the bench as footsteps crunched on the grass behind us. “Hey, here she comes,” she said around a full mouth.

I started to turn, but stopped when I noticed Nash staring. And not at me. His wide-eyed gaze was trained over my head, and if his jaw got any looser, he’d have to pick it up off his tray. “Sabine?” he said, his voice soft and stunned.

Emma slapped the table. “*That’s* her name!” She twisted and called over her shoulder. “Sabine, over here!” Then she glanced back at Nash. “Wait, you’ve already met her?”

Nash didn’t answer. Instead, he stood, nearly tripping over his own bench seat, and when he rounded the table toward the new girl, I finally turned to look at her. And instantly understood why she wasn’t intimidated by Emma. Sabine was an entirely different kind of gorgeous. She was a contrast of pale skin and dark hair, where Em was golden. Slim and lithe, where Em was curvy. She swaggered, where Emma glided.

And she’d stopped cold, her lunch tray obviously forgotten, and was staring not at me or her new friend Emma, but at *my* boyfriend. My kind-of boyfriend. Or whatever.

“Sabine?” Nash whispered this time, and his familiar, stunned tone set off alarm bells in my head.

“Nash Hudson. Holy shit, it *is* you!” the new girl said, tossing long dark hair over one shoulder to reveal a mismatched set of hoops in her double-pierced right ear.

Nash rounded the table and walked past me without a glance in my direction. Sabine set her tray on the nearest table and ran at him. He opened his arms, and she flew into them so hard they spun in a tight circle. Together. My chest burned like

I'd swallowed an entire jar of hot salsa.

"What are you doing here?" Nash asked, setting her down, as she said, "I can't believe it!"

But I was pretty sure she could believe it. She looked more thrilled than surprised. "I heard your name this morning, but I didn't think it would really be you!"

"It's me. So…what? You go to school here now?"

"Yeah. New foster home. Moved in last week." She smiled, and her dark eyes lit up. "I can't believe this!"

"Me neither," Em stood and pulled me up. "What is it we're not believing?"

And finally Nash turned, one arm still wrapped casually around Sabine's waist, as if he'd forgotten it was still there.

"Sabine went to my school in Fort Worth, before I moved here."

"Yeah, before you ran off and left me!" She twisted out of his grip to punch him in the shoulder, but she didn't look mad.

"Hey, you left first, remember?" Nash grinned.

"Not by choice!" Her scowl was almost as dark as her grin was blinding.

What the hell were they talking about?

I'd already opened my mouth to say…something, when Tod winked into existence on my left. Fortunately, I was still too confused by the arrival of Nash's old friend—*please, please* just be a friend!—to be surprised by the sudden appearance of his mostly-dead grim reaper brother.

"Hey, Kaylee, you…" Tod began, running one hand through pale blond curls, then stopped when he saw Sabine and Nash, still chatting like long-lost relatives, while the rest of us watched. "Uh oh. I'm too late."

"Too late for what?" Emma asked, but I could tell from the lack of a reaction from either Nash or Sabine that Em and I were currently the only ones who could see Tod. Selective corporeality was one of several really cool reaper abilities, and now that Emma knew about him, Tod rarely appeared to me alone. For which I was more than grateful—Em was one less person who thought I went around talking to myself when I was really talking to the reaper.

"To warn you," Tod continued. "About Sabine."

"She comes with a warning label?" Em whispered.

I crossed my arms over the front of my jacket. "Well, it can't be sewn into her clothes, or we'd see the outline." Sabine's black sleeveless top was so tight I could practically count her abs.

Emma raised one brow at me. "Catty, much?"

"Well, look at her!" I whispered, both relieved and very, very irritated that neither Nash nor Sabine had given us a second look. A strip of bare skin showed between the low waist of her army-green carpenter pants and the hem of her shirt—an obvious violation of the school dress code—and she wore enough dark eye shadow to scare small children.

And—most grating of all—the look worked for her. And it obviously worked for Nash. He couldn't look away.

"I don't think it's her you have a problem with," Emma whispered. "It's *them*."

I ignored her and turned to Tod. "I take it they were involved in Fort Worth?"

Tod nodded. "Yeah. If you're into really dramatic understatements."

Great.

"Hey you two, care to introduce those of us on the periphery?" Emma called, betraying no hint of Tod's presence. She was a fast learner.

Nash looked up in surprise. "Sorry." He guided Sabine closer. "I'm guessing you've already met Emma?" he said, and the new girl—his *old* girl—nodded. "And this is my…"

Confusion flashed in Nash's swirling eyes, and he dropped his hand from Sabine's waist. "This is Kaylee Cavanaugh."

Sabine truly looked at me for the first time, and I caught my breath at the intensity of her scrutiny. Her eyes were pools of ink that seemed to see right through me, and in that moment, the certainty—the terror—that Nash would want nothing to do with me now that she'd arrived was enough to constrict my throat and make my stomach pitch.

"Kaylee…" Sabine said my name like she was tasting it, trying to decide whether to swallow me whole or spit me back out, and in the end, I wasn't sure which she'd chosen.

"Kaylee Cavanaugh. You must be the new ex."